No Greater Love

To Tina,
Thank you for your
support! In Him with
Love
Kwame 8/8/09

Published by First Fruits Publishing, LLC
www.firstfruitspublishing.com

Subscript taken from THE HOLY BIBLE, NEW
INTERNATIONAL VERSION*. Copyright © 1973, 1978, 1984
by International Bible Society. Used by permission of
International Bible Society.

Printed in the United States of America
Cover photo and Design by, John Honeyblue,
HoneyblueImaging, *www.HoneyblueImaging.com*
Photo location, Teavolve Café & Lounge, Baltimore, MD.
Edited by, Amy E. Roberson
Author Photo by, Quinton Jr.

Library of Congress
Registration Number/Date: Txu001281648/2006-01-10

ISBN 13 978 0 9840618 0 8
ISBN 10 0 9840618 0 0

Acknowledgments

To my parents, Pete and Barbara Conwell thank you for birthing me. And to my Heavenly Father thank You for giving me life.

First, I have to thank my husband Quinton for always loving me unconditionally. You are truly Heaven sent, a special blessing just for me. I thank God for you. To my son, Quinton Jr., thank you for lending your talents in support of my dreams. Remember you are greater than you know; live each day in discovery of your greatness and don't ever settle for less than what God has for you. To my daughter Nia, thank you for sharing your brilliance and for always helping me find the perfect words and phrases. Remember that God has a perfect plan for your life, but you already know that – trust Him always!

To my siblings: Robyn, Kim and Aaron, thank you for allowing me to be the annoying little sister and for loving me anyway. I'm pretty sure that it helped to develop my creative side. To my awesome editor, Amy, thank you for answering the call (email). You have truly added value to this process. Thank you for encouraging me to tap further into my creative self. To John Honeyblue and HoneyBlue Imaging, you know how amazing you are, but I will say it anyway – you are amazing! Thank you for lending your creative talents and visions to First Fruits Publishing.

Finally, to my dear friends, Marie, Darryl and John thank you for always being genuine. I love you exactly the way you are. Your friendships are priceless. So many names so little space – thank you to everyone who has ever prayed for me, encouraged me and believed in me, I am forever grateful. I love you guys!

A very special thank you to Sonny and the entire Teavolve Café & Lounge staff for lending your establishment to First Fruits Publishing for my first official photo shoot.

"If only my anguish could be weighed and all my misery be placed on the scales! It would surely outweigh the sand of the seas,"

~Job 6:2-3(NIV)

No Greater Love
A novel written by Kwanza

Kwanza

Chapter One

The light tapping of the rain against the car window was soothing. Emanuel focused on the road in front of him as he replayed the events of the evening in his mind. Family, friends, and great music -- all the ingredients for a wonderful night, but now all Emanuel wanted to do was spend some much needed quality time with his beautiful wife, Jada. The past few months had been extremely hectic for both of them as Jada worked non-stop preparing for the grand opening of, *Soul Sistahs*, her new jazz club, and Emanuel worked his usual fourteen-hour days promoting Atlantic City's first African American-owned hotel and casino. It had seemed that all of their focus and energy went toward work, which left little time for one another. For six months straight, their days ran into nights, causing all of their relationships to suffer: their marriage, their family, their friendships, and -- most importantly -- their relationship with God. They began their day with a prayer and ended it with prayer, they still felt slightly disconnected, but never losing sight of their many blessings. Amidst all the madness the two came together in the evenings, just long enough to discuss the maladies of the day, over a bowl of cereal, a sandwich, or some other ration that hardly constituted a balanced meal. Spiritually, neither Emanuel nor Jada had the absolute peace that they were used to as they struggled to plan, produce, and meet deadlines. But tonight signified a new beginning for the couple. The launch of the jazz club, and the successful completion of the casino campaign marked the end of long, stress-filled nights and unhealthy eating and the beginning of peace and a renewed commitment to their marriage. They had reached the finish line of their hectic race and now they were preparing to enter a place of peace. After they left the club they both breathed a deep sigh of relief releasing all of the heavy demands that the past months had placed on them. They felt centered and connected. Now all they wanted to do was spend some time alone to serve their God and cater to one another. They both agreed that from this day forward they would no longer allow work to consume them, and in honor of their new found commitment, and in celebration of their successful endeavors, Emanuel and Jada were leaving in the morning for a much-needed two-week spiritual retreat in Colorado. They planned to hike, golf, and sail all day and make love all night. Emanuel could feel his shoulders relax as he thought about the brochure, which featured a spectacular view of the sun rising over the La Playa Mountains, and tall green trees set under a beautiful blue sky. The most mesmerizing photo of all was a scene of the sun setting over a secluded cabin creating an orange hued sky. The images were so vibrant and alive that just the thought of them brought peace and serenity to Emanuel. Emanuel's thoughts, although they felt very real, were in complete contrast to the current scene that played out around them -- heavy rain dancing hard against the asphalt and even harder against the car window. Emanuel flipped the wipers, increasing their speed to keep cadence with the downpour. He looked over at Jada who seemed unfazed by the sudden heavy rainfall, and he smiled because he knew that her peace was a direct result of her faith and confidence in not only God's ability to protect her, but also in Emanuel's ability and desire to keep her safe. Jada looked over at Emanuel; she said nothing, but her smile spoke to his heart and told him all that he needed to hear -- she was happy and in love.

"Did you enjoy yourself tonight?" he asked.

"Tonight was a dream come true," Jada beamed.

"The club is even more amazing than I could have imagined. You and Kay did a great job bringing everything together. I can't believe how many people were there," Emanuel said as he thought back on the crowd.

"I know there were people there that I didn't even know coming up to me and Kay telling us how proud they were of our success."

"No doubt. You two ladies put the C in class. I can tell just by the caliber of people that showed up to support you guys that *Soul Sistahs* is certainly going to be one of those hot spots in the city. What a good looking crowd: businessmen, athletes, and politicians all partying in the same venue."

"Yeah, it was like a red carpet event, minus the paparazzi," Jada laughed. "Everyone looked amazing, but I have to ask what was up with that chick that Khadir had on his arm?"

"Ah man," Emanuel chuckled as he remembered the busty redhead that accompanied Khadir. There were no words to defend his friend and he wasn't even going to try. "She was cute," he offered.

"Babe, come on," Jada twisted her lips, "sometimes cute is just not enough. What strip club did he rent her from?" Jada questioned.

"Actually he met her last week at Bisoes. She's a waitress there."

"Last week, and that quickly she reached the threshold to be presented in front of his dearest friends, on a very special night, for very special occasion?"

"You know Khadir, he doesn't get caught up in all of that. Don't get me wrong, you know that he is happy for you, but I'm sure his focus was more on getting hooked up than impressing anyone."

"Yeah, well the way she had the twins on display and the way they were locking lips I don't think it is going to be too hard for him to get hooked up. I don't know why either of them thought that it was appropriate to act the way they were acting. It was not that type of party or that type of crowd."

"Don't be so hard on him. Khadir means well; his execution just isn't always on point."

"Leave it up to him to always give everyone something to talk about." Jada huffed.

"You know how he is. I don't know why you always invite him to stuff," Emanuel said placing the onus on Jada.

"Because he's your best friend," Jada retorted, "and I know that you love him like a brother. You haven't celebrated anything in the past twenty years without Khadir being right by your side with his chest poked out."

"Like I said he means well. Khadir has a huge heart almost as big as yours, he just has to channel it," Emanuel laughed.

"A big heart maybe," she reasoned, "but he has an even bigger ego. He really believes that he is God's gift to women. I know he's your boy, your brother and all, but he is a dog. He has no concept of commitment. Ever since I have known him I have never seen him with the same girl twice."

"Come on now, that's not fair," Emanuel said trying to defend his friend. "That's a little below the belt. First of all, let's acknowledge that Khadir is genuinely a good guy who God is still working on. Second of all he did bring one girl to two events, remember?"

"Nope, I can't say that I do."

"What about that one girl... dang what was her name?" He asked not really expecting Jada to respond. "Remember the girl that he brought to my parents' 4th of July bash last year and to my birthday dinner?"

"Oh yeah, the 'dancer,'" Jada said making quotes with her fingers. "What was her name?"

"Wasn't it something like Hot Chocolate or Sweet Caramel?" he continued to wonder.

"Hot Caramel!" Jada shouted like she was on Jeopardy or some other quizzical game show. They both bust out laughing.

"Yeah, Hot Caramel." Emanuel tapped the steering wheel as he tried to contain his laughter.

"That doesn't count because the parties were on the same weekend." Emanuel could do nothing but laugh. Jada was hard on Khadir, but Emanuel knew that it was all in love. The truth of the matter was that Khadir was just as close to Jada as he was to Emanuel. The one time when Khadir had his heart broken and he didn't turn to Emanuel for advice, he turned to Jada. And in her natural nurturing way, Jada was able to make sense of how a woman could walk out on a man and never turn back. Khadir's heart didn't hurt any less, but Khadir realized that no matter how successful and good looking he was not all women were satisfied with just being on the arm of a successful and good looking man, especially not a successful and good looking woman. "Now, the crazy thing was," Jada continued, "that she was proud of the fact that she was a stripper. Why in the world would you introduce

6

yourself as Hot Caramel to a group of people that you don't even know? Girlfriend had the nerve to be passing out business cards and everything." Jada shook her head in disbelief.

"Okay, okay. Everyone knows that Khadir is wild. It's a given that he is going to bring some questionable chick to each and every event," Emanuel concluded.

"And if he doesn't bring one with him he's going to leave with one." Emanuel and Jada were silent for a moment each settling into their own memories of Khadir.

"Yeah," Emanuel said thinking of the many questionable girls Khadir dealt with over the years. "She was something else. I don't know what's up with my man when it comes to women. I wish things would have worked out with Brandi."

"Me, too. But Brandi was a powerhouse; she was way too focused to fool with Khadir's immature behind."

"You are sounding a bit judgmental."

"I'm not judging him at all. I am simply saying that your boy had and still has a lot of growing up to do."

"Okay, let's change the subject. I do not want to ruin this beautiful night arguing about Khadir."

"I agree," Jada sighed. "Come to think about it, most of our arguments are either about Khadir or your mother." Emanuel laughed as he thought about the few arguments that he and Jada had over the years, but she was correct every argument they had had to do with either Mrs. Rivers or Khadir.

"Okay now we really need to change the conversation." Jada and the senior Mrs. Rivers had a strained relationship. They were generally cordial to each other, but Emanuel knew better than to try to make sense of the tension between them. "I have to say, by far, that the most amazing part of the night, aside from your beautiful performance," he added because he knew that Jada would call him on it if he didn't, "was when Dr. and Mrs. Rivers got on that stage and things got real jazzy. Did you hear my mom bellowing out *God Bless the Child*? Man, absolutely amazing are the only words that come to mind."

"And your dad on the horn…he – was - out - of - control!" Jada said, emphasizing every word. "But as cool as they are, I tell you I almost fell over when they hit the dance floor." They both laughed. "I didn't know they could get down like that," Jada said jerking her head to the beat that Mr. Rivers played earlier.

"Hey, don't sleep on my parents they have been in the music game forever. I remember as a kid, our house was jumping; they would have music blaring from the speakers. We would dance and sing like we were at the Apollo." Jada loved to hear Emanuel talk about his childhood and growing up in his affluent home. She laughed at the thought of seeing the Rivers family dancing and singing without restraint in their picturesque mansion. "I think that in another life they would have been ranked among some of the greats: Charlie Parker, Miles Davis, Ornette Coleman, Charlie Rivers, and my mother the former Ms. Nora Stone," he said, taking his hands from the steering wheel for a moment and stretching them to the sky signifying their names in lights.

"They were very cool tonight." Jada settled in her seat and smiled at the memory. Emanuel was raised in a very "Cosby" environment; his father was a surgeon and his mother was a judge. The only difference between his life and Theo Huxtable's was the number of sisters -- Emanuel had only one, Nadia who was two years his junior. Instead of growing up in New York City they were born and raised in King of Prussia, Pennsylvania, a suburb outside of Philadelphia. Emanuel was one of those few people who never experienced any real hardship or unhappiness in life. At twenty-six years old, both sets of his grandparents were alive and well, and the only tears that he ever shed was when he was ten and his dog was hit and killed by a car.

Jada, on the other hand, grew up in West Philadelphia. She was raised by her grandmother until her mother "got back on her feet," which, in the hood, was code for 'when she got clean.' This temporary arrangement turned permanent after Jada's mother died of a heroin overdose when Jada was nine-years old. Jada never really knew her father, but it was rumored that he was a neighborhood pimp named Benny. It was never officially stated that he was Jada's father, but after Jada's mother died he made it a habit of coming around more often. The two would sit across from each other at the kitchen table. They never talked to one another; they would just sit and look for any sign of resemblance, something that would solidify in their minds that they belonged to one another. On the surface there was nothing, at least not anything visible to the eye that would confirm their suspicions. Most days Jada's Grandma would sit at the table with them. She would also stare at Benny, but her stare was one of contempt. She was not fond of Benny, and she didn't like the idea of having him in her home. But despite the way she felt about him she believed that he was Jada's dad, and she did not want to stand in the way of Jada getting know him. Jada and Benny would sit at the dinning room table and drink iced cold lemonade on hot summer days and hot chocolate with marshmallows on cold winter days. They never really said too much. Generally Benny would ask a question about Jada's grades and school, and she would respond with the shortest possible response – yes, no, or um-hum. They would sit for about thirty minutes every visit, usually once a week, and when he departed he would leave a roll of money on the table saying, "This is just a little something to help you get by."

Jada's Grandma never said a word, and she never used the money to feed or cloth Jada. Instead, every Sunday she would put the money in the offering basket. She believed that God would provide for them and only He could make that dirty street money clean. Jada was determined not to be defined as the poor daughter of a junky and a pimp, so she set out at an early age to do something with her life. She was always a smart girl and did really well in school, which earned her a full academic scholarship to Temple University. She knew with all of her heart that it was only through God's grace that she received such a blessing. Jada never played the victim role, and she never felt sorry for herself or her situation. She loved life and gave every part of herself to it. Emanuel and Jada were only married for five years, and Jada would tell anyone who would listen that these were the best five years of her life. Emanuel was the best example of a man that Jada had ever seen.

Soul Sistahs was a two-year endeavor that Jada and her business partner Khadijah had undertaken. The two women had been friends since elementary school and they were best friends from the very first day they met. Growing up on Hobart Street in West Philly, Khadijah, who everyone called Kay, lived two doors down from Jada. She sat front row center and bore witness to Jada's turbulent life. Jada would step out of her grandmother's house onto their concrete porch and look at the world around her -- broken and desolate homes and souls. Even as a child Jada was keenly aware of how harsh life could be. She would look past the sunken in faces of dope feigns and see their spirits and before stepping down the front steps of her row house she would pray to God to help heal the souls of those broken. Jada was aware of how hard life could be in the inner city of Philadelphia but she was determined to grow beyond the statistics and attain the life that God had for her. Kay was in awe of Jada's ability to separate herself from the drama that plagued their community. Throughout the years Jada and Kay motivated each other through tough times - puppy love, heartbreaks, and single parenting. When Kay learned at nineteen that she was pregnant, Jada was right there with her -- through the tears, the morning sickness, the heartburn, and the delivery. With help and encouragement from her mother and Jada, Kay was able to graduate from college. Though she had to take a year off, she returned to school and graduated with honors from Temple University with a degree in business. Kay's business savvy combined with Jada's creativity and fearlessness were the perfect ingredients for the success of *Soul Sistahs*. Local magazines and newspapers had begun raving about *Soul Sistahs* months before the club opened its doors. Local radio stations gave out VIP passes to the lucky tenth caller who called in every time the station played Patti Labelle's *Lady Marmalade*, not because Mrs. Patty is from Philadelphia, but because the song included the words Soul Sister. And tonight some of Philly's finest celebrated the opening of *Soul Sistahs*.

10

Jada took a deep breath. "What an incredible night," she said, as happiness settled her heart. She turned to face her husband, the primary source of all her joy, and smiled. With her hand outreached she cupped Emanuel's face and began to stroke his bearded cheek with her thumb. Jada looked at his silhouette, but, in the darkness, she could barely see him. Her eyes sparkled each time she caught a glimpse of his handsome face from the sporadic lights that shined in on them from passing cars. With her head leaned against her seat, she smiled at her handsome husband who seemed to be deep in thought. Slowly tracing her index finger around Emanuel's ear she counted the seconds between the pulses of the one vein that throbbed at his temple.

"What are you thinking about?" she asked. Emanuel looked over at her and smiled.

"I'm thinking about you...me...our baby."

He reached for her flat stomach and rubbed gently. Jada placed her hand on top of his. She was only four months pregnant, but Emanuel had already begun to prepare for their big day. He had transformed one of their spare bedrooms into a beautiful nursery complete with hand-painted *Lion King* characters and the entire *Pride Rock* scene decorating the walls. Although the nursery was adorned with a unisex *Lion King* theme, he could not help but place a child size football with the Philadelphia Eagles logo on the shelf. That small gesture revealed Emanuel's desire for a son, but deep down inside it didn't matter if he had a son or daughter he was overjoyed at the thought of becoming a father.

"Our baby," Jada repeated, "I still can't believe that we are about to be parents," she said. "I would have never dreamed that life could be this perfect: a handsome, successful, and amazing husband; an awesome business; and, a baby." She blushed. "Wow...I am so hungry." Emanuel looked over at Jada and laughed out loud.

"What?" he laughed, "How are you going to go from talking about how wonderful and amazing I am to... you're so hungry?"

Jada also laughed at her ill-logical thinking. "My stomach was growling…and I just realized that I hadn't eaten anything all night."

"I sure hope our child doesn't have your short attention span," Emanuel said jokingly. Jada nudged him with her elbow and laughed.

"Shut up," she whined. The rain began falling harder and faster, making it difficult to see. Feeling nervous, Jada repositioned herself, this time sitting with her back completely against the chair and planting her feet firmly on the floor. The sudden heaviness of the rain made them both slightly uncomfortable. Jada turned up the radio just loud enough to silence the rain. The DJ was playing the smooth sounds of Luther Vandross's, *A House is Not a Home*. Jada hummed along until Luther began to sing:

"A chair is still a chair, even when there's no one sitting there but a chair is not a house, and a house is not a home when there's no one there to hold you tight and no one there you can kiss good night…"

Jada sang in her angelic voice. Emanuel relaxed a little bit as he listen to Jada hit every note just as good as, if not better than, Luther. Emanuel reached over and grabbed Jada's hand; he placed it to his lips and planted a gentle kiss. They made eye contact; Jada smiled at her man and mouthed the words *I love you*. Emanuel smiled back at her and mouthed,

"*I love you to*. He turned to look at the road just in time to catch a glimpse of what appeared to be an animal running out in front of their car. He gripped the steering wheel tightly and turned it hard to the left, causing the car to go into a tailspin. Faced with oncoming traffic, Emanuel turned the wheel again -- this time hard to the right before he lost complete control of the car. The bright lights of an oncoming vehicle blinded him then everything went dark. The only sound that Emanuel heard was

12

Jada's loud, piercing scream echoing in his head as the car rode over an embankment before crashing into a tree.

Emanuel popped up, sweat pouring down his face and his heart racing. It had been a year since that fatal car crash that killed his young wife and their unborn child and just as long since he had slept through the night. Emanuel blamed himself for the accident, and he wished so many times that he had died instead of Jada. He looked over at the digital clock that sat on his nightstand -- it was 3:00 a.m. on the dot. Emanuel leaned over and turned on the lamp. He dropped his head, sank his face in his hands, and sighed deeply. He tried many times at the advice of his parents, his best friend and his therapist to get on with his life, but he just couldn't-- Jada's death left him completely devastated. Emanuel continued to work -- in fact, after the accident all he seemed to do was work. He doubled his list of clients and spent day and night developing advertising and marketing strategies for them. Emanuel was a huge success professionally, but personally and emotionally he was a wreck. Whenever he thought about Jada his heart ached and since she was all that he could think of his heart ached continuously. Emanuel looked over at the picture of Jada that sat on his nightstand; he wished so desperately that he could turn back the hands of time and change that one moment that changed his life. If he were half way in his right mind he would have wished to GOD that things were back the way they were before HE took Jada away. But, so clouded was his judgment by the pain that he didn't want to talk to GOD. In fact, he began to question HIS very existence. Why would the GOD that he was raised to serve do something that HE knew would destroy him. Emanuel couldn't help but wonder that if HE was suppose to be all knowing, why didn't HE know that Jada's death would destroy him. Emanuel could not handle the reality of his life, and he knew that he could not afford to live in a fantasy world so he grabbed onto the one thing that he knew was real and that he had control over - work.

Kwanza

Chapter Two

The loud beeping of the alarm clock awakened Kay. She reached her slim fingers from under the cover and pressed the snooze button. It was 5:00 in the morning and Kay was preparing for her early morning ritual – her one-hour exchange with the alarm clock. It would go off every ten minutes and she would silence it every ten minutes by pressing snooze. She did this until 6:00 every morning, Monday through Friday, except on holidays when she had the luxury of sleeping in. Kay's role as club owner was very demanding and, at times, it threatened to consume her. But being the single mother of a six-year-old son, Khalial, she made certain that their home life was as close to normal as possible. Kay was a dedicated woman who gave herself completely to the things that she loved. Despite the fact that she didn't get home until 11:00 most nights, she rose early every morning to prepare a nutritious breakfast for her baby boy. Every day that Khalial wasn't with his grandparents or father they ate breakfast and dinner together; they called it uninterrupted mommy and son time. But this morning, Kay was feeling a little less like herself. All she wanted to do was stay in the bed and not participate in the day. August 28th, today marked the one-year anniversary of Jada's death and Kay just didn't feel like dealing. She and everyone at *Soul Sistahs* had worked hard for weeks preparing for the event tonight in memory of Jada. Not only had planning the event drained her physically -- it drained her emotionally as well. Her mind was often on Jada, but this week especially Jada was all that she could think of.

Kay could feel her heart heavy in her chest the moment her eyes opened; she closed them as she attempted to center herself. *"Where is my breathing?"* she asked herself in a soft tone almost like a whisper. This was an awareness exercise that she adopted from yoga, a practice that she participated in, in part. Kay often adopted principles that added substance to her life, and although her very 'religious' friends disapproved of yoga, Kay found certain aspects of the ritual to be beneficial, like finding her center. Kay tried to settle into a peace, as one of

15

her self-affirming mantras played repeatedly in her mind, "I can do all things through Christ who strengthens me…I can do all things through Christ who strengthens me…I can do all things through Christ who strengthens me." With every declaration she could feel herself becoming more and more relaxed. Five minutes later, with a new focus and a clear mind, she decided that instead of wasting her first waking hour playing tag with the alarm clock she would crawl out of the bed and start her day. But there was one early morning ritual that she wasn't going to pass by, and that was a greeting to her future husband. Kay reached over to her nightstand and pulled out a picture from the drawer. It was a picture of a handsome man dressed in a police officer's uniform. She kissed the photo and whispered, "I love you." She pretended to hear Malik's voice whisper the words back to her. Malik was Khalial's father, and since their break up six years ago Kay still believed that one day Malik would come around and mend their broken family. After Khalial was born Kay and Malik lasted for two years as a couple before they went their separate ways. Malik was a great father to Khalial and a good friend to Kay. She had never loved another man as much as she loved Malik, and every now and then she cried and yearned for him. She was perfectly prepared to wait for him, no matter how long it took. Malik was a homicide detective for the Philadelphia Police Department. He worked very hard, but, amazingly enough, he always had time for his son. On days when Malik was unable to pick Khalial up, his parents or Kay's mother would help out. Kay had a great relationship with Malik and his family. Now, with Jada gone, Kay's intimate circle consisted of Khalial, Malik, her mother Eva and Malik's parents; they all worked very hard to ensure that Khalial's life and his security were uninterrupted. Not so intimate on the list was her sister, Fatima and her father, Walter, also known as Karim. Kay's number one priority was to make sure that Khalial had the love of family, which was something, that Kay didn't always feel like she had growing up. Kay and her sister Fatima were raised by Eva, but Walter would make the occasional cameo appearance. Eva was too much of a realist to feed her daughters pipe dreams.

Her philosophy was that life rewards those who work hard, and
Eva was a hard worker. It was nothing for her to maintain two
jobs at a time. Eva only had a high school education, but once
Kay and Fatima got older and were able to care for themselves
and contribute to the household income, Eva went back to school
and earned a bachelors degree in psychology. She enjoyed
learning so much that she continued her education and went on
to earn a masters degree in psychology as well. Embracing her
inner intellectual she made it a point to take classes every
semester, even if it was nothing more than a creative writing
class at the local community college. Kay's relationship with her
mother was rocky when she was a child, but as she approached
adulthood the two became very close friends. They had grown to
admire and respect one another as strong, educated women.
Kay's father, Walter, changed his name to Karim Tariq Ali after
he had become a devout Muslim. He had always claimed the
faith, thus his children's names, but somewhere between going
to prison on a petty theft charge and fornicating with Eva to
produce Kay and Fatima, Walter, which was what Kay
continued to call him, had gone from neighborhood stick up kid
to neighborhood activist. He was the founder of a boys' home in
North Philly and was doing great things in his community. After
he found Allah he and Eva realized they were just not going to
work, so they went their separate ways --Eva with the girls and
Karim by himself. Eva had given Karim many chances to play
daddy and provide for them, but whenever things got too
difficult he would run back home to his momma. When Kay was
six years old Eva and Karim split for good. Over the years
Fatima seemed to try harder and harder to be apart of Karim's
life, and she too found Allah and became a devout Muslim. Kay
on the other hand grew more and more distant and attempted to
do everything opposite of Karim. If he looked up, she looked
down; if he said yes, she said no. Kay believed that Fatima only
adopted Islam as a way to stay connected to their father and gain
his approval, which was something that Kay never seemed to
need or desire. Kay was haunted by memories of Karim leaving
their family, and, for that reason, she clung to this fantasy life

with Malik; she did not want Khalial to go through what she went through not having a father in the house. Kay's childhood was not as rocky as Jada's, but it still had its share of dysfunction. When Kay was ten Karim married a woman much younger than him and the two had five kids -- half brothers and sisters that Kay did not acknowledge. Eva married many years later, after Kay and Fatima were grown and left home. She didn't deem it necessary to add any more children to the lot so her two kids combined with Stanley's two kids were enough. Kay didn't acknowledge her mother's stepchildren either; in her mind, her family consisted of her mother, her father, and her two sisters, Jada and Fatima. In fact, Kay was closer to Jada than she was Fatima – thicker than blood - they were soul sisters. Jada would always say that they were probably best friends in heaven who were lucky enough to find each other on earth.

Kay slid out of bed dressed in a pair of boy shorts and a t-shirt. She sat in the middle of her bedroom floor folded her legs and lit a candle. Kay closed her eyes as she meditated, remembering her sister who was no longer with her. She thought about Jada and recalled all of the fun times that the two of them shared together just laughing and clowning about the nothingness of everything. She thought about Jada's laugh and that made her laugh, she thought about Jada's smile and that made her smile. Kay found peace in the memories of her dear friend. Kay and Jada both had a deep love for God they believed every promise that God made was truth. Their main job was to stay connected to Him and that was what Kay tried to do every moment of her life and she knew that Jada had done the same. Jada's philosophy was that life was a gift -- it was part of a greater journey toward growth. She believed that it was up to every individual to live life to the fullest. They often quoted famous philosophers, theologians, and scholars like Lao Tzu Tso, George Bernard Shaw, Mahatma Ghandi, and Ralph Waldo Emerson, and even contemporary "philosophers" like Iyanla Vanzant who coined one of Kay's other sayings -- *Simplify your life*. By the time 6:00 rolled around Kay felt revived and renewed, and she ended her meditation with a conversation to her friend.

Wow… Jada I can't believe that its been a year. I never thought that I would be able to make it a year without you. Every morning when I wake up I pray that this is the day that I would really wake up, wake up from this strange dream that won't allow me to see you, laugh with you, or hear your voice. Even in the deepest part of my knowing I am confused as to how this world could continue to exist without you here, but I know that your spirit is here with me sitting with me even in this moment and I cannot help but thank GOD for the blessing of knowing you. So as I embark on this day, my friend, my sister, I pray that your presence continues to be felt just as strong today in your spiritual as it was in your physical. Rest in peace my sistah.

Kay raised her hands above her head and stretched. She shook off her sadness and stood to her feet determined to have a great day. She went to Khalial's bedroom and peeked in on him; he was sleeping peacefully. She hated to have to wake him up, but the day had to start. She grabbed a bottle of bubbles from his dresser and began to blow bubbles in his direction as she sang a quirky little good morning song that she made up, "Good morning, good morning, good morning mama's baby. Good morning, good morning, it's time to wake up now." She leaned over and kissed his cheek, "It's time to wake up my baby. Rise and shine." Khalial let out a moan and then a groan,

"Aww, Ma. Just a few more minutes, please," he begged.

"Sweetie, it is time to get up. Remember your dad is coming by to pick you up this morning. He's going to drop you off at school today and you need to be ready when he gets here."

"Aww, Ma."

"Come on Khalial you know how your dad gets when he has to wait on you."

"Yeah on your nerves," Khalial joked.

"Ha, ha, ha!" Kay let out an exaggerated fake laugh. "You got jokes hunh." She snatched a pillow from under his head and hit him gently with it. "Just get up man." Kay leaned in and kissed Khalial's cheek. "Up!" she insisted once more before walking through his bedroom door.

"I love you, Ma," Khalial said, just before Kay disappeared from his sight. She stepped back and smiled at her son.

"I love you too," she said, then puckered her lips, kissed the palm of her hand and blew him a kiss, "now get up!" Khalial let out a heavy sigh, and stretched his little arms in the air. The kitchen was filled with the smell and sound of bacon frying as Kay stacked pancakes high on a plate and creamy grits bubbled in a pot. Kay had just finished scrambling eggs as she called out for Khalial. She closed her eyes and took two slow sips of tea. "Lets go, Khalial -- breakfast is ready," she called out in between sips. "Your dad will be here in about twenty minutes." Khalial came into the kitchen dressed neatly in his parochial school uniform. He reached over and grabbed a piece of bacon that sat draining on a stack of paper towels.

"Ma I wish you could come with us to New Jersey this weekend."

"I wish I could too, but I have a very busy night ahead of me at the club."

"Tonight is the party for Auntie Jada right?"

"Yep, that's exactly right." Kay was proud that Khalial would remember such a grown-up occasion. Kay thought about how much she missed hanging out in Jersey with her "would have been in-laws" and she secretly longed for the day when things would get back to normal, when she and Malik would be back together again. It had been four years, but Kay was certain that Malik was only days away from coming back to his senses and realizing that they belonged together. She wanted to be with him, and she was convinced that he wanted to be with her too. Khalial's request was certainly in line with her desires, but she remembered why going to Jersey wasn't an option. "Doesn't Heather usually go with you guys to Jersey?" she quizzed, referring to Malik's girlfriend.

"Yeah, but I would rather have you there.

"Well, I am willing to bet that your dad would much rather have Heather there."

"No. I think dad would rather have you there too."

"Khalial. Why would you say something like that? I thought you liked Heather?"

"She's okay, but I like you more," he smiled, "and I think dad likes you more too."

"Your dad has been dating Heather for two years so I think you ought to get use to the fact that she is going to be around."

"I don't see why it's okay for dad to have a girlfriend and you not to have a boyfriend."

"First of all Dr. Phil," Kay began, "it is okay for both of us to have someone special in our lives. Your dad loves Heather and she loves him. I, on the other hand, am by myself because I choose to be. Thank you very much. Now eat!" Kay demanded, as she placed his food in front of him. Kay sat at the table across from Khalial with her feet up in the chair; she rested her head on her knee and closed her eyes as Khalial blessed their food,

"Lord bless this food we are 'bout to receive. We pray that it no-rich and stren-ten our bodies in Jesus name. Amen." Kay enjoyed her alone time with Khalial. They talked about any and everything that his little six-year-old mind could think to talk about. Kay encouraged him to express his opinions freely, which sometimes left her embarrassed and blushing. Because he was six years old he saw things from his six -year-old perspective, and, quite naturally, his views were different from Kay's. Half-way into breakfast the doorbell rang. Khalial jumped up from the table and raced to the front door of their loft. He stopped in his tracks directly in front of the door and asked,

"Who is it?"

"Dad," Malik announced from the other side of the door. Khalial didn't wait for any other confirmation he began systematically undoing the locks on the door. When the door sprang open Khalial plunged into his father's arms.

"Hey dad."

"Hey man." Malik squeezed his boy tightly and carried him inside. Kay watched their exchange with pride as she began clearing her plate. "What's up Kay?"

"Hey Malik. How you doin'?" she asked in a relaxed dialect.

"I'm good." Khalial let go of his dad and walked back over to his breakfast.

"Dad I will be ready in a few minutes I have to finish my pancakes."

"No problem, man. We have plenty of time."

"You hungry?' Kay offered. Malik looked over the spread.

"Everything looks delicious. You mind if I grab a few strips of this bacon?" Malik smiled shyly as he reached over and grabbed the bacon from the tray. "I forgot how good your cooking was," he said, chomping away.

"What? That white girl aint' feeding you?" Kay joked, taking advantage of the opportunity to point out Heather's perceived flaws.

"Heather is taking care of me just fine." Malik moved in to Kay and whispered, "I need to talk to you about something." His tone was calm. Kay looked over at him trying to read his expression but she could not. The only thing that she could read was that what ever he wanted to talk to her about was serious.

"Okay" she responded. "Hey, Khalial. Why don't you go brush your teeth and make sure that you have everything packed to take with you this weekend," Kay urged.

"Ma, I already checked my bags and I have everything that I need," Khalial whined.
"Well, go brush your teeth." Kay pointed in the direction of the bathroom.

"Okay." Khalial dragged from his chair, through the kitchen, and into the bathroom. Kay was convinced that the boy got slower and slower as he got older.

"So what's up?" Kay asked, although she wasn't sure that she wanted to know. All she wanted to hear him say was that he loved her and that he was leaving Heather so that the two of them could be together.

"I asked Heather to marry me," Malik offered, not wasting any time and without pause for breath or compassion. Kay tried desperately not to appear shocked by his news, but that was a difficult feat. It wasn't that she didn't want Malik to marry, she just hadn't let go of the idea that she would be the one that he would marry one day. Even though he hadn't touched her she felt like she had been assaulted and her body ached all over -- but more than that, her heart ached. His news was like a smack in the face that stung and left her vision blurry. Kay's mind whirled around Malik's words, leaving her dizzy and lightheaded. In a most discreet fashion she gripped the kitchen counter to brace herself because she thought that surely she would crumple right before him. Kay sucked in a deep breath. *"Where is my breathing? Where is my breathing? Where is my breathing?"* she repeated in silence. By the third, '*Where is my breathing*?' she had become more relaxed and clear-headed. "Congratulations. That's great news. I am so happy for you," she said, piling it all on at once, through a strained smile. She released her death grip from the counter and leaned in and gave Malik a big hug.

"Thanks, Kay. It really means a lot to me to have your blessing. I wanted to let you know and make sure that you were okay with it before we told Khalial this weekend. I'm not sure how he is going to take it," Malik said, looking to her for guidance.

"I-I'm sure he will be fine." She stumbled over her words. In her mind she saw herself responding more gracefully, but it took a minute for her physical to fall in line with her mental.

"So do you have any advice on how I should break it to him?" Malik asked looking at Kay attentively as if she could will Khalial to respond positively.

"No, Malik. I don't." He could tell that she wasn't as okay with it as she pretended to be. "You're such a good communicator. I'm sure you'll do fine." She concluded with more attitude than she wanted to display.

"What is that suppose to mean?"

"Nothing," Kay huffed. "I'm sure Khalial will be okay with the news," she offered bringing down her tone a bit. "You just have to convince him that Heather isn't trying to replace me."

"Is that his concern or yours?" Malik asked stepping closer to Kay forcing her to look at him.

"I'm just saying he's a child; he's going to worry about that." Kay offered as she took a few steps back. Malik nailed Kay against the wall with his stare. Although they both tried to ignore it, they knew that there were some unresolved feelings between them. If she had the strength to climb over the wall that she had built around her she would have begged him to reconsider his decision to marry Heather. She would have begged for another chance to make things work between them. She believed that she could love Malik the way he deserved to be loved -- better than any other women in the world. Instead, she retreated behind her insecurities, dropped her head and simply asked,

"Have you guys decided on a date?"

"No we are planning for some time next spring," he offered. Malik knew that Kay wanted to say more. He knew that she was still in love with him, and, although he didn't want to hurt her, he knew that it was over and that there was nothing more he could offer her other than his friendship.

"The spring is always a beautiful time of year to get married." That was the only truth that she was ready to share with him.

"Yeah, Heather always wanted a beautiful April wedding." As he talked Kay could hear the happiness in his voice and it was at that moment, she realized, she had to rethink her future -- a future that did not include her waking up or falling asleep in Malik's arms. On the outside it appeared that Kay lived happily in her own little spiritual bubble that protected her from heartache and pain, but Kay knew better; she wasn't above the drama she had just mastered the art of deductive reasoning and she was always able, after potential heartache, to reason her way back to happiness.

Chapter Three

Emanuel sat at his desk with his eyes glued to the computer screen. But for the glow from the screen the office was completely dark. A cup of cold coffee sat on top of a pile of drawings, sketches, and storyboards that he had designed for various projects. Emanuel was completely focused on the work before him. It was effortless for him to tune out the world around him, but when he was working it was even easier. Emanuel was oblivious to his secretary's tap on his office door.

"Mr. Rivers?" she called out. "Mr. Rivers?" she called again as she pushed open the door. Mona peaked around the door to see Emanuel sitting at his desk. "Mr. Rivers?" Still no response. It wasn't until she flicked on the light that Emanuel acknowledged her presence.

"Mona, please turn the light back off," he demanded as he rubbed his aching eyes.

"I'm sorry. I just wanted to check in on you to see if you are okay."

"I'm fine." Emanuel replied without taking his eyes off of the computer screen.

"Can I get you anything?" Mona inquired.

"No," he said sharply. "I'm trying to focus; I've been working on this slogan all morning."

"All morning?" Mona wanted to say, *"It's only 8:30."* But she refrained and turned off the lights as he requested. She assumed, based on his tired eyes and his 14-hour workdays, that he wasn't getting very much sleep. Mona had been Emanuel's secretary for two years, so she knew the man that he was prior to Jada's death, which gave her the patience necessary to deal with who he had become – aloof, easily agitated, and anti-social. Emanuel could be difficult to deal with at times. Over the summer, during her two-week vacation, Emanuel had gone through four different temps; the ones that he didn't fire ended up quitting. Khadir called Mona, because Emanuel refused to, eight days into her vacation practically begging her to come back to work. And so, she packed up and returned the next day, no

questions asked. Mona was old enough to be Emanuel's mother, and for that reason, it was very difficult for her to not act motherly toward him.

"Mr. Rivers, reading and writing in the dark is not good for your eyes. Why don't you just let me turn on this lamp?" She wobbled her round lumpy body toward the glass console, tapping the base of the lamp with her heavy hand. The light wasn't too bright, but it gave off just enough of a glow so that Emanuel didn't have to strain his eyes to see. Emanuel looked up at her and blinked hard as his eyes tried to adjust. As Mona looked at her boss she could see that he had been crying. His eyes were red and puffy. The sight of him in that state caused her heart to sink. She wished so desperately that there was some way to ease his pain. Emanuel had always been a tall handsome man with broad shoulders and unbelievable confidence, but over this past year Mona watched as he slipped deeper and deeper into despair. "Why don't I get you a fresh cup of coffee?" Without giving him a chance to respond she leaned over him and picked up the cold cup and in doing so she gently placed a hand on his shoulder. "You have a meeting with Greenberg at nine in conference room A. You have about fifteen minutes to get yourself together and be ready to present your advertising strategy." Mona walked out of the office with out looking back at Emanuel; she knew that he heard her because the only time he listened to her was when she was talking business.

Emanuel closed his eyes and rested his head in the palm of his hands; his head throbbed. He rubbed his temples in the hopes of easing the pressure just a little bit. He looked over at the clock on his wall it was 8:43.

"Fifteen minutes," he laughed, "more like two-minutes." Emanuel stood up from his chair his six-foot two-inch frame loomed over the desk. He turned and walked a few steps over to the window and drew the curtains. He attempted to let some light in, but the cloudy April day lacked sunshine -- its gloom did not offer him any escape from the depression that consumed him. Despite the cloudy skies and the lackluster mood of the morning he continued to stare out the window. He watched as busy

Philadelphians raced up and down the city streets to destinations unknown. He wondered how many of them would die before the day was over. How many had plans and appointments scheduled weeks in advance that they would miss because of this untimely, ill-logical thing called death, this death that did not care whether or not you had plans or promises to keep. This death that did not take into account the fact that one was young or old, rich or poor, married or single, happy or miserable. These thoughts brought tears to Emanuel's eyes and placed a lump in his throat the size of a golf ball. He wiped away a single tear before it began its journey down his cheek.

In the conference room Emanuel's confidence was strong. He was direct and exact in his statements, which left Mr. Greenberg and his colleagues in awe and very excited about the proposed advertising campaign. People like Greenberg paid Emanuel a lot of money to sell their products. Lucky for them the same Emanuel that could be found sitting alone and in the dark in his office was not the same Emanuel that would be found in the conference room. Emanuel returned to his office to find his desk completely organized which was a sign that Mona had come in while he was gone and straightened things up. There was also a huge bouquet of flowers placed in the center of his coffee table. Emanuel assumed that the flowers were from his parents. They were always considerate in that way. He walked over and leaned in to inhale the fresh aroma of the flowers. He closed his eyes, and for a brief moment he felt Jada wrap her arms around him, squeeze him hard and whisper, "I love you," in his ear. Emanuel cherished that moment. Jada had always kept fresh flowers in their home, and he was instantly reminded of the many times that he would walk into the kitchen and find her there preparing a vase of freshly cut flowers. She would smile at him and say, "Good morning, sleepy head," all a-grin. Emanuel opened the card and it took only a moment for him to realize that the flowers weren't from his parents. The neat hand written note read

Emanuel,

I pray that all is well with you. I tried calling you, but I guess you didn't get my messages or you were too busy to return my phone calls. I hope you can make it to the club tonight. I think you will be pleased to see how many people want to remember Jada on this day. My prayers are with you and remember that you are not alone. I look forward to seeing you tonight.
In Him,
  Kay

Emanuel closed the card not really giving much thought to Kay's words. It had been months since he had last seen her. After Jada's death he closed himself off from the world. He engulfed himself in his work and made himself unavailable to everyone. He didn't visit *Soul Sistahs* at all, and he stopped accepting and returning phone calls from everyone, unless it was business related. He made excuses to his parents why he was unable to attend their traditional Sunday dinner and eventually they stopped asking, hoping that one day he would come around. Khadir and Nadia were the only two who did not allow Emanuel to shut them out. They came by the house and just hung out even when Emanuel closed himself in his bedroom and slept for days. Khadir and Nadia bought life into his home, and they refused to let Emanuel feel like he was alone.

Emanuel's thoughts were interrupted by Mona's voice coming through his intercom, "Mr. Rivers, there is a Ms. Kay Ali on the telephone for you. Do you want to take it or should I take a message?"

Without hesitation Emanuel spoke in the direction of the intercom, "Take a message Mona. I have a lot of work to do so please don't interrupt me again." He scolded.

"Yes, Sir." Mona didn't realize until the flowers arrived that today was a year to the day that Jada died so she decided to give Emanuel a break and allow him to be alone, which was something that she usually wouldn't do.

Emanuel spent the rest of the morning in his office. He didn't talked to anyone and no one talked to him, and that was exactly how he wanted it. He sat with his chair facing the window; feet propped up on the windowsill as he looked out into the sky from the 15th floor. His mind was completely occupied with thoughts of Jada. He couldn't believe that a whole year had passed since that awful day. Emanuel closed his eyes and attempted to let down his walls, but the pain was too great. He hurt all over, and he felt like he would shatter into a million pieces if he didn't control his breaths, and so he breathed cautiously. Instead of allowing himself to feel that much pain he hardened his heart and mentally crawled back inside himself. Emanuel's door opened abruptly thanks to a commotion between Khadir and Mona.

"What's up E?" Khadir called out in his usual upbeat voice. Emanuel turned his chair around slowly to face his friend who was being closely followed by an angry Mona.

"I'm sorry Mr. Rivers. I told him that you didn't want to be disturbed."

"It's okay Mona." Emanuel stood to his feet and walked toward Khadir. "What's up man?" Emanuel asked as he reached out and engaged Khadir in a long drawn out 'brotha man' handshake. Khadir was like a big kid and it was obvious that he had annoyed Mona. She stood in the doorway with her arms in a knot and eyeballing him hard. If looks could kill Khadir would have dropped dead right there under Mona's stare. He stood behind Emanuel and annoyed Mona even further.

"Thanks, Mona. That will be all," Khadir teased. Mona was in mid-finger-pointing ready to scold stance when Emanuel interrupted her,

"Thank you, Mona," Emanuel said apologetically.

She was always surprised at how quickly Emanuel was able to go from being shut down and shut out to being seemingly up beat and happy.

"Well, can I get either of you anything?" Mona asked returning to a more professional posture.

"You want anything, man?" Emanuel asked.

"Naw, I'm good," Khadir said to Mona in his street lingo. With that, Mona backed out of the office and closed the door behind her.

"So what's up with you E?" Khadir questioned this time in a more serious tone. Emanuel's façade did not fool him.

"Nothing, man. Just working," Emanuel responded. Khadir walked toward the seating area in Emanuel's office and plopped down on the leather couch. Emanuel took a seat in the matching leather chair.

"I have been calling you all day," Khadir continued as he anxiously picked up different items from the coffee table, looked at them, and placed them back to the table.

"I was really busy so I told Mona to hold all of my calls. When you walked in I was just taking a break," Emanuel offered reassuringly.

"That's bull..." Khadir began but was distracted by the huge bouquet of flowers that sat on the coffee table; he reached for the card and began reading it with no thought of how intrusive his actions were. "So are you going?" he asked, referring to Kay's invitation.

"I thought about it, but I already have plans tonight" Emanuel began, being sure to watch his choice of words because he knew that Khadir could be relentless and would call him out in a heart beat if he thought for a minute that Emanuel was trying to dupe him. "Kay just sent those this morning. I didn't know that they were doing anything at the club." Emanuel watched his friend's face to see if he was accepting the story that he was offering, and when he realized that he wasn't he ended his statement with, "but I'm going to try and stop by for a few minutes."

"Cool. I'll go with you," Khadir stated, sealing the plans. "What time are you heading over?"

"Around 6:30, like I said, I have another engagement." Emanuel looked to see if this was pleasing to his friend.

"Okay. Well, I'll swing back by here at around 6:00. We can hang out for a minute then roll up in there together."

"That's cool." Emanuel wasn't completely against going so he figured he would be able to stomach things for 30 minutes. He just wasn't in the mood to have people come up to him every five minutes talking about how sorry they were about Jada's death, how much they miss her, and how wonderful they thought she was. None of that was going to ease his pain. He knew how wonderful she was that's why he married her and he knew that no one in the world missed her as much as he did. Emanuel wondered what kind of tributes would be presented tonight. One thing that he knew for certain was that no matter what anyone said or did it could not come close to capturing the essence of Jada; the closest that he was able to get to her essence was in his memories. Although he wasn't sure what he believed, he wished he had believed in reincarnation that way he could imagine that Jada had returned as a butterfly or some other small creature whose life expectancy was even shorter than Jada's 26 years, but then where was the comfort in that? His thoughts only made him angrier with GOD and there was nothing, absolutely nothing in the world that could change that.

"So how are you doing - really?" Khadir emphasized. Emanuel paused as he wondered,

"Did Khadir even care that he was absolutely miserable without her? Did he really want to hear that he was tired of people asking him how he was doing? Did he really want to know that if he had the nerves he would jump out of his office window to his death to stop the agonizing pain that constantly ran throughout his entire body?" Emanuel knew that Khadir lacked both the patience and care that was necessary to really want to know how he was doing; he was just being polite, so he gave him the polite response,

"It's hard. But, I'm dealing with it." That answer was easier for people to accept. Emanuel looked at Khadir and watched as he registered Emanuel's statement in his mind. Khadir shook his head in agreement after deciding that *I'm dealing with it* was a fair response.

"Yeah, I know that it's hard…" Khadir began. Emanuel tuned him out and finished Khadir's sentence in his mind,

33

"*...but it will get better.*" Emanuel focused back in on his friend just in time to hear Khadir's cell phone ring. Khadir looked at the caller ID before flipping its top and placing the device to his ear.

"Excuse me for one second E. I really have to take this." Without waiting for a response, Khadir stood up and walked toward the window. While Khadir stood with his back to him Emanuel sulked and sighed deeply under his breath.

Hopefully he has to go. Emanuel thought to himself. He listened as Khadir gave a series of okays and um-hums before finishing with,

"I'll be there in about twenty minutes." Emanuel smiled on the inside. "Hey, E. Why don't I meet you at *Soul Sistahs* around 6:30. I have to run to West Philly real quick."

"That's cool. I'll just meet you there." Emanuel stood up and gave Khadir a handshake and an embrace. Khadir walked quickly towards the door, but before Emanuel could breath a sigh of relief he stopped in his tracks, turned around and warned,

"Hey, E. You better be there." Emanuel didn't say a word -- he just nodded his head.

Chapter Four

The atmosphere at *Soul Sistahs* was very peaceful, the dimly lit room added to the setting. The scented candles that adorned every table and countertop sent a sweet aroma of jasmine into the air. Jasmine was Jada's favorite scent; so tonight, it was only appropriate that the environment embodied everything her. There were still photos of Jada, blown up in size, hanging strategically from the ceiling, paintings on the walls, and portraits in a silver frame on each table. Kay made a last minute walk-through ensuring that all was good before the guests began to arrive. She fussed over the smallest of details as she ran her index finger across the base of one of the picture frames that featured Jada.

"Looking good, Ma-ma," Kay said as she smiled at her friend who was smiling back at her. Kay caught a slight reflection of herself in the glass and adjusted her blazer. She was dressed in a gold satin pantsuit and a pair of gold-strapped pumps. She patted her hair down although there was not a strand out of place; she wore it in a fancy ponytail with huge spiral curls and the little makeup she wore gave her a very natural appearance. She looked more like a movie star and less like the bereaved business partner that she was. Kay was excited about the performances that were to come, but she was a bit nervous about her own performance. She was going to sing one of Jada's favorite songs--Sam Cooke's, *A Change Gone Come.*

There was a list of local entertainers and artists who wanted to remember Jada in their own special ways-- some through poetry, spoken word, song, or just kind words from the heart. To most of the artists that were scheduled to perform tonight, Jada was like family. Through *Soul Sistahs,* they were given their first opportunities to perform in front of an audience, that was completely Jada's vision. Kay stood in the center of the room and took in the scene. She was pleased and she knew that Jada would have been pleased also. "Well girl," she spoke to her friend, "this is all for you I hope that you like it." Kay talked to Jada every chance that she got; it was her way of coping with life without her. Kay walked to the table that she had reserved for herself and Emanuel and gave it the once over. A lavender candle burned in the center of the table and the flicker from the candle reflected light across a small 5"x7" photo of Jada that also adorned the table. Kay had planned for the two of them to sit together and enjoy the dedications. She looked forward to seeing Emanuel; it had been months since she last talked to him and even longer since she had seen him. It didn't take long after Jada's death for her to realize that she did not make the cut when Emanuel stood-up his support group. Although they were close when Jada was alive, after her death Emanuel withdrew and Kay could not break through his walls. She was hopeful that tonight she would have a chance to reconnect with him as they shared in Jada's memory.

When Emanuel walked into *Soul Sistahs* he was immediately greeted by a huge painting of Jada. This was the first time that he had stepped foot into the club since her death, and, although this was a celebration of her memory, he didn't expect to see pictures of her looking so vibrant and alive. Emanuel reached out and touched the painting. He ran his hand across the canvas; he moved his fingertips to his lips and then placed them on top of hers. Seeing Jada that close and life-like combined with the faint scent of jasmine in the air made his heart skip a beat. He could feel her presence hovering around him. Emanuel closed his eyes and found comfort in his illusion. He took in a deep breath. In his mind, he enjoyed the feel of Jada's soft hands stroking his face and her soft lips against his lips. He was so taken in by the thoughts of her that he did not hear Kay when she walked up behind him. Her presence only added to his delusion; she became Jada. Her gentle touch on his shoulder was comforting.

"You are so beautiful," Emanuel said, eyes still closed.

"Yes she is." Kay agreed. Her voice startled him. "Hey Emanuel," she greeted as she walked around to face him. Emanuel opened his eyes and was surprised to see Kay so close to him and sadly he was yanked back into reality.

"Kay...hi." Emanuel stuttered. She slid in and wrapped her arms around his waist, gave him a hug, and kissed him on the cheek.

"How are you?" she asked in her raspy voice.

"I'm good." He lied. In reality he felt weak in the knees; it was all much more than he had imagined. Kay stepped back, with one hand still around his waist.

"You look great," she exclaimed.

"You too," Emanuel said without really taking Kay in.

"I'm so glad you were able to make it."

"Yeah I can only stay for a few minutes. I have some work that I have to finish at the office," Emanuel said, offering his excuse early.

"Oh. Okay." Kay tried not to sound too disappointed. "Well I'm glad that you're here." She truly was happy that he was there and she didn't want to ruin the night by asking too many questions too soon. Emanuel's eyes drifted from Kay back to Jada's photo. Kay followed Emanuel's eyes "This guy named Mark painted that for the club right after Jada..." Kay paused, not wanting to say the words as if the mere mention would remind Emanuel that Jada was gone and cause him to mourn all over again - as if he ever stopped. Her pause turned into an awkward silence. Emanuel's sad eyes fell upon Kay. He expected her to say something more, but the look of embarrassment on her face was evidence that she felt like she had said too much already. He noted the sadness on her face and realized that he had not seen a sadder pair of eyes since he looked at himself in the mirror. It dawned on him that someone other than himself was also deeply aggrieved by Jada's death. Kay and Emanuel looked into each other's eyes and their pain connected. Kay prayed that tonight would help them both let go of their heartache as they realized how many lives Jada touched in her short twenty-six years on the earth. "Why don't we go inside and get you something to drink," Kay offered, trying to lighten the mood.

"Sure." Emanuel's distance was very obvious to Kay and she hoped that as the night went on he would be put more at ease. When Kay and Emanuel entered through the curtains that led to the grand room Emanuel was overwhelmed by the dé cor. Everywhere he turned there were photos and paintings of Jada. Photos hung from the walls and the ceiling. Kay watched as he looked at the pictures and portraits, and it was in that moment that she questioned her decision to hang so many. She wished that she had gone with the standard portrait in the club's entrance and maybe just one more in front of the stage, surely that wouldn't have been as overwhelming. Kay led Emanuel through the club, and instead of taking him to the special table that she reserved for them, she him to the bar, hoping that she would have an opportunity to remove the photo from their table before Emanuel would see it.

"Let me see if I remember correctly," Kay thought as she and rested her elbows on the bar, " Max!" she called out across the bar to the short muscular bartender, "Can you get me a cranberry juice," she paused, "on the rocks?" she added with a giggle.

"Actually, I'll take vodka and cranberry juice on the rocks," Emanuel corrected. Kay was surprised-- the Emanuel that she knew never drank alcohol. "It's a celebration right?" he joked, sensing her concern. The bartender placed the drink in front of him. He picked up the glass swished it around and took a long sip. The drink was sweet going down, but Emanuel didn't get the instant relief that he was hoping for so he ordered another. Kay tried not to show her concern. She wanted Emanuel to feel comfortable, but she couldn't help but wonder if he had turned to drinking as a way to help him cope with the loss of Jada, the loneliness, and the pain. Kay had no idea how heartbroken Emanuel really was, but after his third drink in 30 minutes she quickly got a sense of his pain. She hadn't seen him in over ten months so she had no idea how he was dealing with the loss of Jada. Back then she knew that he needed his space so she stepped away and gave him just that. She believed that his family and his closest friends were in a better position to help him. She continued to pray for him and she frequently sent him motivational cards and left motivational messages on his telephone to keep him encouraged. When she started making plans for the memorial event for Jada she really wanted him to be a part of it so she began reaching out to him weeks ago, but Emanuel never returned any of her calls. Little did she know that if it were not for Khadir's persistence Emanuel wouldn't be there now.

Kay walked Emanuel to their table after she was able to get one of her waitresses to remove the photo, but Emanuel did not want to sit so close to the stage. Instead, he requested a seat in the back of the club in a corner. The evening was full of poetry, music, and song. Artists took their turn on stage reciting and singing their renditions of who they thought Jada was, but Kay's soulful rendition of, *A Change Gone Come* was more than Emanuel could stand, and his tears began falling. He was glad that he wasn't sitting in the front for all to see his pain. As Kay sang, he remembered how much Jada loved that song. She would play the old 45 over and over again. The song held a special place in her heart and was the soundtrack to her and her mother's splintered relationship. But oddly enough it was the sole source of the happy memories she had of her mother. When she was a child, before Juanita began using drugs, Jada would sit for hours and listen to her sing the lyrics to *A Change Gone Come*, and Jada hoped that it would. Juanita would stand center stage in the middle of their one-bedroom unit in the projects holding her make believe microphone, singing her heart out. She always dreamed of being a famous singer one day. After her solo Jada would stand to her feet and cheer her mother on; in Jada's young eyes Juanita was already a star.

Emanuel's heart screamed from the pain of missing Jada. He thought that coming to the club tonight would be hard, but he had no idea just how hard. Remembering her in this environment was much too much for him to handle, and after his fourth vodka and cranberry he was finally able to relax – just a bit. He listened intently to the words that Kay sang, and he realized that they spoke directly to his pain. He didn't cry for Jada he cried for himself because just as Kay bellowed, *it had been too hard living*, and *he was afraid to die*. He hated feeling so depressed and hopeless, but, in his confusion, he believed that the pain was his cross to bear for surviving the accident. By midnight, the club had cleared and Emanuel still sat in the very same spot -- head cloudy, despite the fact that Kay cut him off two hours earlier. Kay ordered a pot of coffee hoping that it would speed the sobering process. Long after the last patron had gone Kay and Emanuel sat in the corner and watched as a few employees cleaned the club. The dead air between them was thick, and, although the night was about Jada, neither of them wanted to talk about her or their feelings as they pertained to her. They both were missing Jada like crazy and based on the fact that they were sitting next to one another it was obvious that they were surviving, but they both were curious to know how the other was really doing. Emanuel watched Kay throughout the night as she embraced the guest and contributors to the celebration; she appeared strong. Emanuel, on the other hand, grew terribly uncomfortable every time people approached him and offered their condolences. He watched as Kay worked the room smiling and greeting everyone. The only time she cried was when she sang, which only added fervor to her performance. Emanuel sipped the black potion slowly; the strong aroma turned his stomach.

"So how are you doing?" Kay asked in a caring tone.

"I don't know," Emanuel offered honestly. Yes, he was dealing with the effects of the alcohol, but the heavy-headedness of the libation was small compared to the mixed emotions that arrested his soul.

"Did you enjoy yourself?"

"Ye- yes," Emanuel stuttered. Kay listened as Emanuel tried to recapture the events of the night; his speech was slurred and his eyes were heavy. "Everything was really, really- real …you know?" She didn't know, but she pretended that she did. She was patient and prepared to sit and listen to him as long as he wanted to talk. She could barely make out most of what he was saying and listened very intently as she tried to piecemeal his words. Khadir sorta appeared out of nowhere of course with a woman on his arm. He ordered Emanuel a drink and kept it

40

moving. Kay assured Khadir that she would see Emanuel home safely. Khadir didn't seem too concerned with Emanuel's drinking. Khadir knew that Emanuel needed to relax and nothing could break down a wall like alcohol. Khadir had arrived at the club around 8:00 and was heading out the door by 9:00.

"Well," Kay breathed, "it's getting late why don't you let me take you home."

"I'll be fine," Emanuel replied as he attempted to stand to his feet, but he was unsettled and fell back into his chair.

"Whoa!" Kay extended her arms as she tried to guide his fall. "Why don't you give that coffee a minute to kick in." Emanuel didn't respond; he closed his eyes instead. He tried to will himself to sobriety. He did not like feeling so vulnerable and this made him angry.

"I said I'll be fine."

"I know that you are okay, but it's late and you had a lot to drink. You could hurt yourself or worse than that you could hurt someone else."

"Yeah right," he laughed awkwardly. "I probably drive better when I'm drunk. Hell, I was sober when I killed my wife and my child." He continued to echo a wicked, confused chuckle. Kay immediately realized his true state of mind; he blamed himself for Jada's death. Kay could not imagine the amount of guilt that he carried, so instead of trying to psychoanalyze him she just down played his comment.

"I could lose my club you know…if you went out there and had an accident," she reasoned. "Please just let me make sure that you get home safely." After some urging Kay leaned in and grabbed his keys; this time he didn't put up any resistance. By the time they arrived at Emanuel's house he was more sober than drunk, but still Kay decided to help him inside. Emanuel leaned his heavy body on Kay's small frame; she held him tightly and walked slowly towards his front door. Emanuel fumbled with the keys for a moment before Kay eased them out of his hands. She leaned up against his door, balancing his weight and hers against the hardwood for support. When the lock on the door unlatched Kay and Emanuel stumbled inside.

Kay secured the door and reached for the lamp, which she remembered, sat on the console. Emanuel released his handle on Kay and staggered a few feet to the couch.

"GOD, I feel like crap," he confessed as he hung his head in his hands.

"Yeah you were knocking those vodka and cranberries back like they were going out of style." She laughed; Emanuel laughed too, which frightened him. He, literally, had not laughed in over a year.

"Will you excuse me for a minute... I need to use the bathroom," he said embarrassed.

"Sure, no problem." Emanuel walked slowly, still a bit off balance, but he made it safely to the bathroom. Kay watched him until he disappeared down the dark corridor. She looked admiringly around the beautiful living room. It had been awhile since she had been in the house that Emanuel and Jada called home. She was surprised at how immaculate it was; it still reflected Jada's style even down to the dozen orchids in the crystal vase that sat on the coffee table. Kay took note of everything in the room: Jada's favorite coat which still hung on the coat tree; the set of tiered jasmine candles that sat on the glass console and, the wedding picture of Jada and Emanuel placed in a crystal picture frame. On the opposite side of the console in a similar crystal frame was another picture of the couple, a picture that Kay recognized as the one she took the night that Jada died. Kay looked so intently at the photograph that she didn't hear Emanuel when he came back into the room. He was able to walk up behind her before she realized that he was there.

"Do you remember taking that picture of us?" he asked, appearing a little more relaxed.

"I do," Kay responded, still looking at the photo. She had mailed the picture to Emanuel a few months after the accident, after she tried to settle back into life. "GOD she was so beautiful." Kay said out loud not really expecting a response from Emanuel so she wasn't surprised when he didn't give one. Jada's most amazing feature, was without a doubt, her smile, and in the photograph her smile showed the world that she was happy and in love. Kay looked at both of their smiles and she could not help but feel a heavy sadness in the pit of her stomach. It had dawned on her, in that very moment, that when they smiled for this picture no one knew that three hours later she would be gone, forever. Suddenly a lump rose in her throat and tears filled her eyes. She tried to get herself together; she had made it through the entire day without crying and she certainly didn't want to break down now, not in front of Emanuel. Kay's breaths were becoming shallow, *Where is my breathing? Where is my breathing?* She asked herself in her mind two times before she lost consciousness and fell toward the floor. Emanuel caught her before she hit the floor and carried her over to the couch. Minutes later, although it felt like hours, Kay regained consciousness. She awoke to find herself laid out on the couch with Emanuel kneeled down next to her dabbing a cool rag on her forehead.

"Are you okay?" he asked genuinely concerned. His mint breath invaded her nostrils.

"What happened?" Kay asked as she placed one hand on her fore head.

"You fainted." Emanuel answered as he continued to dab her face with the cool rag.

"Fainted? Oh my God! That is so embarrassing!" Kay closed her eyes and threw her hands in front of her face to hide her embarrassment. "You knock back vodka all night and I'm the one who passes out." They looked at each other and couldn't help but laugh at the irony. Although Emanuel didn't suppress his laughter like he had earlier, he was very aware of the fact that he was laughing for the second time in one night. "It was not that funny," Kay pouted, "Was it?" she questioned, feeling a bit insecure, but before Emanuel could respond he bust out laughing again. Kay hit his arm jokingly. "Stop laughing I could have really hurt myself."

"You weren't going to hurt yourself. I wouldn't have let you fall." The statement forced him back into reality; he heard himself say the words, and he meant what he said, but he was quickly reminded of his inability to protect anyone. With that reality came an attitude adjustment, and Emanuel suddenly became serious again, quickly retreating back behind his four walls: insecurity, disappointment, anger and self-pity. He rose to his feet abruptly and the smile that he had on his face just seconds earlier was now replaced by a stern expression. "It's getting late," he announced. Kay noticed his sudden change in demeanor and agreed that it was late and perhaps she should go. She sat up slowly not quite sure if her equilibrium was in tact or if she would feel dizzy, but she stood to her feet with no problem. Kay gathered her things; bid Emanuel a good night, and left.

Chapter Five

Three short hours after Emanuel's head hit the pillow he awoke, heart pounding and skin sweating. Jada's piercing scream echoed in his ear sounding very life-like. Emanuel sat up in his bed, his silk sheets covering him slightly. His lean, sweaty, muscular body glistened in the darkness. Emanuel closed his eyes to hold back the tears that tried to fall. He always awoke with a keen awareness of how empty his house was without Jada. It was as if every waking moment was a reminder of her absence. He tried to remember if he had ever felt so alone before her death and he had but he never felt the agonizing pain that he was currently feeling. The feeling that he felt now was certain it was very distinct; not only could he feel her absence in their home, but he could also feel the absence of her of spirit on earth. The world was different without her. At first he would pretend that she was just away on business, but after a few nights without her he could no longer kid himself into believing that she would return. It was that truth that made life so unbearable. After a few minutes of trying to get the best grip on reality that he could get, Emanuel began his usual early morning ritual: without turning on any lights, he eased out of bed, shed his sweat soaked shorts, and walked effortlessly through the darkness to the shower. He slid open the glass door, turned the knob to the left until it wouldn't go any farther and stepped inside the small cold space. In the darkness, with hot water beating down on his back, he cried loud and hard. In his anger and sadness he questioned and cursed God. Fist pounding against the wall he called out Jada's name until he strained his vocal cords. Emanuel did this every morning hoping that one day God would descend from His heavenly throne and speak to him. He wanted God to tell him personally why He took his love away. To a sane and less tormented person this kind of thinking would have registered crazy, but for Emanuel this was his life and he felt entitled to an explanation. He wondered if he was being punished for something that he had done in the past. He wondered if it was because of choices that he made as a young man that warranted this karma.

He thought about every questionable act that he had ever committed, every less than Christ-like behavior that he ever displayed. He thought about his years of womanizing, although his actions were minor in comparison to Khadir's, Emanuel still believed that he would have to answer for his actions. During his first year of college, before he met Jada, he dated a lot of girls and slept with even more. Emanuel was not perfect. He had his share of female drama; there were the one-night stands and the late night phone calls filled with tears and confessions from young girls who wanted more from him than he was willing to give. But his most disturbing memory -- the one that haunted him -- was the abortion that he demanded that an earlier girlfriend get because he wasn't ready to become a father. Maybe, he thought, the baby's death was God's way of telling him that he missed the opportunity. Emanuel knew, the moment the doctor told him that Jada was dead, that the baby could not have survived at only four months into conception. He wondered why God even allowed Jada to become pregnant if He knew that the child would not live for even a day. Emanuel could not wrap his mind around his reality; it was inconsistent with everything that he believed that the God that he was raised to believe in would do. The fact of the matter was that, as he saw it, he and Jada had a happy and amazing life and in a blink of an eye, without warning, she was gone. People tried to assure him that everything happens for a reason, and they reminded him that God doesn't make any mistakes, but Emanuel was convinced that there was no reason for Jada's death and that God had certainly made a terrible mistake. He was mad at the world, and he didn't think that there was a person in it that was worthy of knowing his true feelings. He realized that as everyone else had moved past Jada's death they became less and less tolerant of his sadness and more interested in moving him beyond it. His mother had taken a Christian approach and came to his house one afternoon with a group of women from her church. They attempted to lay hands on him and rid him of the mourning demon that had taken over his mind. His father took a more modern approach; he offered his son a prescription of lithium, which he copped from a doctor friend. He suggested that Emanuel medicate himself back to happiness. At Mona's urging Emanuel tried a therapist, but she only made him angrier. Dr. Banks's advice to Emanuel was simply to get over it before it kills him. She tried to convince Emanuel that if he continued to live in his fantasy world then he would slowly but surely lose his grip on reality. After Emanuel's first meeting with Dr. Banks he realized that she, like everyone else, was not interested in hearing what he was really feeling. She only wanted to hear what she was able to deal with. Emanuel understood that he was just mourning and that didn't mean that he was possessed or crazy. He was in pain because the woman that he loved was gone and he didn't think that there was anything wrong with wanting her back. He was sane enough to know that mourning was natural and he questioned everyone else's sanity when they suggested otherwise.

Emanuel stayed in the shower for an hour; the water had long since gone cold, but he didn't care, his tears were warm. With a heavy heart he stood there under the cold water, in the darkness, waiting for God to move. At around 4:00 a.m. Emanuel threw on a velour Sean John sweat suit and prepared to go to the office. He walked toward the door expecting to grab his keys and head out but he quickly realized that not only were his keys missing but so was his Mercedes.

"Man, where are my keys?" He instinctively patted his pants pocket. He thought for a moment then remembered that Kay had driven him home and he had left his car at the club. Emanuel pounded his fist against the front door when he realized that he was stranded in his own home. He paced the floor trying to figure out what he should do. It was way too early to call Kay and ask her to drop off his keys. He thought about calling a cab and having the driver drop him off at the office but again he thought about the early morning hour. In the sane part of his mind he knew that it was too early to wake up the rest of the world. Defeated and out of ideas, Emanuel sat on the couch, legs spread open and shoulders hunched. He did not want to spend his waking hours in this house full of sorrow, but he had no choice. He looked around his living room hoping that he would get a clue of what to do next. He noticed a picture on the floor, and as he walked over to pick it up he was reminded of Kay's little bout with gravity, and he felt the corners of his mouth move toward a smile. He looked at the picture and there was Jada, more beautiful than ever, smiling up at him. He ran his finger across the glass wishing that it were that easy to touch her.

Emanuel plopped back onto the couch he threw his head back and closed his eyes. He could not believe how empty his thoughts were and by default his mind automatically went to Jada and their short life together. Emanuel thought about the night before and how amazing the tributes were-- the singing, the poetry, and the art that decorated the club. His chain of thoughts led him to Kay and her beautiful rendition of, *A Change Gone Come*. She was so talented, just as Jada was, and Emanuel was truly blown away as he sat and watched her behind the piano playing and singing her heart out. Her soft, raspy voice with its neo soul flavor sang each word with dedication and conviction. Tears rolled down the cheeks of almost everyone in the club as they listened to her sing,

> *I was born by the river in a little tent but*
> *just like the river I've been running every*
> *since it's been a long time a long time*
> *coming but I know a change gone come...*

Emanuel was not a singer but he couldn't help but sing the words to the song as he sat there, in the early morning hour, alone,

> *"Its been too hard living, but I'm afraid to*
> *die...cause I don't know what's out there*
> *beyond the sky its been a long time a long*
> *time coming but I know a change gone*
> *come."*

A single tear escaped from his eye and ran down his cheek. He stared at the photo again and studied it. He smiled as he remembered that evening. He and Jada had finally managed to steal a moment away from the crowd when Kay came along taking pictures like the paparazzi.

"Say cheese you love birds."

"Cheese!" Jada said as she wrapped her arms around Emanuel's neck and struck a pose. She was always camera ready. Emanuel smiled as he thought about Jada's beautiful smile, and in that split second he felt whole again and he did all that he could do to hold onto that moment. Emanuel closed his eyes and settled into thoughts of Jada. He imagined that his life was uninterrupted. If this were a normal Saturday morning, at a more decent hour, he and Jada would probably be laying in the bed, just finished making love, which was how they enjoyed most Saturday mornings. Jada would probably be full of energy, as usual, laying on her back and talking non-stop. Emanuel would be half conscious, but completely at peace. Emanuel sighed deeply trying to breathe past the pain of remembering how happy he once was.

Kwanza

Chapter Six

    Kay fell asleep to her nature CD, the sounds of ocean waves were on repeat in her stereo. She slept peacefully and awoke feeling refreshed. Her eyes popped open without the help of an alarm clock, or a ringing telephone. She stretched her arms above her head and spoke out, "This is the day that the Lord has made I will rejoice and be glad in it." Kay yawned loud and the sound echoed throughout her empty loft. Her hair looked like a birds nest on top of her head. She released the clip that was supposed to be holding it all together and ran her fingers through her hair. She twirled her hair into one long twist then secured it to the top of her head with the same clip that she had removed moments earlier. Kay slid out of the bed onto the floor as she prepared to get into her usual morning workout routine. She stretched as thoughts of the night before played in her head. During her drive home last night she couldn't help but think about how Emanuel had gone from laughing and joking one minute to being totally uptight the next. She realized that he was still very much in pain. She remembered how she felt the first few months after Jada's death; she didn't want to eat or sleep, and when she did go to sleep she didn't want to wake up. She thought that Jada's death was going to bring her and Malik back together. He spent a lot of time at her house making sure that she and Khalial were taken care of. He allowed Kay the space to mourn and he was there for her just like he had always been. However, in Kay's desperate state, she mistook his concern for love. One night after Malik had put Khalial down for bed he came into Kay's room to see if she needed anything before he laid down to rest on the couch. Kay was feeling especially disconnected that day; she was emotionally overloaded. She wanted desperately to feel something, and, in her mind, Malik's arms around her holding her tight and close was just the thing to bring her back to life. She leaned in to Malik, and because he did love her he gave her the hug that he sensed she needed. Kay squeezed him as tight as she could and tried to make him squeeze her tighter but she felt nothing. Desperately Kay placed

51

her lips against his and forced her tongue into his mouth. Malik's concern for Kay immediately turned into anger as he aggressively shoved her away from him. Kay dropped her head in embarrassment but oddly enough his rejection was just what she needed to slap her back to life. After making a fool out of herself she realized that she really had to get herself together so that she and Malik could get back to their separate lives.

Kay thought about the fact that she had spent virtually no time with Emanuel over the past year. She thought that giving him some space was a good thing and maybe that would help him deal with Jada's death. Kay sensed that Emanuel had not dealt with Jada's death at all -- not only was he stuck between feelings of anger and depression but he also had a bad case of survivor's guilt. At least that was Eva's diagnosis as she analyzed him from a distance at Jada's funeral. Kay remembered the term from a psychology elective she took in college – survivor's guilt. She tried to recall what else she had learned about the term; perhaps it would give her some insight into how Emanuel was really dealing with the loss. She had so many questions; she wondered if he received any counseling or if he tried dating since Jada's death. Kay thought about all of this as she effortlessly went from one stretching exercise to the next. She stood on her treadmill and pressed a few buttons to get the machine moving. Kay ran at a moderate pace for her 30-minute dance with the treadmill. Fifteen minutes into her routine she welcomed the interruption of the telephone. She pushed the speakerphone feature on her cell phone and spoke breathlessly in the direction of the device, "Hello."

"Good morning, Kay," there was a pause, "this is Emanuel."

"Hey, Emanuel. I knew it was you. What's up?" Kay responded just as upbeat as she always was. Emanuel could hear her smile in her voice and instantly he got a clear visual of her in his mind. Kay pushed a few buttons and before long her fast-paced run turned into a steady walk. She dabbed the sweat from her brow and drank from her water bottle as Emanuel stuttered over his words.

"I, umm...I have some things that I have to take care of today, and I-I realized that my car is still at *Soul Sistahs* and you have my keys." Emanuel stuttered. Kay felt that his stuttering was not due to nervousness but because he didn't really want to talk to her. It wasn't personal -- he didn't want to talk to anyone and she understood that.

"I know. I was going to call you this morning but I figured you were probably still sleeping off those drinks from last night," she said jokingly.

"Well, actually, I have been up for a while." Emanuel responded without acknowledging her joke.

"Really, I thought that those vodka and cranberries would have had you out for most of the day." She laughed again but still he was unresponsive.

"I was hoping that, if it isn't too much trouble, you could drop my keys off some time today so that I could go pick up my car."

"No problem. In fact, I will do you one better. Let me get showered and dressed, and I will be there in about an hour to pick you up and take you to the club to get your car," she said a little less chipper.

"That would be great. Thanks. So, I will see you in an hour?"

"Yup. 'Round about," she responded.

"Okay. Bye." He hung up before she could respond.

Kay finished her workout with some stretching exercises before she jumped into the shower. She arrived at Emanuel's house just before 10 a.m. The beautiful April morning was sunny and bright, but a bit chilly. Kay was comfortable in her taupe *Baby Phat* valor sweat suit. She had her hair pulled back loosely into a ponytail. Her petite figure and the way she was dressed made her look like a teenager. The bounce in her step when she walked caused her ponytail to swing from side to side. Emanuel watched her from his window as she pulled into his driveway, walked up his drive, and rang the doorbell. He didn't know why he stood there watching her from the window; he felt kind of creepy, and when he realized what he was doing he laughed to himself. Kay barely had a chance to remove her finger from the doorbell before Emanuel opened the door.

"Oh. Hey!" Kay said, startled. She was surprised at how attractive he looked. Emanuel was at least six-feet two-inches tall and he towered over Kay's five-foot five-inch frame. He was Denzel brown, with very broad shoulders. His face was stern with a strong jaw line. He wore his hair tapered with an ocean of waves that were deeply defined like the Pacific. His face was covered with a neatly trimmed beard that met his thin mustache at the crease of his smile, a smile that, if Kay remembered correctly, revealed two of the most amazing dimples. His lips were thick and beautiful. Kay was embarrassed by the fact that she was looking at him in this way. The sun was bright so Emanuel squinted as he looked at her, which made him even more attractive.

"Hey," he said.

"Hey," she said through her smile. "Here are your keys." She dangled the keys out in front of him.

"Thanks," he said, taking them in his hand, "would you like to come in while I grab my wallet?" he asked, hitching his thumb in toward his house.

"Sure." Kay walked passed Emanuel without thinking twice about his invitation. "So I would have thought that you would have been hung over this morning." She laughed. "You had like four drinks last night."

"I didn't drink that many, did I?" He felt a bit embarrassed.

"Yup. One after the other." Emanuel grabbed his wallet from the coffee table and began walking to the door. He didn't comment on Kay's last remark because he was too busy trying to figure out if he really had drunk that much, and if he had, he wondered why he didn't feel hung over when he woke up.

"I really appreciate you giving me a lift to my car."

"It's not a big deal." The two walked in silence to Kay's arctic white Mercedes ML350. She pointed her keys in the direction of her vehicle, and with the push of a button unlocked the doors and started the ignition. The drive to the club started off slow there was close to no conversation. The first few minutes were filled with silence, which was interrupted by Kay's growling stomach. She laughed, embarrassed by the loud noises that were coming from her. "Oh," she said, putting one hand on her stomach, "I haven't had breakfast yet." she continued offering a reason why her stomach was talking. Emanuel didn't respond; he just looked at her and smiled slightly. "Usually I would have eaten by now." She twisted her wrist to look at her watch. Emanuel still didn't respond, but he heard a faint voice in the back of his mind suggest,

"Invite her out to breakfast." He took a deep breath and tried to ignore the voice. He continued to sit in silence.

"I don't know what you have planned for today but do you have time for breakfast?" Kay asked. Emanuel contemplated. He thought about how nice it would be to actually sit across the table from someone and enjoy a meal. He thought even further and realized that to have breakfast with her would mean that he would have to converse with her, which was something that he wasn't in the mood to do. When he woke up this morning he declared that today would be a day that he would spend in silence. But before Emanuel could say anything, his stomach growled even louder then Kay's had growled. "It sounds like you are just as hungry as I am," she laughed. Now it was Emanuel's turn to be embarrassed. He held his stomach, but, as hard as he tried, he could not hold in his laughter.

"I guess I am." They looked at each other and laughed out loud. Emanuel felt relaxed, and he realized that he had laughed three times now in two days and each time it was in the presence of Kay. He looked over at her; he didn't say anything. He just wanted to look at her. She was beautiful and vibrant; he wished that he had just a fraction of her happiness. Kay turned up the volume on the radio,

"Oh, my! This is my song!" She snapped her lean fingers to the beat and began to sing, *"Ohhh chile' things are gonna get ea-si-er ohhh chile' things will get brigh-ter."* As Kay sang lively, Emanuel tried hard to contain the faint feeling of joy that had begun to stir in his belly. He couldn't help but think about how the song reminded him of the movie *Boyz N the Hood*. He thought about the scene when Lawrence Fishburn was coming back from fishing with his son and this song came on. Emanuel was having his own moment as Kay bobbed her head and sang so loudly that she drowned out the radio. "Do you remember this song?" she asked in between her singing.

Emanuel thought about bringing up the *Boyz N the Hood* thing but instead he just gave a dull, "Yeah."

"You know what this song always reminds me of?" she asked the question but didn't wait to hear his response. "Remember *Boyz N the Hood*?" She laughed. Emanuel couldn't believe she said that. It was like she was reading his mind. "Remember the part when Lawrence Fishburn…" she began, but Emanuel interrupted

"…and Tre were coming back from fishing."

"Yeah!" they laughed. "And when they got back on the block…" she started again only to be interrupted once more.

"…Doughboy and Chris were getting locked up…"

"For shoplifting!" they said in unison through their laughter.

"Why do we even know that?" Kay questioned as she pulled smoothly into a parking spot in front of Bisoe's. Bisoe's was a soul food restaurant that sat on the corner of 48th and Market Street in West Philly. It was a classic hole in the wall but their food was delicious.

Once in the restaurant Kay and Emanuel were seated in a rickety red booth in the corner. They both scooted in their seats and immediately began looking over the menu.

"Everything looks so good," Kay started. "I think I am going to get me a nice big bowl of hot buttery grits, scrapple, eggs, and toast. Emanuel looked over at Kay and laughed to himself. She couldn't have weighed any more than one hundred and ten pounds but she had the appetite of a woman twice her size. After Kay ordered her "hungry man" breakfast but Emanuel couldn't let her out do him so he ordered the same, plus a stack of pancakes and a side of bacon. They both handed their menus to the nice waitress, who was a rarity at hole in the wall restaurants in West Philly.

"So how have you been?" Kay asked.

"I am fine." He gave his standard response.

"Are you really?" she questioned.

"Yeah." Emanuel offered again, this time trying to sound more convincing.

"This has been a crazy year. In fact, it has been the hardest year of my life." She continued sounding more serious than Emanuel had heard her sound all day. He could tell that there was something more on her mind.

"Yeah. It has been a difficult year." Emanuel agreed. His heart began to pound a little harder and slightly faster. He wasn't sure where this conversation was headed but suddenly he had begun regretting his decision to have breakfast with her.

"I can't even describe how much I miss Jada, you know? Its like I'm dreaming and all I want to do is just wake up." Kay continued to talk; she didn't care that Emanuel wasn't responsive because she knew that he heard her. "You know, I still talk to her." She laughed softly "Everyday. When I'm driving, while I'm shopping… all day, everyday. I talk to her and I know that she hears me." Emanuel looked up at her,

"Was she serious? Had Jada's death bought her to the brink of insanity as well?"

"Do you know that Jada and I have been best friends since we were five years old? She was the smartest and funniest person I ever knew." Kay's eyes were getting glassy. Emanuel didn't say a word. "I remember one time, we couldn't have been no more than eight years old, the same age as Khalial, and we had planned to run away from home." She laughed. Through her laughter a tear rolled down her cheek but she didn't bother to wipe it away. "We were going to go to Chicago and live with the Evans family." Emanuel's puzzled look prompted her to explain further. "Good Times. The Evans family -- James, Florida, Jay-Jay, Thelma, and Michael," she rattled off. Surely he was aware of Good Times. Every black family was familiar with Good Times, even the bourgeois Rivers family. "We thought that Jay-

Jay was the coolest big brother in the world, and Thelma, well she was just too fly." She laughed. "We didn't even care that they lived in the projects. We were just jazzed about the fact that they were a family, complete with mom and dad." Kay talked non-stop until the waitress returned with their meals and even then her mouth moved a million miles a minute as she shared some of her fondest memories of Jada. Emanuel, on the other hand, only listened. He enjoyed hearing Kay talk about Jada. He enjoyed the way she told her stories because he was tired of the recycled memories that played over and over again in his mind. He didn't give a response greater than yeah, un-hunh, and wow because he didn't want to break her rhythm. Emanuel couldn't help but think about how Kay reminded him so much of Jada. They didn't necessarily look alike, but their mannerisms were exactly the same -- the way she spoke, in that hard Philly accent -- an accent that wasn't as distinctive as a New York accent or a Jersey accent, but people picked up on it just the same. Her laugh was even like Jada's -- the way she started with a hearty bellow which quickly faded into a chuckle. Initially their likeness made him uncomfortable, but eventually he found comfort in her familiarity and he realized that he had felt more at peace when he was around Kay than he had all year long.

Chapter Seven

After breakfast Kay dropped Emanuel off at *Soul Sistahs* so that he could pick up his car. She decided to hang out and make sure things were in order for the Saturday night jazz crowd. "Well, thanks again for the lift." Emanuel said as he eased out of her SUV.

"No problem. Thank you for breakfast." Kay smiled, "Next time it's on me."

"Okay. I'm going to hold you to that." Emanuel said trying to appear comfortable but with their connection still fresh they could not stand the weight that a long good bye required and so after quickly running out of words they found themselves in an awkward silence. "Well, I guess I will see you around," Emanuel offered before turning around and walking toward his car.

"Hey, Emanuel," Kay called out, "don't be a stranger. I enjoyed hanging out with you today." Emanuel was speechless. He wanted to say something, anything, but it was as if his words were held hostage so he just nodded his head in her direction, turned, and walked away. Prior to Jada's death Emanuel and Kay spent a lot of time together; Kay practically lived at their house. Emanuel and Jada were Khalial's godparents; Jada was his godmother since his birth, and Emanuel inherited the title by marriage. He understood from the day that he met Jada that Kay and Khalial were her family and he had always treated them as such. Emanuel had never given Kay a second look; he realized that she was an attractive woman; her beauty was obvious, but in his eyes Jada was the most beautiful woman in the world. He never had a reason to look at another woman, especially Kay. Emanuel jumped in his Mercedes and turned on the ignition. His mind wandered back to the cold January morning in 1998 when he spotted Jada in a coffee shop on the corner of 15th and Broad Street in North Philadelphia, just down the street from their alma mater, Temple University. He walked swiftly down the city street braving the cold winter hawk. He was focused; the only thing on his mind was getting out of the cold, but the sight of

Jada made him forget the elements. When he walked by the coffee shop everything seemed to move in slow motion. Jada sat by the window on a stool like a goddess -- legs crossed, body erect -- her confidence was undeniable to all who saw her. Her long, lanky silhouette captivated Emanuel; he had to know who this beautiful woman was. The brisk winter air offered him the perfect alibi to go inside and seek refuge in the coffee shop. Emanuel sat at an empty table right next to Jada, she appeared to be very focused on her reading. He ordered a cup of hot chocolate and pulled out a book trying to appear astute. Emanuel stole glimpses of Jada, but with her face buried in her book she barely noticed him or so he thought. He could tell by her silhouette that she was very pretty, at the least, and based on her clear skin, long hair and lean body he knew that she had the potential to be beautiful. Jada was beautiful, and she was used to guys trying to get her attention, and she was use to ignoring them. Jada pretended to pay Emanuel no mind, but she had noticed him weeks ago on campus. She smiled to herself when she realized all that he was trying to do to get her attention.

Emanuel began his efforts by making little clumsy noises like knocking the saltshaker over on the table. When that didn't work he pushed his heavy backpack from the empty stool beside him onto the floor. When Emanuel realized that that didn't get her attention either he went into a coughing fit, which he thought would surely get her attention. When his hot chocolate really did go down the wrong pipe causing him to choke for real, instead of Jada coming over to his rescue, a tall, skinny waitress appeared tapping his back hard like a mother does when her child is choking.

"You okay?" she questioned with an attitude, like she was mad at the fact that he was choking at her table.

"Yeah…yeah," Emanuel responded, leaning forward trying to get out of her heavy handed reach. "I'm fine."

"You need to slow down on that hot chocolate." She warned. As the waitress walked away Jada couldn't help but laugh at Emanuel's silliness.

"Why don't you just come over, introduce yourself, and ask if you could join me?" she said with a smile. Emanuel looked up at her and realized that she was even more beautiful than he had imagined. He looked behind himself thinking surely she was talking to someone else. "I'm talking to you," she said, eyes peering directly at him.

"Excuse me?" he asked, still not convinced that she was talking to him.

"Hi. My name is Jada," she offered as she extended her hand out to him. Emanuel fumbled over himself trying to get to her.

"Hi. I'm Emanuel." He took her hand gently.

"Well, Emanuel, it is a pleasure to meet you." Emanuel was always a confident guy but there was something about Jada that made him feel like a shy schoolboy; her confidence clearly over shadowed his. "You can join me if you like." Emanuel didn't hesitate to gather his things and make his way to her table. "Emanuel, what a beautiful name. So is God with you?"

"He must be because I am in the presence of an angel."

"How cute." Jada smiled. "I bet you say that to all of the girls."

"Nope. I just made it up just now." He said, proud of his clever remark. Jada smiled at him and from that very moment he loved her.

"So, Emanuel, are you from Philly?"

"Yeah. What about you?"

"West Philadelphia born and raised." She sang stealing a tune from the Fresh Prince of Bel Air.

"On the playground is where I spent most of my days." He continued sticking with the Fresh Prince of Bel Air lyrics. It was rather corny, but Jada laughed any way.

"No. I spend most of my days in the library. What about you?" Jada asked sternly.

"I spend time in the library." The truth was that Emanuel was a marketing and public relations major, which didn't require that he spend much time in the library at all.

"Funny, I've never seen you there."

"Where?"

"In the library."

"Yeah, well, I don't go all the time. I do most of my studying in my room." He smiled.

"So do you work?"

"Work?"

"Yes, have a job?"

"No. I'm in school," he said it as if her question were silly.

"Me, too. But I still have to work." Jada stood up. It was only then that Emanuel noticed the café's name and logo embroidered on her shirt. She gathered her things. Emanuel felt embarrassed. Her statement reminded him that not everyone had the privilege to go to school and not have to worry about working. Without saying another word Jada grabbed a pen from her hair, reached for Emanuel's textbook, and jotted her number on a random page. "Call me sometime." She closed the five hundred plus page book and handed it back to him.

"Okay," he said through his dry lips. Jada gave him another breathtaking smile before she turned her back to him and walked away. At twenty-one years old he had never thought about marriage before, but after five minutes in Jada's presence he knew that he wanted this woman to be his wife. Emanuel searched feverishly through his textbook for Jada's number. Emanuel called her that night and invited her to dinner; she accepted without hesitation. That night at dinner Emanuel learned everything that he needed to know about Jada. He learned that she was as strong as she was beautiful and he admired that. Jada told him all about growing up in West Philadelphia and being raised by her grandmother, but she spared him the details about her parent's struggles -- she only told him that they died when she was young. Jada told him about her friend Kay, who was more like her sister, and Kay's son Khalial. Emanuel learned that even though Jada had earned a full academic scholarship she still had to work to pay for other unrelated expenses like food and shelter. She was offered a room on campus but because of Khalial she and Kay opted to get an apartment together instead. Even after Emanuel dropped Jada off at home he called her and they talked for hours. From that day Emanuel and Jada were inseparable.

Emanuel was exhausted when he left Kay; all of her talk about Jada was emotionally draining. Although he didn't do very much talking he was mentally and emotionally invested in the conversation. He was present in the moment as he laughed and cried on the inside. Now all he wanted to do was rest his head on a pillow and sleep. Emanuel took off his jacket and kicked off his sneakers before he drew the curtains in his bedroom. He stretched across his bed and closed his eyes, but before he could get too comfortable his telephone rang. He let out a heavy sigh and contemplated whether or not he should answer the phone. He knew that it was his mother, his sister, or Khadir -- neither of whom he really wanted to talk to. Hesitantly he reached over in the darkness and answered the ringing phone.

"Hello."

"Hey, sweetheart." Mrs. Rivers's voice said on the other end.

"Hi, Ma. How are you?"

"I'm fine, baby. How are you doing?"

"I'm fine, just a little tired."

" I called you earlier but I didn't get an answer."

"Yeah, I just came back in."

"Where were you?" she inquired.

"I just stepped out to get a bite to eat." Emanuel was a bit annoyed by her overly concerned tone.

"Oh. Well, I was just calling to remind you that our anniversary is tomorrow and make sure that you and your sister are still going to meet us at church and join us for lunch."

"Yeah, Ma. I didn't forget." Emanuel lied. He completely forgot about lunch and his parent's anniversary.

"Pastor Samson is going to be so excited to see you. He asks about you all the time. He said that he has been praying for you." Mrs. Rivers offered. Emanuel didn't respond because he was too tired to come up with a response that didn't include an expletive. So instead he remained silent. Mrs. Rivers picked up on his silence and continued, "We are leaving here at 10:30 to make the 11:00 service. Are you going to ride with us?"

"No. I think I'll just meet you there." Emanuel did not want to be held hostage all day by his parents' schedule He had learned from past experience that he enjoyed the luxury of being able to leave when he was ready.

"Okay. Well, don't be late," Mrs. Rivers warned.

"Don't worry, Ma. I will be on time."

"Did you talk to your sister?"

"No. She called yesterday and left me a message. I just haven't had the time to call her back yet." He yawned.

"Why are you so tired and so busy?"

"Ma…" Emanuel did not feel like answering to his mother like a child, but he knew that her questions would not stop. "I have been very busy at work and I didn't get in until late last night."

"Oh, that's right. They had the memorial for Jada. How was it?"

"It was really nice." Emanuel could feel his head becoming heavy. He wasn't in the mood and he didn't have the energy to talk about the events of last night. "Ma, I have a bit of a headache and I need to lay down. Can I call you when I wake up?"

"A headache? Are you okay?" Emanuel didn't want to worry his mother, which was easy to do.

"Yes, I'm fine. I just got in late last night and woke up early this morning. I'm just tired. I'll call you later."

"Okay, baby. You get some rest. I love you."

"I love you too, Ma," Emanuel said before hanging up the phone. He didn't bother placing it back in the cradle instead he disconnected the call and dropped the phone beside him on the bed, rolled over, and found rest in the middle of the day.

Emanuel slept for hours. When he awoke the sun had set, leaving his room completely dark; the only light he saw came periodically from passing cars. The flashes of light became entertaining; he counted the seconds between each passing car. After Jada's death Emanuel had picked up a few disturbing behaviors and counting had become one of them. Without thought he counted; he counted everything regardless of whether or not he already knew the count. He counted the number of windows in his bedroom, four; he counted the number of smaller panes of glass that were in each window, twelve -- forty-eight in all. He counted the number of tiles in his shower, three hundred and seventy-five. And so he lay there for no reason, counting the number of cars that passed by his house. The counting wasn't a compulsion; it helped him to relax in some strange way. He felt rested and his mind was clear. When the succession of cars became too slow to count Emanuel listened in the darkness at the heavy pounding of his heart. Why is it beating so hard, he wondered. He searched his mind for fear, am I afraid? Emanuel realized that this was the first time in a year that he woke up on his own without the help of Jada's alarming scream. He listened as his heart raced too fast for him to count or perhaps he was too deep in thought to concentrate. His heartbeat along with his heavy breathing was fascinating; it reminded him that he was alive. Despite the ache in his heart and the clear emptiness in his soul, he was alive. He wondered how the heart could continue to beat when it was broken? Emanuel hung his head as he settled back into his role as the desperately saddened widower. And just that quickly he was once again consumed with sadness. He was sure that GOD had miscalculated. How could it be expected that he was to live without Jada? It was impossible, yet here he was heart beating, breathing, conscious, and living. The reality measured against the thoughts in his mind just did not add up. It was distorted and required too much of his energy. And so he laid there in the dark and exactly on cue the tears began to fall and there was nothing that he could do to stop them. He thought back to Kay's confession at breakfast about talking to Jada everyday. He wondered if that really helped her deal with the pain of missing Jada so much. "How silly," he said to his thoughts. "People would really begin to think that I was crazy." He shifted his body turning his back to the window. Suddenly the lights from the cars became less entertaining and more distracting as he could see his silhouette. He didn't want to see himself because that image along with the heartbeat and breathing made him feel too real, which always made him feel guilty when he thought about the fact that Jada was dead, void of a body, a heartbeat, or breath. On his nightstand was a picture of Jada, smiling, and now as cars passed by the lights flashed across the picture giving him a glimpse of her beautiful face, he became desperate for the glances and with each passing car he would say her name. "Jada." He stroked her pillowcase -- the one that she laid her head on which he refused to wash. If he pressed his face just deep enough in the pillow and inhaled deeply he could still smell her. The scent and the image stimulated his senses and he could almost feel her with him. "Jada" he moaned, "I miss you so much." He squeezed the pillow as tight as he could. He took a deep breath and thought for a moment, *"If Jada were here, what would I say?"* He wondered. There was a lot that he wanted to say, but mostly he wanted her to know that he was sorry for failing to protect her. The room was dark but Emanuel closed his eyes anyway and began to talk to Jada.

"Hey Ba-by...," his voice started off shaky, "I-I really miss you," he continued. He took a deep breath followed by a long pause. "I guess you know that I have been having a really hard time here with out you." Emanuel felt very awkward, "I-I am so sorry. If I would have just paid more attention to the road, then..." he paused. "This is silly," he thought and with that Emanuel flicked on the lamp that sat on his nightstand and sat upright on his bed. He clinched his jowls and let out an angry growl then tensed and dropped his head in his hands. The quietness of the night was suffocating. Emanuel needed to get out and break free from the constant state of loneliness. His first instinct was to go to the office, but that feeling was overshadowed by an urge to see Kay again. A trip to *Soul Sistahs* for a night of jazz was just what he needed. Emanuel jumped in the shower and changed into something jazzy. He wore a pair of black slacks, a cream colored silk shirt, and a black leather jacket. He sprayed on a mist of Black and hit the door.

Chapter Eight

When Emanuel walked through the door of *Soul Sistahs* he expected to see the painting of Jada that greeted him the night before, however, in its place was a generic poster, which introduced the artists of the night. A young man, whom Emanuel had never seen before, greeted him at the entrance.

"Good evening, Mr. Rivers," he said, "How are you?" Emanuel was surprised that the young man knew his name and wondered if they had met before.

"H-i-i" Emanuel stuttered over the short word. The young man opened the curtain leading into the club area and motioned for Emanuel to enter.

"Enjoy your night, sir." He smiled displaying a bright set of white teeth, which glowed against his very dark skin.

"Thanks," Emanuel replied. He walked into the club. The room was dimly lit and heavy with patrons. Emanuel made his way through the crowd; eyes focused on one of the few empty tables. He noticed Kay walking around near the bar greeting her guest and making small talk. He couldn't take his eyes off of her. Not paying attention to where he was going, Emanuel walked straight into a waitress knocking over the tray of drinks that she was focused on balancing. With liquid running down the front of his shirt Emanuel apologized profusely,

"I am so sorry." Emanuel thought for sure that the young waitress was going to sass him out but she didn't. Instead, she quickly recovered the glasses from the tray and without hesitation she began dabbing at the moisture from his shirt.

"No problem, Mr. Rivers. I should have been watching where I was going."

"No. I should have been paying more attention," he corrected. "Let me pay for those drinks." Emanuel reached for his wallet but she would not hear of it.

"Sir that will not be necessary." She giggled and with that she quickly turned on her heels and marched back toward the bar. Emanuel was slightly embarrassed although no one seemed to notice his little blunder. He looked back at the table that he was eyeing and just that quickly two people had occupied it. He glanced back over his shoulder and found Kay still smiling and shaking hands with patrons. She wore a loose fitting black dress that hung off one shoulder. Her hair was pinned up in a curly up-do, and big silver earrings dangled from her ears. Emanuel found an empty seat at the bar and quickly took it. He swiveled his stool around to get a better view of the crowd. He admired the couples sitting together on lounge chairs and across from one another at tables. He felt a tinge of jealousy rise up in his spirit but he quickly rebuffed it. He changed his focus and admired the club's décor; it was cozy and elegant. The color scheme was bohemian inspired, heavy velour rich burgundy curtains draped from the walls. Against the surrounding walls were a few lounge chairs decorated with velour and silk throw pillows that complimented the curtains. People stood against the wall while others swayed on the dance floor, and some sat around the bar talking and laughing. A buff bartender leaned over the bar and said,

"Good evening, Mr. Rivers. What can I get you to drink?" Emanuel turned to the bartender expecting the same one, who waited on him last night, but he didn't look familiar and so Emanuel counted one, two, three – three people who he did not know, but some how they knew his name. He figured that there must be a picture of him in the back with a sign that reads, *Fragile. Handle with care*. He could have asked the bartender how he knew him but that was more conversation than he wanted to have so he simply ordered.

"I'll have a cranberry juice on the rocks." He laughed to himself remembering the time, shortly after he and Jada began dating, they were all out on the town celebrating -- Kay and Malik; and Khadir with one of his many lady friends. Everyone was feeling festive and decided to order drinks -- vodka on the rocks, Bacardi on the rocks, gin on the rocks and every other form of hard liquor on the rocks. But when the waitress got to Emanuel he ordered cranberry juice on the rocks and everyone bust out laughing, including the waitress. Emanuel laughed to himself remembering how easy life was back then. He frowned as he thought about how much he missed those times and how much he missed his life. The bartender returned with Emanuel's drink,

"Here you are, sir."

"Thank you." Emanuel sipped his juice slowly enjoying the bitter taste and mouth-watering sting that followed. The music was like medicine seeping into the soul and bringing with it an element of peace. The smooth jazzy sound floated through the air like a warm hug and wrapped itself around him. Emanuel closed his eyes and rode the waves of each melody. It was intoxicating. He tapped his leg lightly like a pianist stroking his keys completely oblivious to the world around him. A beautiful blond interrupted Emanuel's focus when she bumped his hand with her butt as she eased onto the empty barstool next to him.

"Oh, excuse me," she giggled. Emanuel didn't respond instead he grabbed his glass and took a second sip. "This place is awesome isn't it?" she asked, trying to stir up conversation. Without looking at her Emanuel just nodded his head. "I love jazz," she said as she sipped her glass of white wine. Obviously unmoved by Emanuel's lack of interest she continued to talk, "I can only think of one other thing that I would rather be doing right now," she said with a giggle, but Emanuel offered nothing back, not even a smirk. "Are you a fan of jazz?" she asked as she ran her finger around the rim of the glass. Realizing that the woman wasn't going to go away Emanuel turned and looked at her. Her beauty did not surprise him; she looked like a typical urbanite white girl: big breast; long, thick hair; botox-injected lips; and tanned skin.

"Yeah, it's cool" he said reluctantly.

"My name is Jenny. And you are?" she asked extending her hand to him. Emanuel hesitated for a moment; he really wasn't in the mood to entertain. He wasn't there to meet anyone new and he certainly wasn't prepared to engage in nothingness conversation with a stranger. Half-heartedly, he reached out and shook her hand.

"Emanuel."

"Well, hello Emanuel. It's a pleasure meeting you," she said trying to sound seductive; she lowered her voice as her eyes met his. Emanuel turned away and peered over his shoulder looking for an escape.

"Nice meeting you, too." He lied. He was completely uninterested in this woman.

"Would you like to buy me a drink?" she asked as she downed the last drop of wine from her glass. She licked her overly glossed lips.

"Sure. What are you having?" he asked raising one finger to signal to the bartender that he wanted to order a drink.

"Another Riesling, please." She blushed. "I'm feeling all warm inside. I don't know if it's you or the wine."

"I'm sure it's the wine."

"No, I'm pretty sure it's you." Emanuel gave her the once over. It had been a while since he had hung out in a club and by no stretch of anyone's imagination was he a lady's man so her advances dumbfounded him. He looked over his shoulder measuring the distance between him and the front door. "So do you come here often?" Emanuel sipped his cranberry juice wishing that he had ordered something a little stronger. Lucky for him Kay noticed his distress signals from across the room.

"Hey, baby." Kay squealed. "I didn't know you were going to be here tonight." She leaned in and gave him a hug and kiss on the cheek. Emanuel took a quick assessment of the situation and realized that Kay was trying to give him a way out and away from this woman who was sitting way too close for comfort.

"Hey... baby," he stuttered, "I wanted to surprise you. I just got here a few minutes ago." He leaned in and returned the gestures. Kay squeezed between the two and nestled between Emanuel's legs facing the woman. Emanuel wrapped his arms around her waist and kissed her neck, completely unnecessary, but Kay enjoyed it.

" Hi, I'm Kay-- Emanuel's girlfriend. And you are?"
"Jenny."

"Jenny? We don't know a Jenny. Do we babe?" she asked looking over her shoulder in Emanuel's direction.

"Nope. She was just about to leave."

"Yeah," Jenny offered, "I was just about to leave." And just as quickly as she appeared she eased out of her seat and raced through the crowd. When she was well out of earshot Kay and Emanuel bust out laughing.

"What was that about?" Kay asked turning to face Emanuel.

"I don't know. I think she was trying to hit on me," he said innocently.

"Don't you know that as fine as you are, you can't just come popping up in here by yourself and not expect these single women to pounce on you like a lion going after its prey." Kay laughed at her obvious exaggeration. Kay's compliment wasn't lost on Emanuel he heard it and was flattered. "At least she was cute...you could have been approached by that one..." she said, pointing with her pinky finger at a large, less than feminine looking woman who sat eyeballing Emanuel from across the bar. "I wouldn't have been able to help you with that one, brotha." Kay laughed again. Emanuel dropped his head in embarrassment. Neither Emanuel nor Kay realized that she was still in his embrace. "You owe me big time," Kay said poking his shoulder jokingly.

"Whatever you need just say the word." Emanuel lifted his hands in surrender then without thought he placed them back on her waist "I'm just glad you recognized my distress."

"Yeah well that's part of my duties. Besides you looked like you were about to run for the door."

"I was!" he said through his laughter. Kay threw her head back and laughed hard. "You're not in the county any more, Mr. Rivers., These city women are very aggressive nowadays so the next time you decide to pop in here on a Saturday night do yourself a favor – come with Khadir. He certainly knows how to handle the ladies."

"I have to remember that." Emanuel smiled as peace settled over him. His eyes locked with Kay's. It was as if they wanted to say more, but they both refrained. Kay's eyes softened and she took her bottom lip into her mouth, something she often did when she was nervous --a small gesture that only added to her beauty. It was at that moment that Emanuel realized that she was still positioned between his legs and he still had his hands on her waist. It all felt very natural, and to his surprise, he was comfortable and he didn't want to let her go. It felt good having her that close to him but he couldn't ignore the subtle feeling that was telling him that the two of them in that small space was not appropriate. Kay must have been having like thoughts and they both snapped out of it at the same time.

"Well," Kay said as she began to back away from him, "what brings you out here on a Saturday night anyway?"

"I don't know. I was kind of in the mood for jazz." Emanuel said as he shifted his upper body in a dancing motion.

"Jazz or vodka and cranberry juice?" Kay asked referring to the glass that sat in front of him.

"Actually this is just cranberry juice. Despite what you may think I don't drink all of the time. Last night was an exception," Emanuel said, taking his first shot at being honest.

" Of course it was." Kay continued to joke, but Emanuel was not amused.

"No, really. I wasn't sure how I was going to deal with all of the excitement last night and I thought that a couple of drinks would help me relax."

"A couple of drinks?" Kay questioned "How about four or five."

"Okay, okay so you're right. I had more than a couple," Emanuel responded recalling the events of the night before. He took a deep breath to escape his embarrassment. "By the way, I wanted to thank you for putting that together for Jada -- everything was beautiful."

"Well, Jada was beautiful. I wouldn't have had it any other way." Kay noticed something leave Emanuel's eyes. She recognized the deep sadness. "I was just really happy that you were able to make it." She tried to recover. "Everyone worked so hard to make the night special."

"And it was," Emanuel concurred. "It was very special." He smiled.

"A bit of an emotional roller coaster though." Kay rolled her eyes toward the ceiling. "Jada was always the organized one. She had a real knack for attention to detail."

"You did a great job, Kay. I think you paid great attention to detail."

"Thank you," she smiled "One minute I was crying, the next I was laughing and in between there were tears of joy," Kay said, remembering the ups and downs of the night before.

"I wish I could say that I know what you mean, but I basically cried all night. It's been a very long time since I cried tears of joy. As I think about it, the last time I cried tears of joy was when Jada told me that we were having a baby." The words escaped his lips before he had time to think them away. A part of him wanted to unleash and tell Kay all about his pain. He felt like she would understand, and tell him that what he was feeling was okay. But the part of him that was silenced by his family and friends was afraid to open up. That part of him was tired of feeling rejected so he willingly embraced isolation. "I can't believe how sad I am."

"Well, I guess we will have to do something about that." Kay said as she reached out and removed a piece of lint from his shirt. "Sadness is a difficult emotion to manage. It seems to come out of nowhere. You can remember something sad that happened a long time ago and the moment you are reminded of it you are right back in that place as if time had never passed." The conversation was quickly becoming more serious than Kay wanted. She knew that there was a word from God that she needed to share with Emanuel, but she also knew that God would offer her another opportunity, so she took Emanuel's hands in hers,

"Come dance with me."

"Oh, no." Emanuel protested.

"Come on." Kay tugged at him a little harder. "You owe me remember." Kay looked over her shoulder, "you see that guy against the wall in the dark suit." There were several men against

the wall in dark suits. "I think he likes me, but I don't like him."
She said sounding like a little girl. "I pretended to be your
woman to get you out of a sticky situation so now I need you to
pretend that you are my man." Kay said rolling her neck.

"Kay, you can't be serious."

"Oh, but I am." She said and turned her back to him and
danced seductively against him. Emanuel placed his hands on
her waist. She leaned her head back against him.

"I have been telling this guy that I have a man for
months, and what better way to get him off my back than by
pretending that you are my man." Kay all but dragged Emanuel
to the dance floor, but this time, he put up little protest. The
musician was playing a slow tune that Emanuel recognized, but
couldn't quite recall at that moment. He and Kay found a place
on the dance floor, she wrapped his arms around her waist and
rested hers on top of his shoulders; they swayed to the music.
Kay moved in closely against Emanuel pressing her body against
his. Emanuel grew increasingly nervous. His mind flashed back
to a year ago almost to the day when he and Jada shared a dance
on this very dance floor. He suddenly became light headed and
his mind raced in a panic, the events of that night looped in his
memory at an accelerated rate of speed causing him to feel
dizzy.

"I'm sorry, Kay. I'm not feeling too well." He stepped
aside.

"Do you need some water, or something?" Kay noticed
that Emanuel was sweating profusely. "Hey, let's sit down." She
led him back over to the bar.

"Max, a glass of water please."

"I am so sorry. I don't know what came over me," he
said before he drank his water. Immediately Emanuel began to
relax a little more. Kay recognized the act as a panic attack
because she had experienced the same symptoms after her breakup with Malik. She knew that all he needed to do was relax. So
in her motherly way, she reached over and began to massage his
shoulders.

"So you were in the mood for jazz, eh." She flashed a sweet smile. And just that quickly she put him back at ease.

"Yes." Emanuel smiled embarrassingly. He did come to the club for the music, but mostly he wanted to see Kay, there was a part of him that wanted and needed to be around her. "Okay, so you must think that I am the biggest idiot ever. First you have to drive me home because I drank too much and now this. Can I buy you a drink?"

"You could, but your money is no good here."

"Why not?"

"Because you own half of everything in here." Kay smirked.

"I don't understand."

"You do realize that you inherited Jada's interest in the club?" The look on Emanuel's face showed Kay that he had no idea what she was talking about. So she continued, "After Jada's death..." Kay paused, even after a year the words were thick coming from her lips and it became even more difficult to say them in front of Emanuel. "You inherited her share of the club. You are equal owner with me." Emanuel hadn't really paid much attention to the business side of things. The thought of the club never crossed his mind. After Jada passed he vaguely recalled his attorney saying something about *Soul Sistahs*, but there were a whole lot of people telling him a lot of stuff and even now he still had not given his attention to those matters. He was too busy trying to manage the basics like remembering to breathe when everything in him wanted to die. He didn't want to concern himself with business, at least not tonight, so he made a mental note to himself, to check into it on Monday. In the meantime all he wanted to do was enjoy the night in the company of the only person that he actually yearned to talk to.

"Well, let me rephrase that...would you join me for a drink?" he said through a dimpled smile.

"Absolutely." Kay smiled back at him. "Max!" she called out to the bartender.

"Yes."

"We would like a bottle of white wine." She ordered without conferring with Emanuel. "Can you send it over to us in VIP along with a couple of menus."

"Yes, ma'am."

"VIP? Are we doing it like that?" Emanuel asked.

"Emanuel, you're the owner. Where else would you sit?" Kay took Emanuel's hand in hers; he didn't resist her and like a little child he let her lead him. Kay plopped down on the couch hard causing her feet to fling in the air, but she was so beautiful that it didn't take away from her elegance. "This is the first time I sat down all night." Kay exhaled. Candles burned on the table in front of them as they sat together being sure to maintain a friendly, non-intimate, space between them. Emanuel admired her bare shoulder, tanned the color of bronze. He licked his lips as thoughts of kissing her shoulder entered his mind. One of his favorite things in the world was to kiss Jada's narrow shoulder before laying his head on it. Everything about Kay reminded him of Jada even down to the smallest detail like the barely there diamond nose ring. Kay laid her head back on a silk pillow. The live jazz music playing in the background was very relaxing. Emanuel watched as Kay sat with her head back and her eyes closed. Under the dim lights Emanuel couldn't help but notice how much Kay resembled Jada. He watched her carefully for any glimpse of Jada and when he saw it his heart filled. His mind began to play tricks on him and right before his eyes Kay became Jada. He watched in amazement and great pleasure as she transformed. The young waitress that Emanuel collided with earlier arrived at their table with a bottle of wine and two menus. "Thanks Lydia, can you give us a few minutes."

"Yes, ma'am." Lydia disappeared back into the crowd.

"Have you eaten anything today?"

Emanuel thought for a minute and realized that he hadn't eaten anything since breakfast. "Not since we had breakfast."

"Well, our chef is a master in the kitchen. What will you have?"

Emanuel looked over the menu, but it required more thought then he wanted to give it. "I don't know. What do you recommend?"

"His lamb meatballs over spaghetti in a white sauce are to die for." Kay offered without hesitation. She raised her hand high and signaled to the waitress. Kay placed the order and poured two glasses of wine. She handed one to Emanuel and kept the other one for herself. "Here's to Jada."

"To Jada." Emanuel echoed, then took a short sip. "Earlier you said that there was this guy trying to hook up with you. What's that all about?"

"Oh, I don't know. This African guy comes to the club every weekend and he tries to stir up small talk. He's asked me out a few times and I keep telling him that I already have a man. But he says, in this thick accent that I can barely understand, 'I never see you with anyone,'" Kay laughed as she tried to duplicate his accent.

"So, I take it that you really don't have a man in your life?"

"Nope." Kay sighed and sipped her wine.

"Why not?" Kay thought for a moment then laughed under her breath, no way was she going tell Emanuel that she was waiting for Malik to take her back. Reality set in as she was reminded of the news that Malik broke to her the other morning – he and Heather are getting married. So instead of sharing with Emanuel the desperate details of her life she simply said,

"I don't know. I guess between Khalial and the club I really don't have time. So what about you? Dare I ask if you have dated anyone?"

"No." Emanuel responded sharply. He wasn't angry by Kay's question, he just felt like asking it was a way of saying that he needs to move on.

"Do you feel like it's too soon?"

"Really, I haven't thought about it."

"You haven't thought about dating or whether or not it's too soon?"

"Neither."

"So how are you doing?"

"Things are fine. Just working like crazy."

"Yeah I hear you're a real big shot in the PR and advertising world."

"I do alright." He was modest.

"Alright? Landing Randolph Emerson's big Atlantic City venture is more than alright."

"How did you hear about that?"

"Good news travels. Besides, it's the nature of the business to know whose who."

"Yeah, well, I don't know if I am listed amongst the who's who."

"Well, that's the thing -- you're not supposed to know. It's a title that others give you." Kay crossed her ankles and turned to face Emanuel taking a more serious posture. "Not only are you one of the who's who of Philly, you are listed amongst the who's who across the entire tri-state area and that is no easy feat with New York less than a few hours away." Kay assured. Emanuel thought about her words; that really was the last thing in the world that he was trying to do – make a name for himself. But he was good at what he did and without much effort he was a creative genius. "Your reputation has exceeded you." Emanuel took no pleasure in Kay's compliment. He looked towards the stage at the tall, dark music man playing his trumpet, his jowls blown up like the great Gillespie. The rough sound of music escaped from his instrument and engulfed the room.

"He is incredible," Emanuel said referring to the musician.

"Yes he is. You're pretty good at changing the topic." Emanuel dropped his head and smiled.

"We don't have to change the topic." Emanuel looked Kay right in the eyes giving the impression that he was confident. "We can talk about whatever you want to talk about." He took another sip of wine.

"Anything?"

"Anything."

"Even Jada?"

"Even Jada." He said with a shrug of his shoulders.

"Okay." Kay thought for a minute. "I know that I really miss her." She paced herself. "I can only imagine what you're feeling and what this past year has been like for you." Kay settled more deeply in her seat. "Last night as I listened to everyone talk about Jada it just reminded me of how much of a blessing she was to so many people. You know?" Emanuel would have agreed with Kay's assessment but she lost him with the term blessing. He wasn't sure how he would have described the effect that Jada had on those people who wanted to remember her, but he wasn't prepared to call it a blessing. *If she was a blessing,* he thought to himself *then why was she taken away?*

"She touched a lot of lives." Emanuel rephrased his agreement.

"Yes she did." They both settled into their own thoughts of Jada. "Does it make you uncomfortable to talk about her?"

"No." He lied.

"Because you look a little uncomfortable."

"I'm not uncomfortable at all." He spoke in almost a whisper. In fact this was the most comfortable he had been all night, but he wasn't going to tell her that. "So if you want to talk about Jada? Let's talk about Jada. What do you want to know?" he asked shifting his body to face her.

"Um, let me see. How are you dealing with life without her?"

"I'm not." Emanuel responded instantly without thought.

"What do you mean, you're not?"

"I mean I'm not. It's like I know that she is gone because I don't see her or feel her, but it's like my mind is playing tricks on me because I just don't know deep down inside that she's gone." What he said made absolutely no sense to Kay but she listened anyway without interruption. "Since that day I haven't slept through the night; I haven't gone through one day without missing her like crazy; my heart aches continuously. I swear one day it's going to explode, that is if my head doesn't explode first." Emanuel rambled on, and to his surprise Kay didn't flinch at his confession; instead she listened very intently. He could see the compassion in her eyes. "So, yeah," he said as a matter of fact "basically, I'm not dealing with it."

"I know what you mean. I didn't realize how huge a part she played in my life until I woke up that next morning and I couldn't call her." Kay said looking out into the dim distance. "I never lost someone who was that close to me. For months, no matter how hard I tried; I just couldn't seem to get myself together. There was no peace, only a huge void in the world that left the entire universe off balance. So it seemed."

"Yeah that's about the size of it. That's how I feel everyday. Like my world is off balance."

"But even in the midst of the unbalance we have to learn how to honor God's rhythm."

"Is there a rhythm to this madness? Because it all just sounds very calypso."

"Well calypso is music too." Kay nudged his arm in an attempt to lighten the mood. Kay's eyes locked with Emanuel's. "I was so worried about you. I knew that if I was missing her so desperately then you must have been insane with grief." Emanuel's eyes lit up,

Did she really know how I felt? Did she know that he had gone insane? He wondered to himself. "So how did you deal with it?"

"Well at first I was in complete shock so I didn't feel anything, but then a few days, after the funeral when things started to settle a bit I was so angry."

Angry with God? Emanuel wondered to himself and waited on edge for her next words.

"So angry with life and what it meant. She was so young and so beautiful. You know. The last time I talked to her she was so happy." Kay exhaled letting out the tinge of anger that tried to set in. "The fact that someone could be here one minute and gone the next... forever." Tears filled Kay's eyes but she never took her gaze off of Emanuel. Then with one gentle blink the tears released and rolled down her cheek. Emanuel's heart felt heavy in his chest and grief rose in his throat. He swallowed hard refusing to cry in front of Kay. "If only my anguish could be weighed and all my misery be placed on the scales! It would surely outweigh the sand of the seas," she said poetically. Emanuel held on to every word.

"If only my anguish could be weighed." Emanuel repeated. " That's beautiful. Did you write that?" Kay giggled despite her tears.

"No. I'm not that good."

"Who is that?"

"Job." Kay laughed even harder.

"Job?" Emanuel questioned.

"Job- from the bible, the book of Job, old testament, between Esther and Psalms. Surely you are familiar with the book of Job."

"Of course I am." And he was, it had just been some time since he heard it referenced. The months following Jada's death just about every Christian that he came across referenced the book of Job. "*You ought to read the book of Job,*" they said, *"he lost everything but he never cursed God."* Emanuel was familiar with the story of Job, but it had been some time since he read it, or any part of the bible for that matter.

"You should read it. It is a phenomenal story."

"Phenomenal. That's a pretty strong description."

"I'm just being honest. It's this series of dialogue between Job and his friends. And Job wants to know why he has lost everything and he goes through this period of mourning -- this period of questioning God." Emanuel didn't want to be interested in what she was saying, but he was,

Could it be that Job questioned God? He wondered to himself, but dared not ask.

"Then God answered him." Kay said excitedly as she took on a loud, bold voice, "Who is this that darkens my counsel with words without knowledge?" Emanuel was on edge with anticipation. "Would you discredit my justice? Would you condemn me to justify yourself?" Kay exclaimed. "Phenomenal, I'm telling you. You have to read it." Kay reached for her glass and took a short sip. Emanuel was very interested in the story of

81

Job and he wanted to know how it ended, thinking that somewhere in the tale would be the answers to his questions. "So if you don't mind me asking, did you get any counseling to help you cope with losing Jada?" Kay felt like the question may have been too personal, but she wanted to know and something told her that Emanuel wanted to share. Kay's voice was calming; she had a way of speaking that was non-threatening and that helped Emanuel open up.

"I went to two counseling sessions, but I didn't think that they were helpful."

"Why not?" Kay asked. Emanuel laughed a nervous laugh as he thought about the reasons why he didn't find counseling helpful.

"I don't know. I just felt like everyone was telling me that I was wrong for feeling the way that I was feeling. It was like no one understood why I was sad." Emanuel replayed his response in his mind he thought it to be elementary but he hoped that Kay understood what he was trying to say.

"It was probably just too soon. Sometimes people really don't know what to say or how to say it and they can come off sounding a little insensitive."

"I suppose." Emanuel was over the conversation. He didn't want to talk about his counseling sessions.

"Mourning can be a long, fragile process." Kay said in her best psychologist voice. "You know, I really wanted to be there for you." She said more seriously. "I tried calling you for months after." Emanuel didn't realize that he had hurt her; he was too busy trying to manage his own pain to think about the possibility of his actions hurting anyone else. "I was trying to figure out what I had done. Why you were so angry with me."

"I wasn't angry with you. I was angry with life; with God." Despite his attempt at transparency Emanuel didn't want that to slip out, but like a professional listener Kay didn't skip a beat.

"Yeah, I got that revelation a few months later. I realized that you needed your space to find your own way of dealing with things." Emanuel appeared deep in thought. "Did you know that there are something like five stages of mourning? There's denial, anger, depression, guilt and…" Kay looked towards the ceiling for the answer to the fifth.

"Bargaining," Emanuel added. Of course he knew; he had been in continuous rotation from one stage to the next.

"Yeah, bargaining." She lowered her voice as she realized that he probably knew better than most. "So where are you in the process?" she asked.

Emanuel took a quick inventory of his emotions. He had been teetering between anger and guilt, but at that moment he was feeling more angry than guilty. Emanuel prepared to answer her question, but his words could not get around the lump that filled his throat. Still committed to not crying in front of Kay he focused on holding back his tears, as he forced his words out.

"I am angry as hell." His words were exact and Kay could hear the contempt in his voice. Emanuel's heart was so heavy that it pulled his head down to his chest. Kay reached in, cupped his chin in her hand and lifted his head up. "That night just keeps playing over and over again in my mind. I keeping thinking that if we would have just stayed at the club a little longer or left a little earlier than we could have avoided the accident all together and she would still be here. Or, if I would have just hit the damn deer and not tried to swerve to miss it."

"Emanuel, you can't do that to yourself. We never know why things happen the way that they do but you can't go on beating yourself up over something that you had no control over."

"That's just it…I did have control over it. I was the one driving the car."

"Yeah, you had physical control over the car but you didn't have control over the situation. You can't blame yourself."

"I don't blame myself…I blame God." His voice cracked. "Why would He even put her in my life…if…if He knew that He was going to take her away from me so quickly?" Emanuel's words were broken. "Five years Kay? That's it?" His voice was strained. Kay could tell that he was trying to hold back the tears. She didn't want to see him cry, not because she didn't think that a man was suppose to cry, but because she knew that he didn't want to, and he didn't have to. His pain was evident and if she looked hard enough she could still see, as Smokey Robinson sang, the tracks of his tears.

Kay reached over and took Emanuel's hands in hers. "Emanuel I know that you are hurting, and as bad as I miss Jada I know that it doesn't even measure up to you missing her. But what gives me solace is knowing that everything is purposed according to His perfect plan. Just think that maybe God didn't put Jada in your life for you to experience tragedy; maybe He put you in her life so that she could experience joy. Jada was always happy, but when you came into her life you gave her joy." Kay's words were like a revelation and Emanuel's mind began to wrap around the concept. He had never considered that possibility, but still it didn't make him feel any better. Kay wrapped her arms around Emanuel; she could feel his warm tears drop on her bare shoulder. He didn't cry loud or hard but his tears were continuous and free flowing. And true to the nurturer in her, Kay sat there in silence; she rubbed his back gently and let him have his moment, knowing that it would soon pass and it did.

Long after Emanuel shed his last tear and the last patron left the club the conversation got lighter and eventually there was more laughter than tears. At around two o'clock in the morning Max locked things up leaving Kay and Emanuel in the club. They talked until they both fell asleep. It was unclear who fell asleep first, but it was obvious that they both were exhausted. There they lay in a peaceful slumber, Kay's head on Emanuel's shoulder, her legs tucked up under her thighs, and his arm around her waist for the second time that night.

Chapter Nine

Kay woke up early Sunday morning but not as early as Emanuel. When his eyes opened just after six a.m. he was unbelievably well-rested. He looked down at Kay who, at some point during the night, had moved her head from his shoulder to his chest. With her head snug against his chest, her right hand resting on his shoulder and her right thigh cocked on his leg Kay slept peacefully. Emanuel could not resist the urge to touch her and with his free hand he gently stroked her face. He was slightly ashamed of what he was feeling. In a different lifetime under different circumstances he would have kissed her without hesitation, but he understood the inappropriateness of that action and opted to ease from under her and go home instead. Emanuel immediately recognized the feeling of jubilee that settled in his heart; he was feeling better than he had in a very long time and he was well aware that his newfound joy was a result of spending time with Kay. When he arrived home he felt refreshed and revived with more energy than he knew what to do with so he put on some work out gear and began to lift weights. Emanuel's body had always been well-sculpted. Even during the months after Jada's death, when he was too depressed to get out of bed, his body didn't seem to lose its tone and every muscle remained perfectly defined. He began his workout routine with weightlifting, followed by sit-ups, push-ups, and ending with a short run. Emanuel threw on a sweat jacket, grabbed his Ipod, and headed out the door. He browsed through his music selection scrolling past Kirk Franklin, Fred Hammond, and Tye Tribbet he chose to program a hip-hop mix and the first artist out of the shuffle was DMX. The beat blasted through his headphones as he started his jog. His Nikes pounded the pavement heavy as the rough and rugged sounds of DMX played through his headphones. Emanuel's breathing was strong. He breathed in deep through his nose and breathed out hard from his mouth. He was in a familiar place -- his confidence was renewed, his mind was clear, and he was conscious of the life flowing through his body. His run was refreshing, and with every step he felt himself feeling more and more free. He mentally checked his vitals: heartbeat strong, breathing steady, mind clear --all was well, and in that brief moment he was happy to be alive. Emanuel thought about the possibilities of finding love again and he debated with himself over the moral dilemma of falling in love with his deceased wife's best friend. His mind was busy with thoughts of life and death, love and like, Jada and Kay -- and he decided that he wanted to live, and he wanted to explore love with Kay. He realized that it had only been two days, but when he woke up this morning with Kay in his arms he felt whole and he felt like he was back in this thing called life. For the first time in a year, Emanuel's thoughts were happy, and he looked forward to seeing Kay again. Emanuel turned his attention from matters of Kay and tuned into the words that DMX rapped in his ears, *I know only I can stop the rain with the mention of my saviors name – Jesus!* DMX called out through the headphones. This was the last place that he expected to here from God. Annoyed by even the mention of His name Emanuel turned off his device. He was a few steps away from his house so he began to walk as a part of his cool down exercise. As Emanuel approached, he noticed Khadir standing at his front door. He watched as Khadir rang the doorbell and peered in through the side window. He laughed on the inside because only Khadir would think it appropriate to look into someone's home through a side window.

"What's up, Khadir," Emanuel called out breathlessly.

"Hey. E." Khadir turned around startled. He did not expect Emanuel to be out and about so early on a Sunday morning. Khadir immediately recognized the gleam of hope in Emanuel's eyes. He looked clearer than he had in months. "What's up?" Khadir asked expectantly. "What's going on?" he asked again, not giving Emanuel a chance to respond to his first question. Emanuel didn't respond to either question, instead he walked up to his friend, shook his hand, and gave him a playful hug, which ended with Khadir in a sweaty headlock. "Come on, man!" Khadir pulled away, "That's just nasty." He wiped Emanuel's sweat from his face. "What's up with you? Why are you out running and playing this early in the morning?" Khadir could visibly see a change in Emanuel his eyes -- they were brighter and his posture appeared stronger. Emanuel wiped his sweaty brow with the back of his hand.

"What's up with me? What's up with you?" Emanuel turned the question back to Khadir. "What are you doing at my house this early in the morning." Emanuel joked – he never joked and this made Khadir even more suspicious of Emanuel's behavior.

"Stop playing, man. For real, what's up?'

"Nothing. I got up early this morning and I felt like a run." Emanuel explained as he unlocked his front door.

"You just felt like a run?" Khadir questioned suspiciously. This annoyed Emanuel.

"What do you want, Khadir?" Emanuel asked as he walked through the front door; Khadir followed closely behind him.

"I don't know the last time you went running. Is everything okay?"

"Besides the fact that I tragically lost my wife and child a year ago this weekend?" Emanuel said sarcastically, meaning for his words to sting. "I feel great! Excuse me for wanting to take a run." Emanuel stormed towards the kitchen. He grabbed a bottle of water from his refrigerator and stood there drinking it with the refrigerator still ajar.

"E, I apologize. I just wanted to make sure everything was good." Emanuel didn't respond. He slammed the refrigerator door shut as a sign to Khadir that his apology wasn't going to be accepted that easily. "Come on, E. You can't blame me for prying. I mean you've been walking around here for a year like a zombie, now all of a sudden you're light-hearted, kidding around and all. It was just strange."

"Strange? Why is me being happy strange?"

"It's not strange that you're happy; it's just strange that you are so happy, so quickly, after being so solemn for the past year. I mean dang I just left you Friday night at the club drinking your sorrows away."

"Well, I guess I drank myself to joy." Emanuel outstretched his arms and smiled. "Look, I'm sweaty and I'm tired. What do you want?"

"I just wanted to drop off this card for your parents. I can't make their anniversary brunch so I was hoping that you could give them this little card for me." Khadir handed Emanuel an off-white envelope.

"Sure. No problem."

Khadir thought that perhaps Emanuel met someone at the club the other night and maybe that was why he was feeling and acting a bit more like himself. "So how was Jada's memorial at the club Friday?" He asked trying to change the topic, but also wanting to get some information.

"The club was cool, aside from the fact that, as you mentioned, I drank way too much."

"Yeah, you were pretty wasted when I left. How long did you stay?"

"I don't even know. Kay ended up bringing me home."

"Kay?" Khadir asked slyly. His mind was going a million miles a minute.

"Yeah," Emanuel said with a smile on his face. A real smile not one of the faux smiles that he had been masquerading with over the past year.

"So, how is she doing?" Khadir asked being sure to watch Emanuel's expression as he spoke.

"She's great." Emanuel said looking out into the distance -- a sure sign in Khadir's mind that he was into Kay.

"Great?" he questioned.

"Yeah."

"Great?" he asked again.

"Yeah, man. She's good. What?" He knew his friend too well and he knew where he was going with his line of questioning.

"I'm just saying. A brother doesn't usually say a female is great unless they got something going on. I mean she was looking real good the other night. Good enough to make a brother forget all of his woes." Khadir watched Emanuel register what he was saying. Emanuel just laughed.

"Naw, man. It's not like that. We just hung out; I enjoy her company. That's it." Emanuel wasn't ready to share the mixed feelings that he was having about Kay with anyone, especially not Khadir. Besides, he was the last person to talk about who was hooking up with who. He had a hard enough time keeping up with his own love life, but that didn't stop him from prying into Emanuel's.

"Again," he sighed and shrugged his shoulders, "I'm just saying she's a hottie. You better watch yourself."

"She's cute." Emanuel said trying to sound disinterested, but he lingered too long in thought, which said more to Khadir then Emanuel wanted to convey.

"I hope you know what you're doing. I mean she is Jada's best friend."

"I know who she is man." Emanuel stood up from his seat, and walked towards the kitchen again. *Why was he even still here?* Emanuel thought to himself and at the same time the words escaped from his lips. "Why are you still here?" Emanuel yelled out to his friend from the kitchen. Five minutes ago Emanuel was happy thinking about life's possibilities, and just that quickly Khadir had rolled in and shook his fragile world. Emanuel didn't go into the kitchen for any reason in particular; he just wanted to get away from Khadir. While he was in there he realized that he hadn't eaten a thing all morning so he grabbed an apple and returned to the living room and took his seat again.

"Oh, now I can't even come over and hang with my boy unless I have a reason?" Khadir laughed as he reached for Emanuel's apple. "Sure, I'll have an apple. Thanks." He took a bite. "I'm just putting two and two together. Friday you weren't happy, now today you're happy. The only thing that has changed over the past year was that you hung out with Kay. So, tell me what's up because my common sense suggests that your nose is open." Khadir laughed.

"Only you could come up with some idiotic logic like that. Friday, I was unhappy; today, I'm happy -- so I must be sleeping with Kay." Emanuel mocked.

"I never said you were sleeping with her. I'm just saying that I think you are feeling her. That's all I am saying."

"So what if I am? Would that be wrong for me to enjoy being around her?" He asked, half wanting Khadir's advice.

"I'm not saying that you can't enjoy being around her, but what you can't do is try to hook up with her."

"Okay, let's talk about this for a minute," Emanuel began. "What if we were attracted to each other?"

"E, she's Jada's best friend. That wouldn't be cool on any level."

"But it's not like it's impossible or even immoral."

"Impossible, no. Immoral – perhaps."

"Okay, not that I even think that you have the authority to even talk about morality, but I'll entertain you for a minute. What would be so wrong with it exactly?"

"E, she's Jada's best friend." Khadir repeated. "Jada was your wife. You were intimate with Jada, and if you were seriously pursuing a relationship with Kay then I would think that at some point you would be intimate with her, too. It's like hooking up with sisters. Man, that's not your style. That's my style, but it's not yours."

"Since when did you become the moral police on dating?" Emanuel joked trying to lighten the mood.

"Man, you know what I'm saying. Women, especially beautiful women, they got a way of making you forget all of the rules. The next thing you know you're waking up in a stranger's bed with handcuffs on your wrist, dried wax on your chest, and lipstick kisses all over your body. And the worse part is, you don't have a clue as to how you got there!" Emanuel and Khadir both burst out laughing.

"Khadir, you are a sick man. Only you can wake up in some mess like that."

"E, trust me. Stranger things have happened." Emanuel couldn't do anything but shake his head and wonder why he thought that he could have a real conversation with Khadir. If nothing else, Emanuel knew that Khadir would always offer some great comic relief.

Kwanza

Chapter Ten

Kay only had two glasses of wine, but for the life of her she could not remember the latter part of the night. She remembered sitting on the couch, sipping wine, laughing and joking with Emanuel, but she did not remember falling asleep. When she woke up at around seven thirty, the club was empty and cold, and aside from the stiffness in her neck she felt refreshed and well-rested. Kay gathered her things and headed home. The drive into the city was quiet and her mind, like the streets, was empty; she enjoyed the serenity. Kay, who was never a big fan of driving in Philadelphia's usual heavy traffic, enjoyed the solitude of the morning, free from the distractions of loud and booming car stereo systems, double parked drivers, and hurried pedestrians. She admired the scene as the sun crept over the tall narrow buildings, leaving an orange hue splashed against the rooftops. She stopped at the red light even though there was not another car on the road. In the stillness of the moment she thought about the night before and the time that she spent with Emanuel; it made her smile. Kay took her right hand off of the steering wheel and placed it up to her nose. She could smell Emanuel's scent. She closed her eyes and inhaled deeply. Embarrassed by her actions Kay opened her eyes and looked around hoping that no one had seen her. She laughed to herself. "Get it together mama," Kay said softly. The light changed to green and Kay slowly pressed her foot on the gas. She tapped the steering wheel to an eclectic beat that played in her head. Kay arrived home just in time to drop her purse and rush to answer her ringing telephone.

"Hello," she said, breathless.

"Hey."

"Hey."

"This is Emanuel."

"I know," she laughed. "To what do I owe this early morning phone call?"

"I just wanted to check to make sure you made it home safely. I felt kind of awkward leaving you asleep at the club this morning but…"

"But not as awkward as you would have felt waking up with me?" Kay said half jokingly.

"No, that wasn't it at all. I just woke up early, as usual, and you looked so peaceful that I didn't want to wake you." Emanuel's reasoning was partially correct; he didn't want to wake Kay, but more than that he didn't want to have to deal with the uncomfortable scene – the two of them waking up in each others arms.

"Yeah, right. Maybe you were just embarrassed by your morning breath." She joked, laughing hard at her wisecrack; Emanuel laughed too, but not as hard.

"Very funny," he said sarcastically.

"I can't remember who fell asleep first, you or me." Kay made the statement hoping that Emanuel would elaborate. But in his usual elusive way Emanuel responded,

"I think we both dosed off at the same time." He lied. He knew exactly what happened -- Kay was in the middle of telling one of her favorite stories about her and Jada and she must have yawned twenty times in between before she fell asleep mid-sentence. Within minutes her precious head was slumped on his shoulder. He didn't disturb her; in fact he enjoyed having her there, and given the circumstances – the feelings of peace and comfort-- he too settled in for a moment's rest. He could have eased from under her and gone home, but the truth of the matter was that he wanted to be right where he was with her in his arms. And although that desire brought shame in the morning, at that moment he needed to breath, and being with her helped him breath.

"I guess I didn't realize how tired I was. So what can I do you for?" Kay jokingly asked.

"Well, I was calling…because, umm…I was wondering…if you don't already have plans for today…if you would like to go with me to my parent's church?" Emanuel stumbled distractingly over his words. Kay listened intently trying to make sense of what he was saying. "I haven't been to church in a really long time, but they are celebrating their 35th wedding anniversary and its a really a big deal to them. My mom thought that it would be nice if the family gathered for church service." Emanuel explained. "We are going to brunch afterward. I just thought that maybe you would like to go." Emanuel rambled on.

"I would love to go." Kay said without giving it a second thought. "What time should I be there?"

"Service starts at eleven o'clock, but I can swing by to pick you up between ten and ten-fifteen?" Emanuel's uncertainty turned his statement in to a question.

"Sounds good," Kay responded. Emanuel wasn't quite sure what time she was agreeing to. "Do I need to bring a gift?"

"No, it's not that kind of gathering."

"Well, I won't feel right showing up empty handed."

"Really, it's not like that. Nadia and I chipped in to send them on a weekend retreat -- in Jersey."

"Who retreats in Jersey?" Kay questioned sarcastically. Emanuel didn't know if she was for real or if she was joking, therefore he didn't know if he should be offended. His silence triggered her thoughts. "Just kidding," she added, freeing Emanuel to laugh. "Well, I will be ready around ten," Kay concluded.

"Ten it is," Emanuel agreed.

"See you then." Kay hung up without saying good-bye but that didn't offend Emanuel he was too busy trying to remember to breathe through the anticipation of spending yet another day with her. He placed the telephone gently in its cradle and smiled. Kay did the same. As soon as she hung up the phone she began peeling off her clothes. She hummed the same eclectic tune out loud as she walked to her bedroom. "What to wear...what to wear?" she wondered as she mentally went through her closet, checking out her wardrobe. "Should I wear a dress?" she asked herself as she slid out of her panties. "Maybe I'll just wear a skirt suit," she thought. "I'm definitely not going to wear pants." She concluded as she turned on the shower. Kay wrapped her hair in a loose bun then reached for her pink shower cap, which hung on the bathroom door. She took a swing of mouth wash and swished it around as she looked at herself in the mirror. She was pleased with the image that was reflecting back at her. She gently ran her fingers across her neatly arched eyebrows before spiting the mint-flavored liquid into the sink. The shower was steaming hot just the way she liked it and her body relaxed instantly. She closed her eyes and talked to God. "Lord, thank You for waking me up this morning and watching over me as I slept last night." And then she thought *Thank you for who I slept with last night* She smiled then instantly felt ashamed. "Forgive me, Lord. I thank You for Your grace and mercy. Thank you Jesus for restoring my soul daily. Great is Your wonderful name. I give You all of the honor and the glory and the praise, forever and ever. Amen."

Kay climbed out of the shower and wrapped herself in a fluffy towel. She walked through the cloud of steam to her bedroom. She couldn't explain the excitement that she felt in her belly. For years she hadn't even entertained the idea of being with any man other than Malik. But here she was, after spending only two days with Emanuel, thinking about him non-stop. A part of her wanted to believe that she was excited about going to church, but she could not deny the subtle feeling of joy that ran through her soul as she thought about seeing Emanuel. There was something very strange and almost frightening going on between them, and although she hadn't really taken the time to think about it she recognized it, and she was sure that it had something to do with the fact that they were spending so much time together. Kay hummed out loud as she lotioned her yoga-toned, petite body. It was during this small space in time that she questioned her emotional self. *Could I have feelings for Emanuel?* She asked herself, *or am I just enjoying his company?* He was such a huge part of her life when Jada was here and she felt that maybe she was just excited about being in that familiar place that his presence put her in. After a bit of reasoning and self-reflection, Kay settled on the fact that she was just enjoying his company, and she chastised herself for thinking that it was or could have been anything more. Besides falling asleep in his arms last night she really didn't have any other indication that this weekend was about anything more than two old friends getting reacquainted to share in the memory of someone who meant the world to them both.

Kay stood in her walk-in closet trying to decide what to wear. Her clothes were arranged neatly by color codes: beige, taupe, and browns hung together followed by black, gray, and blues. She changed into no less than five different outfits before she finally settled on an A-line khaki skirt and matching blazer. She grabbed a pair of brown four-inch Santana pumps. Her make-up was very natural including her lipstick, which was more like a sheer brown gloss. She whipped her hair up into a neat bun with a few tresses hanging from either side.

Kay paced the floor from her kitchen to the window as she waited for Emanuel to arrive. She could feel butterflies swarming about in her stomach as the clock got closer and closer to ten. She tried to silence the butterflies by talking to herself, which was something that she did often. If she had girlfriend issues that she needed to work out then she would talk to Jada, as was the case Friday morning when she learned that Malik and Heather were getting married. Whenever she was feeling desperate for Malik she would rehearse her, *I'm still in love with you,* speech which was something that she recited at least five times a week. The feelings that she had for Malik were very real to her and often after watching a love story or hearing a love song she craved him even more. This generally kicked her imagination into overdrive and all she could do was fantasize about the life they should have had together. Sometimes she even fell into a self-imposed moment, like when she planned her usual home-alone movie night, where she would overdose on love stories like, *Love Jones, While You Were Sleeping,* or *The Notebook.* Those nights usually ended with Kay crying herself to sleep, sick over thoughts of missing Malik. But just as much as she talked to Jada and Malik she talked to God. She knew without question that it was in His word and His presence that she would find answers to all that vexed her. She knew and

97

believed that God was her ultimate supplier and in Him and Him alone was her peace, but sometimes she choose to deal with things in the flesh and it was then that she made decisions out of fear. He was the only one who could really help her get through whatever situation she was dealing with. But right now, she chose to approach life in the flesh because she was enjoying the thoughts that she was having about Emanuel and she liked how it made her feel. She knew that her thoughts were inappropriate but she didn't want to be appropriate right now; she wanted to feel the strong desire that she was feeling and secretly she wanted Emanuel to feel it, too. Kay recognized her lustful state and the sensible part of her began a monologue that she didn't want to entertain.

Would it really be so wrong if I had feelings for him?. . . I mean he is a man. . .a very attractive man. . .and I am a woman. . . a fairly attractive woman. . . It wouldn't be completely impossible for us to be attracted to one another...I mean human nature alone can draw us towards attraction. Kay reasoned with herself out loud, hand gestures included. *But he was Jada's husband... and Jada was my best friend... they were in love with each other ... she married him... she made love to him... and she was having his baby. Those are enough reasons why I need to get over it – even if I am attracted to him.* Kay was feeling good about her rationalization. She was beginning to feel like she put her mind back on track. *Emanuel and I are just friends, nothing more. What kind of hooch would I be if I sleep with him? Oh my God, did I just think it let alone say it out loud. Could I sleep with him? Absolutely not!* She scolded her own thoughts. *He is so fine though.* She said emphasizing the word fine. Kay's mind quickly flipped back and fourth. *Those lips,* she remembered as she licked her lips. *Those arms,* she smiled, *his chest...* She closed her eyes for a brief second as a wave of heat shot from between her thighs and out in different directions from her head to her toes and settled back between her thighs. Kay squeezed her legs together tightly and moaned, "What in the world is wrong with me?"

The ringing doorbell interrupted Kay's thoughts. Her body still hot from lustful thinking, she knew that she needed to say a prayer for herself.

"My God my God," she began "please give me the strength…to be around this man and not make a fool of myself. Let me enjoy the day and be forever mindful of the fact that Emanuel is my friend and was my best friend's -- my sister's husband." When Kay felt that she said all that she could say on the matter she closed her prayer with a loud "Amen" as if the louder she said it the more power it would have.

Emanuel rang the doorbell a second time and as he waited for Kay to answer. He watched the tranquil Sunday morning activity on Kay's street. His Kenneth Cole shades protected his eyes from the spring sun. He watched as two older women talked to one another, one from her porch and the other from the sidewalk. Emanuel couldn't hear what they were saying, but he assumed that they were talking about the beautiful weather and the early Sunday service that the woman standing on the sidewalk was either going to or returning from, based on what she was wearing, a lavender spring dress accented with chiffon and a huge lavender hat tilted to one side. Kay opened the door in what seemed like slow-motion and there Emanuel stood looking finer than ever. Kay swore to herself, that he looked more and more attractive each time she saw him. She likened her desire for him to the desire she had for something forbidden -- like a chocolate cake when she was fasting from food or a pair of designer shoes when she was fasting from shopping. The mere smell and sight of it caused moisture to drip from her lips, and that was how her body responded to Emanuel. The mere smell and sight of him caused moisture to drip from her lips; she squeezed her legs together tightly. Emanuel wore a pair of chocolate brown slacks and a cream colored silk shirt covered by a chocolate brown leather jacket. The dark brown against his caramel-colored skin was beautiful. Kay's smile was sufficient on the outside, but on the inside she was doing cartwheels and smiling like a Cheshire cat. She realized immediately that the prayer that she sent up moments earlier had not yet processed through the prayer line because she could feel the heat between her thighs renewed.

"Hey, Kay." Emanuel leaned in and gave Kay a gentle hug and kissed her cheek. "Are you ready?" he asked in a confident tone. Kay was afraid to even look at him; in fact, she held her breath when he hugged her because she didn't want to breathe him.

"Yup, I'm all set." Kay turned her back to Emanuel as she locked her door. With her back still turned to him she looked up toward the heavens and asked under her breath, "Help me Lord."

Chapter Eleven

During their drive to church Kay couldn't help but notice how comfortable Emanuel appeared. He talked non-stop the entire ride only pausing long enough to laugh, and allow Kay to acknowledge his statements. Emanuel didn't talk about anything important or anything in particular which was fine by Kay because she spent the twenty-five minute car ride inhaling his intoxicating scent and trying to talk herself out of the lustful thoughts that were swirling throughout her mind. As the doors of the sanctuary opened the choir greeted Emanuel and Kay in song, *Faithful... Faithful, Faithful is our God*. The words reverberated with great volume seemingly bouncing off the walls. Emanuel felt as if the choir was mocking him with their confession. Immediately Emanuel regretted his decision; he wished that he had met his family at the restaurant after the service instead of agreeing to attend church. But it was too late; Mrs. Rivers had already spied him and she threw up her hand to signal her location. He looked over at Kay thinking that maybe he could persuade her to turn around and leave with him, but she had already begun to sing along with the choir,

"Unleashing the harvest God promised me take back what the devil stole from me and I rejoice today for I shall inherit it all." The choir sang in full unison. Kay looked over at Emanuel and smiled. He didn't want to be rude, but he could not muster a smile, not even the faux smile that he had mastered over the past year. So instead, he raised his finger in acknowledgment of his mother's signaling. Emanuel took Kay's hand in his and guided her towards the pew where his parents and sister were seated. Mrs. Rivers did a double-take when she noticed Kay walking hand in hand with Emanuel.

"Is that Jada's friend?" Mrs. Rivers asked with a nudge to Nadia's side. In her typical indiscreet way Nadia turned to the back of the sanctuary.

"Um-hum." Nadia breathed through twisted lips.

"I wonder what this is all about."

"I don't know, but I'll find out." Nadia's investigative mind had already begun to gather clues. Their emotions were mixed concerning Emanuel and Kay and their happy glances quickly turned into confused stares. Nadia watched with a critical eye as Emanuel and Kay walked down the aisle. She was very aware of how chivalrous Emanuel was towards Kay. She took a mental note when he gently placed his hand on the small of her back and motioned for her to take a seat. And when Emanuel waited for Kay to be seated before he sat down Nadia's suspicion only escalated. She was all for chivalry, but Emanuel appeared to be far too attentive to Kay. Kay sat next to Nadia and offered her a greeting,

"Hello."

Nadia didn't say a word she just smiled and nodded. Mr. Rivers, who seemed unfazed by the entire scene, continued to tap his knee as he sang along with the choir. Emanuel leaned over Kay and his sister to kiss Mrs. Rivers on the cheek.

"Happy anniversary, Ma," he whispered.

"Thank you son." She smiled. He tapped his father's shoulder then playfully tapped Nadia on the side of her head.

"Hey, big head."

"Shut up." They behaved like two children. Just as Emanuel and Kay settled in their seats the choir finished singing and Pastor Samuel approached the podium causing the congregation to stand to their feet.

"Amen, Amen!" An older saint cheered from behind Emanuel for no apparent reason.

"Good Morning, Church," Pastor Samuel greeted. "It is truly a blessing to be in the house of the Lord this morning." Emanuel tensed in the midst of all the Amen's and Hallelujahs. "Before I get into the word I want to send up a special blessing to Charlie and Nora Rivers. Congratulations on thirty-five years of marriage." People clapped and patted the couple on their shoulders in congratulations. "You know it takes a special kind of love to make it through thirty-five years." Again, the congregation responded with a series of *Amen's* and *yes, Lords*. "Love…" Pastor Samuel began, "It takes a patient kind of love."

"Amen"

"Kind love."

"Hallelujah!"

"A love that is not envious, a love that is not boastful, not proud. I tell you it takes a special kind of love." Emanuel shifted in his seat, the words reminded him of his wedding day because Jada had included that very popular scripture in her wedding vows. It brought tears to Emanuel's eyes then, and today was no different. Emanuel poked at his eyes trying to dry his tears before they could fully develop. He swallowed hard as his breathing became faint. Pastor Samuel continued,

"Love is not rude, it is not self-seeking, it is not easily angered; love keeps no record of wrongs. Love does not delight in evil but rejoices with truth. It always protects," and with that Emanuel completely zoned out.

Love protects. The words repeated in his thought, reminding him of his inability to protect the one person whom he loved the most. Pastor Samuel continued with his message, but it was all a blur to Emanuel.

"Always trusts… always hopes… always perseveres. Love never fails." Pastor Samuel ended with a hearty congratulations and the congregation stood to their feet and cheered for Mr. and Mrs. Rivers. Emanuel stood up out of respect for his parents but inside he felt great envy. Emanuel braced for an hour-and-a-half of *thus said the Lord,* and so on, and so fourth. He half-listened to Pastor Samuel's high-energy sermon and watched with disinterest as he spoke on the word of God. He couldn't completely zone out because he was distracted by the older woman behind him, she said *Amen* over one hundred times, Emanuel was sure of it. He fidgeted in his seat trying desperately not to jump up and run for the doors. Emanuel winced every time the Saints shouted *Amen* or *Praise the Lord*. He could feel his spirit stirring inside, and he believed it was because of the uneasiness he felt listening to people praise a God that he wasn't sure he believed in, and whom he had no faith in. He felt like he was in the Twilight Zone surrounded by everyone shouting and dancing for the Lord. Unable to completely zone out, Emanuel began focusing on insignificant things like how many times the pastor said 'saints' through out his sermon. He counted, *'listen saints...'*

"One."

'Saints, God said...'

"Two."

'Hear me saints...'

"Three."

Emanuel sat stiff-backed throughout the entire service relaxing only briefly when Kay leaned into him and asked if he was okay. He gave her a halfhearted smile and nodded his head, "I'm fine," he said.

After the long agonizing hour-and-a-half service Emanuel was more than ready to go and he all but ran out of the church. Kay took notice of his uneasiness but she didn't comment on it. She knew that the pain he felt from the loss of Jada ran very deep, but she had no idea how deep. Kay's focus was completely on Emanuel so she paid little attention to Nadia's judgmental eyes watching her every move. Nadia and Kay had never been close, and they had nothing in common but Emanuel. As far as Kay was concerned Nadia was nothing more than Emanuel's little sister, and at this stage of their relationship that fact was rather insignificant. Nadia, on the other hand, didn't put anything past Kay. She knew the power of a woman's allure and sex appeal, and based on that she was fairly confident that Kay's interest in Emanuel was deeper than just a friendship.

Emanuel's parents chose a quaint little restaurant in Center City. The room was filled with the usual Sunday morning after-church-crowd. A lean Middle Eastern man greeted them at the door and immediately seated them at a round table in the middle of the room. Kay and Nadia sat on either side of Emanuel; his parents sat across from him. Despite the fact that Kay knew Emanuel's parents fairly well that didn't minimize the nervousness she felt in her belly. With all eyes on her, she felt like a girlfriend who was meeting the family for the first time. She had spent a lot of time with Emanuel and his family on many occasions prior to Jada's death so she attributed the tension in the air to their confusion about her current relationship with Emanuel, and Kay was certain that that was why Nadia was eyeballing her.

She noticed that Nadia didn't have much to say to her, but that didn't stop her from cutting her the evil eye every now and then.

"So how are you doing, son?" Mr. Rivers asked in an attempt to break the uncomfortable silence.

"I'm fine, pops. I've just been really busy with work and all." Emanuel offered

"What about you, Kay," Mr. Rivers continued, "How are you?"

"I am fine sir." Kay nodded and smiled. "Happy anniversary." She offered as a reminder of the occasion and why they were there.

"Thank you, dear." Mr. Rivers responded.

"Thirty-five years, hunh? Wow, that's amazing!" Kay said in a tone that clearly showed she was trying too hard.

"Yep, thirty-five wonderful years." He smiled and took Mrs. Rivers's hand in his. Emanuel pretended to read the menu and didn't comment. He couldn't understand why some people got thirty-five beautiful, uninterrupted years while others barely make it through five. He sipped his ice water, hoping that it would help him swallow his contempt.

"So, what's the secret?" Kay asked.

"I don't know," Mr. Rivers began, "If I had to guess I would say that communication is the key," Mr. Rivers offered. "What do you think Nora?" He turned the question to Mrs. Rivers who was surprisingly quiet.

"I agree. Communication is very important." Emanuel laughed on the inside; he thought that it was amusing how people believed that anything in life was more than pure luck. He shrieked at the idea that things were blessings, fate, or destiny. Emanuel drank from his glass again, this time taking a long, hard sip.

"That's what I always hear couples say," Kay interjected. "Communication."

"So, what about your parents, Kay. Are they still married?" Mrs. Rivers questioned.

"No. My parents never married . . .well, at least not to each other," Kay corrected, "but they are both happily married now." Kay fumbled over her words.

"Humph." Mrs. Rivers huffed with attitude causing everyone at the table to look in her direction.

"So, how is your son?" Mr. Rivers inquired.

"Khalial is great."

"I bet he is getting big."

"Oh, yeah." Kay felt ridiculous about feeling so nervous. She wished that she could shake it off. She couldn't understand why everyone was acting so uptight, and why it didn't seem to faze Emanuel at all.

"Are you and Khalial's father planning to marry?" Mrs. Rivers pried.

"No, ma'am." Kay couldn't help but laugh at Mrs. Rivers' question. She didn't think it was appropriate to even go down that road with the Rivers family. They did not need to know that Malik choose a wife and that it wasn't her.

"Why not?" Mrs. Rivers continued. Kay looked over at Emanuel as if to say, *Please get your mother*. But Emanuel was too busy studying the menu.

"Well," Kay began nervously, "Malik and I are good friends and we are great parents; we just didn't make the best couple."

"Kind of like your parents, hunh? Interesting." Mrs. Rivers said as she stirred her tea. Kay could hear judgment in her voice. Kay didn't want to be disrespectful, but she could not hide her irritation. She took a deep breath and as quietly as she could she exhaled.

Lord, please give me peace. She prayed silently. She didn't realize how difficult Mrs. Rivers was. There were times when Jada would complain about her, and Kay would encourage her to show love no matter what. Right now Kay was trying very hard to take her own advice.

"I guess the apple doesn't fall far from the tree," Mrs. Rivers said digging in even deeper.

"I hope not," Kay snapped.

"Nora, stop questioning the girl so she can look over the menu and see what she wants to eat," Mr. Rivers said lightly. He was the only one who seemed concerned and even embarrassed by Mrs. Rivers's interrogation. Emanuel and Nadia both sat there without saying a word. Nadia seemed to be enjoying it, but Emanuel on the other hand was completely unresponsive.

"So, you think that your lifestyle is acceptable?"

"Excuse me?" Kay retorted. All of her peace and patience was lost on Mrs. Rivers's nastiness.

"I just find it hard to believe that you would think that it is okay to have babies out of wedlock."

"With all due respect, ma'am," Kay huffed perfectly prepared to be escorted out of the restaurant after she checked Mrs. Rivers "this is not about what I think is acceptable or not, this is just life, and sometimes in life people fall in and out of love, and in the midst of them falling in and out of love blessings happen. For my mother and father, it was my sister and I. And for me and Malik, it was Khalial." Kay lost her momentum when the waiter approached and asked if they were ready to order. Mr. Rivers lifted his index finger to signal that he was ready, but Mrs. Rivers in all of her bossiness interjected,

"Please give us a few more minutes." The waiter looked at Mr. Rivers for his concurrence, as it was not standard in his Middle Eastern custom to take direction from a woman. Mr. Rivers nodded and the waiter turned and walked away.

"So you have surmised your sin as a blessing?"

"There is no sin but that which is common to man." Kay was exhausted. This verbal duel was taking its toll on her. If she knew that Mrs. Rivers was going to tongue bash her the entire afternoon she would have politely declined Emanuel's offer to join them, especially since he was now sitting there oblivious to what was going on around him.

"Are your parents Christians?"

"My mother is; my father practices Islam."

"Islam?" Mrs. Rivers questioned in a loud tone.

"Yes. My father is a Muslim."

"So, that means that he doesn't believe in God?" Mrs. Rivers continued in a tone like she had just outted Kay in front of the town's people.

"Oh, no. My father, like all Muslims, believes in God, they just refer to Him by a different name."

"Well, I know those Muslims don't believe in Jesus," she said with great certainty.

"Actually, they do," Kay corrected. "They believe that Jesus is a prophet just like Mohammed. My father is very spiritual and I believe that his path will one day lead him to God. But that is my father's path, his own walk that will one day make sense to him, and I know that God will accept him with open arms." Kay concluded. The last thing she wanted to do was defend Walter, but she refused to let Mrs. Rivers condemn him to hell. Mrs. Rivers stiffened her posture. She was slightly embarrassed by her ignorance in that area and her embarrassment made her defensive.

"So, what exactly does that mean… exactly? Does he believe that Jesus died for his sins? Because you know that the word says, *'that no man cometh unto the Father but by Me,'* she said proudly. "So if he has not accepted Jesus as his personal savior then," she huffed, "it doesn't matter how 'spiritual' he is," she said, making quotes with her fingers around the word spiritual, "that's not going to get him into heaven." Mrs. Rives concluded.

"Well, Mrs. Rivers. Thank God you aren't the final authority."

"Ma," Emanuel chimed in, as if someone just woke him from a deep sleep. "Kay joined us for brunch to celebrate your anniversary."

"Exactly. She joined us." Mrs. Rivers barked as if that made Kay free game.

"Yes, at my invitation." Emanuel said firmly. "I did not invite her here for you to ask her a million questions." Kay was happy that Emanuel finally spoke up, but for some reason she didn't get the sense that he was speaking up on her behalf. "Believe it or not," Emanuel continued, "there are some people in the world who choose not to serve your God."

"Only a fool could deny the power of God," Mrs. Rivers said raising her voice causing patrons at nearby tables to look over at them.

"Yeah, well, the world is full of fools, and depending on who you ask you may be surprised to find out that you are on the wrong side of the aisle."

Mrs. Rivers was confident in her anger towards Kay, but when Emanuel spoke she seemed a bit more undone.

"I know you aren't siding with her." Mrs. Rivers's voice was quivering.

"Ma, there is no side to take because quiet frankly I don't care one way or the other about God, Allah, Budda or any of it."

"Emanuel!" she exclaimed, "You better watch your mouth. You will not sit in my presence and disrespect God." Mrs. Rivers chastised him like he was a child. Emanuel gave a sly smirk, but he didn't respond. He could not say for sure what wrath would fall upon him if he disrespected God, but he knew from experience the consequences that he would have to face if he disrespected his mother. "I don't know what has gotten into you since Jada died. You walking around here mad at the world." Mrs. Rivers went on and on. It was apparent that she was furious. "You need to get over it. It's over. Jada is dead, and you need to get over it." She concluded harshly.

Is this the support that Emanuel has had to help him through this past year? Kay wondered to herself. *No wonder he is still so unhappy.* Kay felt like she needed to say something in Emanuel's defense, but before her lips could form the words Nadia chimed in,

"Ma, that was unnecessary. How could you be so insensitive?"

"I am just being honest."

"Yeah, when all he needs is for you to be understanding." Mr. Rivers scolded. He was usually a man of very few words, and one would be hard pressed to catch him raising his voice, but if there were ever a time when he needed to raise his voice it was at that very moment. Mrs. Rivers's words had cut through everyone in earshot like a jagged edged sword. Without saying a word, Emanuel pushed his chair from the table, stood to his feet, and pushed his chair back in; Kay looked up at him confused.

"Dad... Mom -- happy anniversary. I'll call you guys later." He said unbelievably calm. "Kay, are you ready?" He looked at her and it was in that moment that she noticed a deep sadness in his eyes. Kay did not hesitate for a moment. She quickly got out of her seat and gathered her things, but before she could push her chair in or say her goodbyes Emanuel was half way out the door. Still in shock, Kay and Emanuel drove the entire thirty-minutes to her house in complete silence. Mrs. Rivers's words haunted Kay as they echoed repeatedly through out her mind.

"Jada is dead get over it." Did she really say that? Kay thought to herself. Kay looked over at Emanuel who appeared to be outside of himself. She could only imagine what was going on in his mind at that moment. His calmness frightened her because that was an indication that he had completely disconnected. She would have felt better if he yelled, screamed, and cursed. Kay could not bring herself to speak. There was so much that she wanted to say. She wanted to assure him that God is great, mighty, merciful, and faithful like the choir sang. She wanted him to know that God was not in the business of causing people pain just for the heck of it. She wanted to tell him that his mother was wrong. She wanted to hold him and cry with him and scream with him.

Emanuel pulled in front of her house; he was completely silent. Kay hesitated and searched her heart for the words that she should speak. She didn't want him to go home and have to deal with his pain alone. They sat in silence for a few minutes dealing with the events of the day in their own way. Kay could have smacked Mrs. Rivers for the ignorant comments that she made. She could not understand for the life of her why she said those mean and hateful remarks to her only son about the woman that he loved.

"Wow," Kay sighed. "I am very sorry that you had to deal with that. I hope you know that your mother is wrong."

Emanuel said nothing.

"You don't have to get over it; you have every right to be sad and mourn as long as you need to," she began but Emanuel interrupted her.

"Look, I have to go. There are some things that I need to take care of." Kay knew that he wasn't being truthful. All he wanted to do was go somewhere and cry alone.

"Emanuel, I don't think that you should be alone. Actually, I don't think that I want to be alone either. Why don't you just come in and we can hang out. I can prepare lunch and we can just talk...or not...whatever you're comfortable with." She was right, Emanuel didn't want to be alone because that was the only time that he felt like he could be his lonely and miserable self. Kay refused to take no for an answer, and after some urging she finally convinced him to come inside and have lunch with her. He was tired of the emotional roller coaster that he had been on for the past year, and it felt good to have an option other than going home alone.

Chapter Twelve

Kay and Emanuel sat spread out on the floor, backs against the base of the couch, looking at old pictures. Half eaten sandwiches and half empty glasses of iced tea sat on the coffee table in front of them. Emanuel half-looked at the photos; he had seen them many times before and most of them were ones that he and Jada had in their own photo album. The once sunny skies had quickly become cloudy; Emanuel didn't want to spend the day alone and Kay wanted nothing more than to be with him. Heavy rain played as background music to an almost peaceful evening. The evening wasn't completely peaceful because Emanuel was emotionally drained; the fiasco with his mother earlier was enough to cause an emotional relapse, and he was grateful to have Kay there as a buffer between him and loneliness. Emanuel was very relaxed, so much so that his eyes were heavy and his heart was light. He half listened as Kay pointed at every picture and told a story around each. Kay laughed as she told tales of herself and Jada causing all sorts of mischief as young girls growing up in West Philly. Emanuel tuned in to every other word because what he really wanted to do was lay his head down and rest. Kay pointed at a photo of her and Jada at their senior prom; black and orange balloons hung in the background representing the colors of their alma mater, Overbrook High School. Kay and Jada posed in the middle of the photo dressed in lavender and turquoise satin gowns respectively, not exactly their best look, but Emanuel figured that in 1995 the dresses were probably quite fashionable. Kay laughed out loud as she remembered that night.

"Oh my gosh," she began as the photo jogged her memory, "this night was the best night ever. Malik and I got into a huge argument, and I decided that I was not going to go to my prom. Jada would not hear of it. She dumped her date literally hours before he was supposed to pick her up and we took a cab to our prom." Kay laughed as she remembered her friend. Emanuel peeped over her shoulder at the photo and Jada's huge, bright smile instantly greeted him. He inhaled deeply and closed

113

his eyes. Even in a still photo, in that hideous prom dress, she had the power to take his breath away. Since Jada's death he hadn't looked at the photos because he couldn't stand the pain of seeing her look so alive. Everyone told him, "*You have to keep her alive in your memory,*" but Emanuel didn't have a problem with remembering her. His memories of her were vivid; he remembered her far too easily. Occasionally, when he was alone in his bedroom or anywhere in his house he would get a faint smell of her perfume, and he believed that if he closed his eyes tight enough he could feel her near him. It was in those moments when he thought that he would lose his mind. He had resolved that if losing his mind would somehow put him in her continuous presence then he would embrace its loss.

Emanuel's iced tea sat in a puddle of water created by its own condensation; the once ice cold drink had become warm leaving water droplets running down the glass like sweat. He looked at Kay's silhouette and took a mental note of how perfectly beautiful she was. Emanuel could not deny how much at peace he felt when he was around her. She reminded him so much of Jada -- her clear skin, her silky hair --and her soft lips. He watched them part as she spoke; he watched them curl slightly in the corners when she smiled. Her beauty mesmerized him. He wanted to touch her, and he wanted her to touch him. He wanted her to rest in his arms so that he could hold her just as he had the night before, but this time he wanted it to be intentional. He couldn't take his eyes off of her and he watched her full lips as she spoke and he wondered, *If I lean in to kiss her, would she kiss me back?* He thought about what Khadir said earlier and questioned what he was feeling. *Is it wrong for me to feel the way that I feel about her?* Emanuel rested his head on the seat of the sofa and listened to Kay reminisce. With his eyes heavy he followed the length of her neck, the contour of her shoulder. He smiled at the small, colorful butterfly tattoo on her back -- Jada had the same mark. Everything that the two of them had done had a story behind it and the matching tattoos were no different. After Kay had Khalial she was feeling heavy, heavier than a young woman should have felt after giving birth to a

114

healthy baby boy. She was feeling unprepared and unsure of herself so Jada convinced her to get a tattoo by suggesting that a butterfly represents a new birth and that Khalial was also symbolic of a new birth, not only his own but hers as a woman that God entrusted to raise one of his angels. Emanuel focused all of his attention on her shoulder. In that small freeze frame he recognized Jada clearly. Emanuel licked his lips; his mouth watered at the image that was before him. Without any further thought Emanuel leaned over and rested his lips on Kay's bare shoulder. Being that close to her was more than he could stand, and he became blinded by his desires. He closed his eyes and breathed her in deeply. Kay paused in her speech, and her heart skipped a beat. She dropped her head and closed her eyes, not to find her breaths or meditate but to take in the moment and allow her body to enjoy what it was feeling. She didn't want to listen to reason she didn't want to think things out; she just wanted to let go and simply live in the moment. Feeling completely uninhibited, Emanuel found his nerve and began to place soft, gentle kisses on her shoulder. Kay didn't say a word, and with every peck she became weaker. Kay moaned softly under her breath. Emanuel slowly worked his way up her neck then to her cheek and chin before finding her lips. He gently sucked her lips like they were his own taking them into his mouth playfully. Kay opened her eyes; she wanted to see him, and she wanted him to see her. She gently placed her right hand against the left side of his face and looked into his eyes; they were distant and dark like an endless pool of water -- it was as if she could see directly into his soul. She bit gently on her bottom lip and looked at him. This was the moment when one or both of them were supposed to pull back and say something wise like, '*What are we doing?*' or '*We shouldn't be doing this*' or most importantly – '*What about Jada?*' But neither of them said a word. Their eyes and souls connected, and there was nothing that could stop the energy that was flowing between them. Kay leaned in and Emanuel met her midway, placing his lips against hers. With his left hand placed gently on her neck he brought her in closer to him. Emanuel took Kay's bottom lip seductively into his mouth before he slipped his thick, sweet tongue in hers. Kay sucked it softly then hard. Emanuel wrapped his hands around her waist and pulled Kay closer. She climbed on top of him. Emanuel's mind swirled around leaving him dizzy, and with his lips pressed firmly against Kay's lips he could feel her breaths going into his lungs, breathing life back into him. Emanuel let out a heavy moan as he pulled her closer to him. The desire to make love ran deep and neither of them could control it, nor did they want to. Emanuel ran his hands up Kay's shirt. The feel of her soft skin against his hands was overwhelming and his body responded. Kay reached down to his pants and began to undo his belt and then his button. She was like a woman opening a present from Tiffany's knowing that in just a few moments she would have in her hands a treasure.

Kay had her hand on Emanuel's zipper when the loud ringing of the doorbell interrupted their rendezvous; it startled them both. It was as if they were shook from a dream when Khalial's small voice called from the other side of the door

"Ma! Ma, it's me!" he called out. Heads cloudy and confused, Kay and Emanuel both jumped to their feet and placed their hands over their moist lips trying to hide the evidence of their kiss.

"Oh my, it's Khalial!" Kay said frantically. Emanuel reached out to her and placed his hand on her shoulder -- the same one that he had kissed moments earlier.

"Kay," he looked at her, his eyes more peaceful than she had remembered. "Relax. Open the door and relax." Kay was afraid to open the door; she didn't want to have to explain to Khalial and especially Malik why she was there alone with Emanuel. The doorbell rang again. Heart racing, Kay backed away from Emanuel towards the door, her eyes still on him. Emanuel sat down on the couch and adjusted himself. His heart was pounding against his chest so hard that he thought that it would burst. Kay paused at the door and took a deep breath before opening it. As soon as she cracked the door open just a little bit Khalial burst in and jumped in her arms forcing her back a few steps.

"Mom!" Khalial wrapped his little arms around Kay's neck. He tried to kiss her cheek but she turned away from him in embarrassment.

"Hey, sweetheart." Kay beamed. She squeezed her son a little tighter hoping to compensate for not allowing him to kiss her. Kay swung her baby boy around in the air paying no attention to Malik who stood there in his rain-soaked clothes holding Khalial's backpack. Without invitation from Kay, Malik came inside and closed the door behind him.

"Mom," Khalial pulled back from his mother and smiled his slightly bucked toothed smile. "Dad and Heather are getting married." He sounded happier than Kay had expected.

"That's wonderful." She looked up at Malik; he gave her a thumb up, Kay smiled but she wasn't quite sure how she felt. She expected Khalial to give Malik some grief for his decision to marry Heather.

"I'm going to be Dad's best man. I get to wear a tuxedo and everything!" Khalial could hardly contain his excitement. "Aint that right, dad?" Khalial asked Malik for confirmation.

"That's exactly right. You're going to be my best man and you get to wear a tuxedo." Khalial spun around awkwardly as his feet tangled.

"See, Mom."

"That is really cool, Khalial." Kay embraced her baby boy again. Khalial peered over Kay's shoulder and spied Emanuel sitting still and quiet on the couch, perhaps hoping that he wouldn't be seen. "Hey, Uncle E," Khalial called from his mother's embrace. Kay's guilt-filled eyes immediately met Malik's. Khalial wiggled from his mother's arms and ran over to Emanuel. Not quite prepared to deal with the situation, Emanuel stood to his feet in embarrassment.

"Hey, man," Emanuel said as he kneeled down to hug his little godson. Malik cut Kay a suspicious look, which caused her to drop her eyes and scratch her head. He walked past her and went over to Emanuel.

"What's up, E?" Malik said, extending his hand out to shake.

"What's up, Malik?" The two shook hands. "Congratulations on the engagement."

"Thanks, man. So how are you doing?" Malik asked in a sympathetic tone, remembering that this was the weekend that they had the tribute for Jada at the club.

"I'm good. Thanks for asking."

"It's been a long time."

"Yeah, it has been."

"So, what brings you by?"

"Well…I…um…," Emanuel began before Kay interrupted him.

"He just stopped by to thank me for organizing the memorial event for Jada on Friday." Kay offered and stood between the two men. She wrapped her arm around Khalial who looked about all smiles completely unaware of the awkward situation that was developing around him. It didn't take long for Emanuel to take the hint.

"Yeah," he continued, "I just stopped by. In fact, I was just about to leave."

"You don't have to leave Emanuel. I still need to talk to you." Kay talked as normal as she could given the circumstances. She wanted Emanuel to stay because she didn't want their beautiful night to end this way.

"Give me a call later…either at home or at work tomorrow…you do still have the office number. Don't you?"

"Yeah, I do, but I'll probably give you a call at home later. We can finish talking about…what we were talking about." Neither Kay nor Emanuel were natural in their exchange, and Malik knew that something was going on and in one guess he was willing to bet that he knew what it was.

"Okay. That sounds good. I'll wait for your call." Emanuel gave Kay a hug and a kiss on the cheek, which under normal circumstances would have been perfectly fine, but considering the night's earlier events the once simple act was sloppy and awkward. Emanuel breathed in Kay's aroma; it would have to sustain him until he could hold her again. He knew that he held her too long, but as far as they both were concerned it was hardly long enough. Emanuel gave her one last squeeze before letting her go. "Kay thanks again." Kay couldn't take her eyes off of Emanuel; she wanted so desperately to continue the night that they started. Reluctantly, Emanuel turned his attention away from Kay. "Malik, congratulations again. And you little man," Emanuel turned his attention to Khalial, "maybe we can get together and hangout sometimes."

"Maybe you can come over and I can kick your butt in boxing on PS2."

"Oh, man! Is that a challenge?" Emanuel threw fake jabs at Khalial. Malik was not comfortable with the thought of Emanuel coming to the house and hanging out with Khalial or Kay.

"Come on, Khalial. Emanuel is much too busy to play video games with a six-year old. Aint that right?"

"Naw, I always have time for my godson. You tell me when and I will be here." Emanuel smiled at Khalial, but he took notice of how uncomfortable his presence was making Malik though he couldn't understand why with him being engaged and all. Emanuel walked over to the couch and retrieved his coat. "You guys have a good night. Kay, I'll talk to you later. Malik, it was good seeing you, man." Emanuel extended his hand to shake Malik's and Malik obliged. Emanuel turned his attention to Kay; his eyes connected with hers once more before he walked out the door. Emanuel's exit changed the atmosphere in the room; the tension wasn't any less suffocating but it was more directed. Kay knew by the way that Malik was looking at her that he believed she owed him an explanation.

"Hey, little man," Malik said to Khalial without taking his eyes off of Kay, "why don't you go in your room for a minute while I talk to your mom alone." Khalial obeyed his father without argument; he gave his mom a final hug before grabbing his backpack and disappearing down the corridor towards his bedroom.

"What was that about?" Malik questioned.

119

"What are you talking about?" Kay asked slyly as she walked further into the living room and began picking up the pictures from the floor.

"This whole scene. Lights down low, pictures on the floor, you coming to the door all flushed and nervous."

"Malik, you are being ridiculous."

"I hope that I'm being ridiculous."

"What is that supposed to mean?" Kay was angered by his accusations.

"It means that by the look of things I would say that you and Emanuel seem mighty cozy."

"First of all, you are completely out of line. My business is not your business."

"I'm just saying. If it is what I think it is, then it's foul."

"Who asked for you opinion, Malik?"

"Are you kidding me? You are sitting here in the dark doing God-knows -what with your best friend's husband and I'm the problem? I just hope that in all of your meditation, yoga, and self reflection you realize that it is not cool for the two of you to hook up." Malik sounded angrier than his rights allowed.

"Whatever, Malik. How dare you waltz up in here just days after proposing to Heather and question me about what I may or may not be doing." Kay stuffed the photos in their holding chest and slammed it shut signifying the end of that conversation. "Clearly you've moved on."

"So, what is this about? Me asking Heather to marry me?"

"What?" She looked at him like he was speaking Greek. "First of all, it hasn't been about you for a long time so get over yourself. And second of all, I am happy that you and Heather are getting married." She lied. "I couldn't care less." She hoped that that little declaration would add validity to her statement. Kay spun hard on her barefooted heels and turned away from Malik. She stomped towards her bedroom, but before she disappeared completely she looked over her shoulder and said, "You can let yourself out." And with that, Kay disappeared down the dark corridor.

Chapter Thirteen

Emanuel maneuvered effortlessly through the light Sunday evening traffic. His body was still excited from his exchange with Kay. He replayed the events over and over again in his mind. He could still taste her on his lips; she was sweet like peaches, he laughed to himself. There was not another thought in his mind. Usually his thoughts were plenty and they competed for his attention but not tonight. Tonight his mind was on Kay and Kay alone. He turned on the radio, and of course the sweet melodies of no other than Maxwell reverberated through the speakers. Maxwell moaned and crooned in his Prince-esque tone. He sang something about all the things he should have said that he never said, and all the things he should have done that he never did. Emanuel instantly related to the words. He wished that he would have waited Malik out and stayed with Kay a little longer to do and say the things that he wanted to. The sky let out a constant mist of rain, which fell and rested on his windshield. He drove slower than usual, but he didn't mind because it gave him time to think. Usually, while driving down the Schuylkill Parkway during a downpour, his mind would be plagued with thoughts of that dreadful night, but on this night things felt different; things were different. It was raining outside, but inside he was feeling all of the joy that comes with sunshine. He tried to give the road his undivided attention, but it was useless as his mind continuously wrapped around thoughts of Kay. He could still feel the weight of Kay's firm thighs on top of him. There was a ball of excitement in his belly as he thought about all of the possibilities that a life with Kay would bring. He wondered for a second if he was moving too fast, but it felt so good that he didn't want to question it.

"This is the perfect night to cuddle with the one you love." The DJ breathed in his deep voice.

"You are right about that," Emanuel agreed.

"Let's keep it going with Luther Vandross's, *A House is Not A Home*." The opening melody seeped through the speakers, but before Luther could belt out a single note Emanuel turned off the radio. He had not been able to listen to that song since Jada's death. Whenever he heard it his heart ached, and tonight he was feeling way too good to allow something like reality to disrupt his fantasy. The truth of the matter was that Emanuel spent most days trying to avoid the many, subtle, everyday things that reminded him of that fatal night and how much he missed Jada. Driving at night in the rain on the Schuylkill was one such event that generally would cause him to revert back to sadness. Still there were other subtle things that he could not avoid: a familiar laugh in a crowd or the scent of her perfume, Clinique's Happy - - her favorite fragrance. The memories of that fatal night were haunting and he had never been able to escape them, not even for a minute, until now. With the sounds of Luther Vandross echoing in his head he didn't have a choice but to think about that night -- that song played the entire time while the vehicle spun and flipped even after it hit the tree. Luther didn't sound as good mixed with the sounds of screams and screeching tires. As he thought about it, that fatal night felt similar to tonight. He was so relaxed; his mind was so clear. It had been a great night, and out of now where his world all but came to an end. Emanuel thought about how beautiful that night was and how amazing Jada looked. Before the doors opened for the evening and their guests began to arrive, Emanuel, Jada, Kay, and the rest of the *Soul Sistah* family joined together in prayer and a toast; that was the last time that he prayed. Despite all of the excitement of the night Emanuel still remembered the speech that Jada made with glasses raised in the air and tears in her eyes, Jada started,

"I just want to thank all of you guys for making this night a dream come true. I am humbled by this opportunity. I thank God for blessing me with a family that gives me all the love and support that a girl could ask for. I thank you all for your hard work and dedication to the success of *Soul Sistahs*. This started out as a dream that my sister and I…" she winked at Kay, "wrote out in middle school, and here we are living in the reality of that dream. I thank God for my amazing husband," she turned to face him as he rubbed her back in support. "Emanuel, I could not have planned a more perfect life. Thank you for being the man that God has called you to be. You make me so much better." He kissed her gently and wiped away the tears that dropped from each of her eyes. "To my family, Mr. and Mrs. Rivers, Nadia, Khadir, and to Mr. and Mrs. O'Connor – Mrs. Eva O.," she giggled "and Mr. O., you are like my parents and I love you as if you were." She blew them a kiss. "Thank you all for showing me what a family is supposed to look and feel like." She turned back to Emanuel for him to catch the other tears that escaped. And just like the perfect husband Emanuel wiped each tear away. "And to my sister," Jada continued, "Khadijah, what can I say, other than I love you." Jada shook her head gently trying to knock back the tears, "I'm going to ruin my make-up!" Everyone laughed. Kay stepped up and dabbed a napkin gently across Jada's eyes. No sooner than she wiped Jada's tears a stream of tears rushed down her face causing them both to cry. Unable to wipe her own tears away, with one hand wrapped securely around the microphone and the other wrapped around a champagne glass, Jada used her shoulder to wipe her tears. She exhaled hard before continuing, "Khadijah, you really are the brains and beauty behind this whole operation." Kay shook her head in disagreement; she credited Jada's persistence as the reason why *Soul Sistahs* even existed. "You know that next to my husband, you are the second most important person in my life." Kay placed her free hand to her lips and blew Jada a kiss. "To my *Soul Sistahs* family and all of my friends, I thank God for each of you." She leaned closer to Emanuel. "So, here's to God's grace, His mercy, and the blessing of vision. God bless us all, and God bless *Soul Sistahs*." Everyone raised their glasses and toasted; the harmony of glasses clinging was the perfect celebration song. Jada was beaming that night. There were only two other occasions that Emanuel could remember seeing her lit up as brightly-- the day they got married and the day she found out that they were going to have a baby.

Tears filled Emanuel's eyes leaving his vision blurry. He turned the radio back on. He turned the volume up just slightly and listened as Luther's velvet voice resonated through the speakers and filled his car completely, *A room is still a room even when there's nothing there but gloom.* Emanuel attempted to sing along with Luther, his voice heavy and his speech broken. Unable to catch a beat he sang, "…but a room is not a house and a house is not a home when the two of us are far apart and one of us has a brok-en heart…now and then I call your name and suddenly your face appears, but its just a crazy game when it end… *it ends in tears.*" Emanuel and Luther finished together although Luther's voice was much more elegant and polished. Emanuel could feel the words in his soul. He spent many nights acting out the lyrics to that great love song. If someone would have said to him years ago that his life would become so dismal so quickly he would have denied them; likewise, if someone would have told him last week that today he would be so happy and hopeful he would have dismissed them because in his mind he was closer to death than life. Emanuel realized how fickle one's feelings really were. And without thought his mind or his spirit reminded him, *To everything there is a season, and a time to every purpose under heaven: A time to be born and a time to die; a time to plant; a time to pluck up that which is planted; a time to kill and a time to heal; a time to break down, and a time to build up.* He breathed a laugh. "Why do I remember that?" he asked himself out loud and just as quickly as he asked the question the spirit of the Lord spoke to his spirit saying, *Because son out of the issues of the heart the mouth speaks.* Emanuel was reminded that God is true to his word. He would never leave him or forsake him because although he felt far removed from God's love he was still a child of God. Unprepared to re-embrace his once firm faith in God, Emanuel shook his head hoping to shift his thoughts. He drifted into thoughts of him and Kay. His mind was dark and cloudy at first but then it became very clear. He looked over at the passenger side where she *sat*. Through his imagination he was able to envision even the smallest details of her; she sat sideways looking at him adoringly. He looked at her. She placed her hand on is inner thigh and caressed him. His leg warmed beneath her *touch*. With Kay sitting beside him he felt completely at peace. He smiled at the mirage that sat in the seat next to him. He listened to Kay's soft voice,

"*I had a great time tonight.*"

"So did I." He replied to the empty seat,

"*What was your favorite part?*"

"Holding you in my arms." He said without hesitation. *Kay giggled.* Emanuel pulled into his driveway. He *looked at Kay* and smiled. He imagined that they would spend the night in each other's arms. His mind could not begin to compose a scene of them making love because all he desired was to lay in her arms and rest. As he pulled into his driveway he compressed the remote to open his garage. "Will you stay with me tonight?" he asked. She smiled and softly responded,

"*Yes.*"

Emanuel compressed the remote to open his garage and parked. *Kay followed closely behind him* as he led her through the garage into the house. As soon as he opened the door his ringing telephone immediately pulled him back into reality. Sure that it was Kay, Emanuel turned off the fantasy and happily stepped into reality. He rushed to answer the phone and took a deep breath to collect himself before he spoke. He noticed the blinking red light on his answering machine indicating that he had four new messages; he was certain that the messages were from his mother, father, and sister, in any sequence, betting the Nadia probably called twice.

"Hello." He answered the phone with the calm and confidence that used to be his norm, but lately he was mostly anxious and unsure.

"Hey, Emanuel." Nadia's voice was a sudden irritation to Emanuel's ears. "I've been calling you all day. I was beginning to worry about you. Where were you?" she rambled on.

"Nadia," he said with disappointment in his voice. He looked back at Kay, but his hallucination of her was fading from view. He blinked hard trying to hold on to the fantasy.

"Are you okay?" Nadia's voice pulled him further and further away from his thoughts.

"Yeah," he stuttered.

"I've been trying to reach you all day. I called you like a zillion times." She exaggerated. "Did you get any of my messages?"

"No."

"No? I called like a million times."

"Yeah, well, I guess I lost phone reception." He lied, only to realize too late that her next question was going to be *Where were you?* -- and true to her meddlesome ways she asked on cue,

"Where were you?"

"I was at a sports bar downtown." He lied to her again.

"Which sports bar?" Nadia was relentless with the questioning; she was certainly her mother's daughter and law school only seemed to enhance her interrogation skills. He felt like he was being cross-examined.

"Um, Dave and Busters." He named the first establishment that came to mind.

"Were you with Khadir?" The easy answer would have been yes, but he knew that a call to Khadir had certainly been part of Nadia's search efforts.

"No," he said, angry with himself for allowing Nadia to hook him into a web of lies.

"Were you with Kay?"

He thought for a moment and smiled remembering the time that he had spent with Kay. He wanted desperately to get off the telephone with Nadia and get back to those thoughts.

"Nadia, I think I am losing you," he said pulling the phone away from his mouth and adding some background noise.

"Hunh?" She began speaking louder into the receiver.

"I can't hear you. You're breaking up."

"It must be the rain. Let me hang up and call you back!" she continued to yell.

"What? What was that?" Emanuel yelled back, pulling the phone away from his mouth and ear. "I didn't hear --"

He cut himself off mid sentence and depressed the button to end the call. "What was that I couldn't hear you?" He laughed to himself, pleased with his antics. And with that, he closed his

eyes and rekindled his thoughts of Kay. He looked back and
there she was again smiling at him. "Come lay with me?" he
asked. Of course she didn't resist; this was his fantasy. Emanuel
walked through the darkness to his bedroom. He stretched
himself across the bed and secured his pillow in his arms and
hugged his makeshift Kay. He remembered that she was just as
soft and warm. And with the scent of her perfume still fresh on
his fingertips he closed his eyes and inhaled her deeply. His
thoughts were interrupted once again when his telephone rang.
He was sure that it was Nadia calling back, but he checked the
caller ID anyway. RIVERS, NADIA, the small screen displayed.
He ignored it. Moments later his answering machine picked up
and a woman's computer-generated voice began, "You have
reached 877-" she announced Emanuel's phone number. He
hadn't bothered to create a personalized message. Up until a few
months ago he still had the message that he and Jada created
together -- a sweet message that let anyone who called their
home hear the joy of life in their voices. But Mrs. Rivers,
without discussing it with Emanuel, decided that it was time to
erase that message so that he could move on and without his
okay or knowledge Mrs. Rivers erased the message.

Emanuel was too deep in fantasyland with Kay to listen
to the message that Nadia left. He was sure that she would begin
with a statement about the weather and how it was messing up
phone lines everywhere, then she would apologize for their
mother's behavior at the restaurant and then she would probably
end with questions concerning him and counseling. His family
had insisted that he see someone and discuss his feelings. But he
didn't see the point. His feelings were his feelings, and as far as
he was concerned they didn't need to be discussed with anyone -
- especially some stranger. Emanuel squeezed the pillow tightly
and began to whisper, "You feel so good in my arms. So good."
He closed his eyes and settled comfortably in that moment. Not
long after, his telephone rang again and again. He read the caller
ID to see who it was -- ALI, KHADIJAH. He shifted from
snuggling with his pillow and sat up in his bed, back against the
headboard. "Hello," he said, trying to sound normal.

"Hey," Kay's soft voice echoed from the other end.

"Hey," he responded back.

"Are you busy?"

"Nope," he said like a three-year old making a popping sound off of the "p."

"So, what are you doing?"

"Nothing." He whispered.

"Nothing, hunh?"

"Nope." He popped again. "Just sitting here doing nothing."

Kay laughed loud in his ear. Emanuel had never seemed more relaxed. He was silly and funny, and she loved it. Emanuel closed his eyes to catch the sound of her voice in the air. It made him feel closer to her.

"So, you're not thinking or anything?" Kay teased.

"My mind is going a million miles a minute." He laughed, "I'm always thinking that's one of my problems."

"Just one of your problems." She quizzed.

"Yeah, just one." They both laughed. They had expected things to be awkward after the kiss, but, surprisingly, things seemed more comfortable than ever.

"Well," Kay began, "I guess there's nothing wrong with spending time in thought."

"That depends on what you are thinking about."

"Of course. It's like the word of God says," she began, despite the realization that Emanuel wasn't susceptible to the word of God, "Whatever things are pure, whatever things are just, whatever things are lovely…think on those things."

"I have to remember that the next time I am thinking less than pure, just, or lovely thoughts," Emanuel joked. "Speaking of lovely," he continued, finding the perfect opportunity to take the focus off of God, "I had a lovely time with you tonight."

"Ditto," was all that Kay could say. She didn't want to say too much more even though everything in her was overjoyed. She thoroughly enjoyed the time she spent with Emanuel but she didn't want to appear too eager or anxious even though in her double-minded state she was both.

"Ditto." Emanuel repeated analyzing the short word. Of course Kay picked-up on his cynicism and felt compelled to respond further because she sensed that he wanted and maybe even needed to hear more.

"What I mean by ditto is – I had a great time with you tonight, and I hope to do it again." She giggled like a little girl.

"Ditto." Emanuel responded this time being the one who didn't want to say too much.

"I can't seem to think about anything else. The entire 60-second scene keeps playing over and over again in my head," Kay whispered as her thoughts once again replayed the scene. Her heart dangled in her chest making her breathing shallow. "It may be too early to tell, but do you have any regrets?"

"No. No regrets," he said without hesitation. "What about you?"

"Absolutely not," she said more emphatically than she wanted to. "The only regret I have is that it ended so abruptly."

"Me too," Emanuel said as he stroked his pillow, still pretending that Kay was beside him. He held the phone close to his ear.

"I have to say that you are a great kisser." She immediately felt embarrassed by her words.

"You are too. Your lips are very delectable. I could have kissed you all night."

"All night. I think I would have liked that," Kay responded, thinking about just how much she would have enjoyed it. Emanuel held on to her every word and envisioned her soft lips parting with each utterance. He nestled between his sheets and held onto everything even tighter -- the phone, his pillow, her words.

"Do you think that Malik suspected anything?" He dared to ask.

"Yeah, he did. He actually questioned me about it after you left."

"Really?" Emanuel was surprised.

"I just had to remind him that it doesn't matter what he thinks. He needs to remember that he is engaged and he doesn't have any say when it comes to my lov--," she stuttered, ". . .my life."

Emanuel heard what Kay was about to say, but he didn't want to embarrass her so he just let it go. He couldn't ignore the smile that came across his face.

"So, he's engaged, huh?"

"Yup. Apparently so." Kay tried to sound unconcerned but he wondered how she really felt about Malik moving on. He remembered Jada mentioning that she thought that Kay was still in love with Malik, but that was over a year ago. He wondered if she still had feelings for him.

"So, when is the big date?"

"I don't know. We didn't really get into the details. He just told me Friday morning when he came by to pick up Khalial, but with all that was going on I really haven't had time to think about it."

"You didn't have time to think about it," Emanuel repeated. "Have you thought about it now?"

"No, not really." Kay shrugged it off.

"So, you're cool with him getting married?"

"Yeah. Why wouldn't I be?"

"I don't know. I just don't want to be your rebound guy," Emanuel said jokingly.

"Rebound guy? Never that. It is over between Malik and I."

"Why did you guys break up anyway?" Emanuel was sure that Jada mentioned it to him before, but he couldn't recall.

"I guess we just grew apart. One day he decided that this wasn't what he wanted... that I wasn't what he wanted."

Kay paused as she thought about the reality of their breakup. Kay carried a façde of confidence, but Malik was her weakness and having him leave her the way that he did made her feel unbelievably insecure. She had never completely gotten over him. Being around him was like irritating an old wound, never allowing it to heal. She was still so in love with Malik that the very thought of him hurt her heart. And this evening was no exception. Yeah, she was caught up in the details of her and

Emanuel, but every time she was around Malik something inside
of her yearned for him; leaving her feeling very vulnerable and
very insecure. Kay knew that she needed to move on but up until
tonight it seemed impossible. Other guys that she dated never
seemed to measure up to Malik. The guys either looked good on
the outside but had no personality; or they were busted on the
outside and had all of the personality in the world. Emanuel was
the first man who even came close to making her forget about
her feelings for Malik. Emanuel sensed that Malik was a heavy
topic for Kay, and tonight he wanted to keep things light.

"Well, it is truly his loss. A man would have to be
beyond crazy to not want you." Emanuel said.

"Thank you. That is very flattering."

"So, what are you doing?" Emanuel asked as he settled
his mind and prepared himself for a lively conversation.

"I'm not doing a thing. I'm just happy to have this time
alone to talk to you."

" What do you want to talk to me about?" Emanuel
flirted.

"I don't know. I just want to hear the sound of your voice
in my ear. I don't want to talk about anything deep. I want to talk
as if we are meeting for the first time. What's your favorite
color?" Kay and Emanuel both laughed at her question. They
both agreed that that was as basic a question as you could get.

"Wow! My favorite color..." He laughed again as he
thought about his response. This question reminded him just
how weird he could be at times. As one who was not quite
comfortable with his creative side he always felt that he needed
to make excuses for how he thought. He was aware of the fact
that as the creative type he had always seen things differently,
but the logical part of his being always felt the need to explain
himself and to be understood. But Kay's question was too simple
and his response was just as simple, there was no real
explanation for such a question.

"My favorite color is green."

"No way?"

"Yes, really. I know what you're thinking -- who chooses green as their favorite color?"

"No, I wasn't thinking that at all. My favorite color is green!" Kay laughed. "And not just any green, but every green. I have not seen a green that I didn't like."

"Me either." They laughed.

"I started liking green back in kindergarten. In the morning the teacher would always play music from the Muppets, and I would look at that album cover with Kermit sitting on top of a car. All of the characters were on the cover of course, but I only had eyes for Kermit. I was totally in love with Kermit the Frog. Maybe that's why my love life is so shabby; my first crush was a frog!" Kay's analogy was completely ridiculous, but it was hilarious and Emanuel laughed harder then he had in a long time. "Do you remember the Muppets?"

"Of course, I remember the Muppets. Kermit was the man -- I mean, the frog." He burst out laughing again. "If you loved Kermit the Frog then you would have loved me. When I was in third grade I took a class picture, and I had on a green turtle neck -- it was exactly the same color and texture as Kermit the Frog. It was itchy as all get out, but it was my absolute favorite sweater. Maybe I should pull it out and see if it could make you fall in love with me." Emanuel joked. He could not believe that he was having this insane conversation about Kermit the Frog and the color green, but he was enjoying it. Talking to Kay was effortless, and he enjoyed every silly moment of it. He laughed so hard that his side ached. Kay laughed lightly as she listened and enjoyed the sound of his laughter.

"That is so funny. You have to show me that picture."

"I will the next time you come over; I will show it to you."

Kay and Emanuel talked and laughed all night. When the sun started its creep over the darkness and the birds began chirping, life was signaling to them both that a new day was upon them. Now, instead of struggling with thoughts of death, Emanuel struggled with the thought of having to disconnect from Kay. He felt like a schoolboy experiencing love for the first time. The thought of hanging up the telephone caused him great angst. All he could think about was when he would have the opportunity to be with her again. He watched the clock and the sky as time ticked by. He knew that it was only moments before they would have to say good-bye. At five-thirty Kay's alarm clock rang telling her that it was time to start her day. Despite not getting any sleep she felt refreshed and ready for whatever the day had in store for her. Kay stretched and let out a heavy sigh,

"Well, that's my cue."

"No," Emanuel whined playfully, "just a few more minutes."

"I really don't want to hang up, but I have a very busy day ahead of me. If I start out late I will spend the whole day trying to play catch up," she said regretfully.

"I know." Emanuel spoke regretfully through his stretch. "I can't believe we talked all night. I haven't done this since…" He tried to recall the last time he stayed on the phone all night. It was the day he met Jada, but instead of saying that he settled for, "I hadn't done that in a very long time."

"Well, I have never done it…you were my first," Kay smiled through her words.

"Can I see you later?"

"Yes," Kay responded quickly barely giving him time to get the words out.

"Do you want to do lunch?"

"I can't do lunch; we are taking inventory at the club today, and that will probably last into the late afternoon."

"What about dinner?"

"Dinner sounds great."

"I don't know if I can wait until dinner. Would you mind if I stopped by the club to see you?"

"Yes, I mind," Kay laughed, "I will be in sweats all day and I'm sure that I am going to look a hot, dusty mess," Kay joked. "By dinner I would have had a chance to clean up and make myself beautiful."

"You are always beautiful."

Emanuel closed his eyes trying to capture an image of Kay as evidence of his statement, but Jada's face appeared instead.

"Yeah, well let's stick to that story." Kay joked. "So, dinner tonight. You and me."

"I look forward to it."

"Me too."

"Enjoy your day."

"You too." For the next few moments they said good-bye, neither of them really wanting to end the conversation.

"Okay. Bye."

"Bye."

Emanuel regretfully pressed the talk button to disconnect. He held the phone to his heart. He inhaled deeply trying to fill his lungs with confidence and exhaled hard releasing all of his insecurities. He listened to the early morning music of birds chirping, trees swaying in the gentle breeze, and the sound of tires rolling across the distant highway. He was confident that today was going to be a great day, and for the first time in a year he was looking forward to being a part of it.

Chapter Fourteen

Emanuel decided to take a break from his usual anxiety-filled morning so instead of rising with the roosters and beginning his day in haste, he chose to take in the morning news over a cup of coffee. There was no thought of death or loss, only thoughts of Kay and how much he had enjoyed spending time with her over the past few days.

When Mona arrived in the office at eight-thirty she was surprised to find Emanuel's office empty and uninterrupted. Typically, she would have come in to find him waist deep in work and already three-plus hours into his workday. Mona tried to relax as she pushed back disturbing thoughts about where Emanuel could be. She feared all year that he would do something to hurt himself, and, coming off of the one-year anniversary of Jada's death, it would not be too far-fetched that today would be the day that she get that phone call. Mona closed her eyes and began to speak to God for Emanuel's safety. At ten o'clock Emanuel came waltzing through the lobby smiling a huge dimpled smile. He walked up to the front desk all a-grin.

"Good Morning, Mona," Emanuel announced in a cheerful tone. "Do I have any messages?"

"Yes sir, Mr. Rivers." Mona replied in a surprised voice, not taking her eyes off of him as she reached for the stack of messages that she gathered from telephone calls and emails.

"Thanks," he said collecting the stack from her. He whistled some unfamiliar tune as he looked over his messages and continued to waltz towards his office. Mona followed closely behind him. She was surprised to see him in such a pleasant mood, but she thanked God for it.

"How are you today?" Mona queried.

"I'm wonderful!" Emanuel exclaimed.

"Wonderful?" Mona questioned. *How does one go from sad and gloomy on Friday to wonderful on Monday? It's usually the other way around.* "Would you like a cup of coffee?"

"No thanks, Mona. I'm fine." Emanuel plopped in his chair causing it to swivel from side to side. "What do I have on my calendar for today?" He continued looking over his messages deducing, in his mind, those that needed his immediate attention and those that he could respond to at his leisure.

"Let me check."

Mona disappeared from his office for a split second to gather his daily calendar from her desk. Normally she would have had that information in her head appointment by appointment and all of the details, but this morning was different; the time that she would have spent memorizing his calendar she spent in prayer, which she decided was certainly time better spent. Mona raced back to his door within seconds. "Sir," she began breathlessly, "you have a ten-thirty with Myers; a twelve o'clock with Greenberg; a two o'clock with Winfrey…" she said reading off the list of his day's events.

"Is that with Oprah Winfrey?' Emanuel joked, but Mona didn't get it.

"No. Johnson Winfrey," Mona corrected.

"Mona, it was a joke. I was kidding." Emanuel gave her a smile.

"Oh!" She said and cracked a faux smile. "And there is Randolph Emerson's dinner party, six-thirty at the Hyatt Regency on Penn's Landing," she continued. This was the only meeting that Emanuel jotted down.

"Thank you, Mona."

"You're welcome, sir."

"Do I have the option of bringing a guest?" he asked.

"Yes sir. You plus one." Mona smiled to herself. *A woman* she thought, *I should have known.*

"Great," Emanuel said without further explanation.

"Is there anything else, sir?" Mona's voice trailed into a whisper.

"Yes, one last thing. Lighten up." Emanuel smiled.

That was certainly a change. He was usually the one walking around all uptight, Mona thought, but she simply smiled and responded with a pleasant and professional,

"Yes sir. Let me know if you need anything else."

"I certainly will."

And with that Emanuel reached for the telephone and began dialing Kay's cell phone number. He didn't think that she would be too jazzed about spending the evening at a bourgeoisie gala, but he hoped that she would be jazzed about spending time with him.

He practiced what he was going to say to her as the phone rang, however, once she answered the phone all his cool was gone as he fumbled over his words.

"Hello." Kay answered on the fourth ring.

"He- hey- hello there," Emanuel said feeling like an idiot.

"He- hey- hello there, yourself," Kay mimicked. "I thought that I was supposed to call you."

"You were but something kind of important came up. I was invited to an event that one of my clients is hosting. I forgot about it, but it's one of those things that are good for business you know."

"Yes. I know about those kinds of meetings."

"So, I was hoping that instead of going to a restaurant for dinner you wouldn't mind joining me for a night on the town?"

"Ooh. . . a night on the town," Kay cooed. "That sounds fancy. Do I have to get all dolled up?"

"Wel-l-l" Emanuel stuttered, "It is a rather formal affair, but you always look beautiful so what ever you decide to wear will be perfect."

"Yeah, nice try," Kay laughed in the phone. "What are you wearing?"

"I have to wear a tuxedo."

"A tuxedo? Emanuel, if you are wearing a tux then I have to be red carpet-ready. It's not like I can just throw on any old thing."

"What I mean is that I know you are going to look beautiful no matter what you wear."

"Well, thanks for the vote of confidence, but it takes some work to pull off red carpet, fancy, bourgeoisie, beautiful. What time is the event?"

"It starts at six-thirty, but I planned to pick you up at six."

"Six." Kay looked at the clock on her wall. "Okay, I think I can get fabulous in eight hours," Kay laughed. In her mind every event was a networking opportunity and networking was her second line of business. As far as she was concerned a room full of Philly's finest was a great place to promote *Soul Sistahs*.

Emanuel made the best of his day. He counted down every minute in anticipation of the six o'clock hour when he would pick Kay up and enjoy a night out on the town. Mona prepared his tuxedo and scheduled a driver to pick him up at five-thirty. She was thrilled to learn that he was taking a date to the event, but her feelings were mixed when she learned that his date was Kay. She recognized the potential disaster that such a situation could cause but she reasoned that if Kay had what it takes to put a smile on Emanuel's face then who was she to question it.

Chapter Fifteen

Kay walked quickly through The Gallery mall. She had scheduled a last minute pedicure and manicure at Perfectly Pretty Salon and Day Spa. But first she had to stop by and grab her favorite lemonade from Chick-fil-A.

"A large lemonade, please?" She searched her oversized hobo bag for $2.83 for her drink. She tipped her bag to the side and listened as all of the change fell to one corner. The older Asian cashier looked at her intently waiting for her to pay so that he could complete their transaction. "I'm sorry," Kay smiled, feeling slightly embarrassed. "I know I have the exact change." The man nodded his head in her direction and smiled at her. *Darn my need to always pay with the exact amount of change. Why don't I just give the man three dollars and call it a day?* She continued to dig for pennies. Relief fell over her as she pulled out a handful of change and counted three quarters, a nickel and three shiny pennies. "Seventy-five, eighty, one, two, three." She placed the coins on top of the two dollars that lay on the counter; she felt a sense of accomplishment, but the cashier was not impressed. He gathered the money, handed her the drink, and went to the next customer.

Kay licked her dry lips before she wrapped them around the straw and took a long sip of the bitter beverage. Before she could finish her swig she heard a familiar voice call out her name.

"Hey, Kay." It was Malik walking arm-in-arm with Heather. This was the first time that she had seen the two of them together since Malik announced their engagement.

"Malik, Heather... Hi." She swallowed prematurely and spoke through the liquid that threatened to strangle her. She tapped her chest hard. "Oh, my! It went down the wrong pipe." She giggled awkwardly. "How are you guys doing?"

"We're great!" Heather responded despite the fact that Kay's eyes were on Malik. Kay couldn't bear to look at her. She knew that eventually she would have to embrace Heather but she wasn't quite there yet. It annoyed Kay that Heather was already speaking of her and Malik as "we". *We're great!* Kay mumbled under her breath. But then again everything about Heather annoyed Kay -- her perfect lips, her wavy sandy-blonde hair, her big green eyes, her perfect size six. Kay wished that she hated Heather for a reason that made sense, but she didn't; she hated her simply because Malik loved her. She wished that Heather was mean or arrogant, but the truth was that Heather was as sweet as pie and Malik chose her. She even wished that she was narrow-minded enough to hate her simply because she was white, but no. Her hatred for Heather was fueled only by Malik's love for her and the fact that she was so perfect and she knew that she could not compete.

She looked at Heather with a half-hearted smile on her face. "Great," the word forced itself through Kay's strained teeth. With Malik standing before her looking so happy and so fine and Heather looking amazing Kay suddenly became aware of how homely she looked. Heather's green eyes stared right through her like an x-ray exposing all of her insecurities. Kay stole a glimpse of her reflection in a store window and her once street-chic ponytail, torn jeans, and RUN DMC t-shirt suddenly felt awkward and all wrong.

"So, how are you doing?" Malik asked, as he remembered the angry exchange they shared the night before.

"I'm fine," Kay said flashing a fake smile. "I was doing inventory at the club today," she offered, not so subtly in an effort to explain her grungy appearance.

"What brings you to the mall in the middle of the day?" Malik asked.

"I should be asking you the same question." Kay said with a tinge of anger in her voice, but she didn't want to carry on in front of Heather. Kay hated playing the role of the scorned Baby Mama, but she just couldn't seem to get past her feelings of rejection. Kay took a deep breath and tried to talk her feelings down. She was preparing to spend the evening with a great man so why was she allowing Malik and Heather's happiness to bring her such misery. "I'm actually going to a Randolph Emerson event tonight at Penn's Landing." Kay didn't feel like she needed to say anything more, the name Randolph Emerson spoke for itself.

"Randolph Emerson! Wow!" Malik was impressed just as she expected him to be. "You're hanging out with the crè me de la crème. How did that happened?" Kay wondered after the situation last night if she should share the details about going to the event with Emanuel. She knew that it would get a reaction out of Malik but that wasn't what she was looking for. She didn't want to make Malik jealous especially not of Emanuel. She wished that there were another tall, good-looking guy to flaunt in Malik's face. So she decided to just keep it simple. "Business is good," Kay replied. "I just came to get my nails done. I don't want to sit across from Mr. Emerson and his rich friends with my nails all busted." Kay flashed her free hand, which was rough and dry from lifting boxes in the cellar all morning. "What about you? You're never off during the week."

"Well, today is a special day," Malik began as he laid adoring eyes on Heather. Before he could finish his sentence Heather chimed in --

" It's our anniversary," Heather said looking into Malik's eyes.

"Anniversary?" Kay was confused.

"The anniversary of our first date."

Since when did he start celebrating frivolous anniversaries-- first date, first kiss, first whatever.

Kay twisted her lips and looked Heather up and down.

"Yeah, but after we tie the knot there will be only one anniversary that will really matter." Heather wrapped her arms tighter around Malik's forearm displaying her huge diamond engagement ring.

"Oh, my!" Kay stepped back as if the sparkle from the light hitting the rock blinded her. It was official. Malik had really moved on. Kay sized up her competition one last time and took a deep breath as she realized that it was really over between her and Malik. She suddenly reverted back to the feelings of rejection that she tried so desperately to avoid. They were the same feelings that she felt the day her father left and when Malik walked out on her and their relationship. And now with Malik standing side by side with Heather it was another reminder that he didn't want her. Despite the tossing and turning in her belly and the ache in her heart Kay did what she does best -- she smiled, held it all together, and said, "What a beautiful ring, Heather. Congratulations."

"Thanks, Kay." Heather leaned in and hugged her. "That really means a lot coming from you." Kay's arms were pressed to her side by Heather's embrace. It was more than Kay was ready to handle so she wiggled free from Heather and stepped back.

"Yeah, well, I don't want to be late for my appointment." She looked at her bare wrist where her watch should have been without acknowledging the awkward embrace.

"It was good seeing you two." Kay threw up her hand and waved a half-hearted goodbye. Kay walked quickly in one direction while Malik and Heather strolled in the opposite direction in love. Kay slowed down just long enough to sneak one last glance at Malik and Heather as they walked through the mall hand-in-hand. She hated that their happiness caused her heart to ache, and she promised herself that she would fast and pray pass this insecurity as soon as she had the time, but for now she had a fancy party to prepare for.

Kay rushed home from the mall; she dashed throughout the house trying to gather her thoughts and her clothes for tonight's event. When Emanuel called to invite her to attend the gala with him, her mind instantly started whirling around what to wear. It was during her wine count at the club that she decided on the form-fitting gold gown that she purchased off the clearance rack at Felines Basement's months earlier. Kay would have loved to be able to get her hair and make-up done by a professional, but she just didn't have the time. So when Fatima called her on her cell phone in the middle of her pedicure and asked if she could stop by to talk, Kay convinced her to bring her make-up kit. Fatima was a natural artist when it came to make-up; she didn't wear it herself, but she was a pro at applying it. She had always dreamed of going to beauty school, but

marriage, children, and her Muslim faith interrupted her plans.
Kay had already showered and was wrapped in her robe when
Fatima arrived at the house.

"Hey, mama," Kay said as she embraced her little sister.

"Hey." Fatima was so beautiful not even her hajib could
hide her beauty. Her skin was flawless, and her huge hazel eyes
were like fine jewels. Making beautiful babies was the one thing
that Eva and Walter got right. Kay watched as Fatima got
comfortable and began unpacking her make-up kit.

"Do you want something to eat or drink?" Kay offered,
always hospitable.

"I'll take something to drink. Do you have any apple
juice?"

What an odd request Kay thought to herself.

"Sure." Kay quickly headed towards the refrigerator. "Do
you want ice?"

"Yes, please," Fatima said politely.

Kay grabbed a glass, filled it partially with ice, and then
filled it to the rim with apple juice. She glanced over at the clock
on her range it was four-thirty. She made a mental note to
herself; she would give Fatima exactly one hour to talk about
whatever it was that she wanted to talk about. Kay sat in a chair
directly in front of Fatima and prepared herself for a makeover.
Fatima dabbed some white cream in her hand before massaging
it onto Kay's face. Kay closed her eyes, and relaxed for the first
time since she got the call from Emanuel.

"So, what's going on? How are my nieces and
nephews?"

"They are doing great." Fatima took a long sip from her
glass. "I'm sure Eva already told you that I am expecting again,"
Fatima said rubbing her tiny belly. Kay popped her eyes open;
she didn't want to appear shocked but she was.

"Actually, she didn't. I talked to Ma' briefly this
afternoon to see if she could pick up Khalial for me. She didn't
say a word about you being pregnant. Congratulations." Kay was
not quite convinced that it was as happy an occasion as it was
the first, second, and even third time that Fatima got pregnant,

the fourth and now fifth times were just too much in Kay's mind, but who was she to judge.

"Thank you." Fatima beamed. "I'm barely three months." Kay was speechless she couldn't believe how happy Fatima was. Kay closed her eyes as Fatima applied foundation. Fatima already had four small children all under the age of six so Kay could not bring herself to be completely happy for her. Kay believed wholeheartedly that children are blessings -- but in moderation. She wished that Fatima had been a little more selective in her choices. Kay wanted to tell her just that, but she didn't want to get into it with Fatima. She was an adult; she was married; and it was her life. So Kay sat back in her chair and listened as Fatima shared the tattered tale of how she found out that she was pregnant and how happy Raheem was when she told him the news. Kay could only imagine what Eva said when she found out - now that was a story that she couldn't wait to hear.

"But that's not what I wanted to talk to you about." Fatima's eyes got brighter than usual. "I have been seriously considering going back to school." Fatima waited for Kay's reaction. She expected Kay to be shocked initially, and she was.

"Wow! That's great. What are you going to go to school for?" Kay was afraid to ask.

"I want to practice civil rights law."

"Civil rights law." Kay had to repeat it because she couldn't believe her ears. Fatima always wanted to do things the hard way. Kay recognized the stupidity of her next statement and if she had been talking to anyone other than Fatima she wouldn't have felt the need to point out the obvious.

"So that means that you will have to go to college and then law school." Kay knew the answer, but she wasn't convinced that Fatima realized exactly what her plans entailed.

"Of course, it does." Fatima laughed. "I've already signed up for some classes at community." Kay could have tried to process Fatima's plans in their entirety but instead she chose to focus on one detail at a time. Kay rewound the conversation in her head and repeated it to herself. *She wants to go to college, she wants to practice civil rights law, she has already signed up for some classes at community*. Kay could have asked all of the important follow-up questions, but she just didn't have the time so instead of saying anything that would have dragged the conversation on any longer than she had time for she simply replied,

"Fatima that is awesome."

Underneath all of the madness Kay heard Fatima say that she had signed up for college classes; that was a great start and Kay was proud of her little sister. Kay didn't want to say anything to discourage her, but she couldn't help but wonder how she would manage such a task with four, now five kids in tow. And, as if Fatima could read her mind, she began to explain her plan,

"I know that it is going to be difficult with the kids and all, but I know that I can do it."

"Fatima, I think that you can do whatever you set your mind to." Kay gave the appropriate big sister response.

"Raheem said that he would support it as long as I find someone to watch the kids while I'm in class."

Kay's heart dropped, she was sure that Fatima was going to ask her to watch the kids and she was just as certain that she would have to say no. Fatima's children were four of the most beautiful kids that anyone has ever seen, but they were more work than Kay was used to.

"So, who are you going to get to watch the kids?" Kay didn't even want to discuss the fact that Raheem didn't offer to watch them.

"That's the thing." Fatima leaned back. "My classes are at night and I was hoping that you could talk to Eva for me," Fatima said squinting her eyes, trying to dampen the look that she knew Kay was going to give her. "Maybe she could help me out by watching the kids a few evenings out of the week."

"And you want me to talk to her about that?"

"Un- hunh." Fatima gave an immature response.

"Fatima, I think that is a conversation you need to have with Eva."

"I know, and I will, but if you mention it to her first you can get her to think about it so then when I mention it to her she would have had enough time to reflect and have a real conversation with me and not just flip out the minute I ask." Fatima always used Kay as a buffer between her and Eva. Even when they were little Kay would ask the hard questions first. She would, get hit with all of the verbal darts that Eva would throw before she took the time to think about the question and come up with a well thought out response. Her response was usually still no, but after a little reflection it was a kinder, gentler no.

"Okay, I will do it, but you know that you are going to have to have a well thought out plan. Eva is not going to support any half-hearted pipe dreams."

"I don't know why she always get so bent out of shape when I ask her to watch my children. She watches Khalial all of the time without question," Fatima retorted as if you could compare the two.

"Actually, she watches Khalial sometimes but only after I have exhausted all of my other resources. Furthermore, Khalial is six-years old and it's only him. Fatima, you have four babies and another one on the way. That's a lot to ask of anyone even Eva." Kay realized that perhaps she had said too much when Fatima dropped her head and let out a heavy sigh. The last thing that Kay wanted to do was discourage her sister so she changed her tone quickly. "But this is a big deal," she reasoned, for her own good as much as Fatima's. "Eva will have her reservations, but if you show her that you're serious I'm sure that she will support you. I'll talk to her tomorrow." Kay didn't believe a word she just said. She knew Eva too well and so did Fatima, but if Fatima wanted to pretend that their mother would jump at the opportunity to watch her grandchildren while her daughter, who never finished anything, went back to school, then Kay would pretend too.

"Thank you." Fatima beamed. "This is going to be so great!" Fatima reached down and hugged her big sister's neck tightly. Kay couldn't understand for the life of her why Fatima was so clueless when it came to taking care of her business. She was certainly Walter's child. If there was a difficult way to do things then she was going to do it. She enrolled in the school of hard knocks on purpose and she had the bumps and bruises to prove it. One thing that Kay knew for sure was that if Fatima wasn't her sister then she would not be bothered with her, she was just simple enough to fall off of Kay's radar.

"So, how are you doing with this make-up?" Kay asked exasperated. "I have a big night ahead of me."

"What's occasion?" Fatima queried as she brushed a sheer gloss over Kay's lips.

"I have been invited to attend a fancy dinner party this evening." Kay smiled as thoughts of Emanuel entered her mind, pushing out the foolishness that Fatima laid on her.

"A fancy dinner party with who?"
Kay hesitated. "Well, you know this past weekend I had the memorial service for Jada at the club."

"Yeah, I know. How did it go?"

"It was great. The club was packed. Emanuel even showed up."

"Oh, wow. How is he doing?"

"He's great." Kay responded trying not to disrupt her painted lips. "I mean as good as can be expected." Kay digressed. "We kind of hung out a bit afterwards and so he invited me to go to this dinner party with him tonight." Kay braced herself for Fatima's response.

"Cool." Fatima didn't flinch. "All done." Fatima announced with one final stroke of blush across her cheeks. "What do you think?" Fatima held an oval-shaped mirror in front of Kay. She was breathless. Kay was convinced that this was Fatima's calling. Forget law school. Make-up was her true talent.

"Fatima. You are incredible. You should skip law school and go to beauty school. You have a real talent when it comes to makeup."

"Yeah, right. I enjoy it, but how can I do someone's make-up when I don't even wear make-up."

"Girl, look at my face. What do you mean, how can you do make-up? Just like this!" Kay said adamantly as she looked past the mirror at Fatima.

"I suppose."

After Kay finished admiring herself in the mirror she turned back to Fatima's comment about her evening plans with Emanuel.

"Cool. Is that all you have to say about me hanging out with Emanuel? Surely, you are going to say something about the two of us spending time together."

"What else should I say? You and Emanuel are going to a dinner party. What?" Fatima was clueless.

"Nothing." Kay laughed under her breath.

"You guys are still friends, right?"

"Of course we are."

"So, what do you expect me to say? What, do you like him or something?"

"Or something." Kay smiled.

"Well, who knows? You two may get married and have a bunch of babies of your own." Fatima said rubbing her tiny belly for effect. Kay could only shake her head; there was no response for such an insane statement. Kay quickly changed the subject and lured Fatima into talks of Walter. Although Kay didn't make it a point to talk about their dad she was curious to know how he was doing. Besides, after her verbal dual with Mrs. Rivers about Walter's faith he had been on her mind. Kay thought about the statements that she made in defending him and she quizzed Fatima to be sure that what she claimed was accurate.

"So, how is Walter?"

"Dad is great." Fatima always called Walter "Dad," a title that as far as Kay was concerned he lost when he walked out on them. "I was just at his house over the weekend. The kids are wonderful -- Hadassah is great; Dad just received honors from the Mayor for the work that he's doing with the schools. They are all doing really good."

"Good," Kay groaned. Fatima had given her more information than she wanted to know; she had never been concerned about Hadassah, the twenty-something-year-old-woman that Walter called wife. But oddly enough Kay did find herself feeling a bit proud of Walter's recognition by the mayor.

"Dad asked about you and Khalial. He really misses you guys."

"Yeah, well, he knows where I live. If he really missed us he would come visit."

"Yeah, right. He's not convinced that you would even let him in if he knocked on your door."

"Neither am I," Kay said with a laugh, but she wasn't kidding.

"Khadijah, you should really give him a chance. Dad is different. He is nothing like the man that he was when he was with Eva. Hadassah has been really good for him. He is healthy and happy. You probably wouldn't even recognize him." Fatima smiled. "You'd be proud of the man that he's become." Fatima concluded with a certain confidence.

"Yeah, whatever." Kay shrugged off Fatima's statement; there were too many things in her statement that annoyed Kay, especially the insinuation that Eva was some how responsible for Walter's shortcomings. It didn't take long for Kay to realize that she wasn't as open to have a conversation about Walter as she thought. Fatima recognized her discomfort and decided to change the subject.

"So, how is Malik doing?"

"He's fine." Kay said with very little energy.

"I hear he's getting married.' Fatima was almost sympathetic.

"Where did you hear that from?"

"Dad."

"What does he know about it?"

"I don't know. He said that he bumped into Malik on 69th Street and he told him that he was getting married. Dad asked him if he was marrying you." Fatima burst out laughing. Kay cut her an evil eye. She did not see the humor in it.

Why, she wondered, *would it be so ridiculous in Fatima's mind for Malik to marry me?*

149

Fatima didn't recognize Kay's irritation and true to her clueless self she continued, "He should marry you." For a minute Kay thought that she was trying to make up for her hurtful comment, but no. Fatima was just getting started. "I mean, after all you are the mother of his son. What man wouldn't want to be with the woman who gave him his first son?"

Kay looked at her sister in complete disbelief; she searched her eyes for a sign of life, but she got nothing but a green-eyed blank stare from her sister. Kay could have taken the time to school Fatima on proper conversation etiquette, but she was much too annoyed to entertain anymore of Fatima's conversation. She replayed the events and deduced that Fatima hadn't said one thing that made any good sense during the whole hour that she was there. She had a beautiful night ahead of her, and she didn't want to upset her spirit trying to talk sense into Fatima.

"Well, I need to get dressed. My limo will be here any minute." Kay embraced her sister, offered her a cheek kiss, and escorted her to the door.

"Don't forget to talk to Eva," Fatima reminded her just before Kay closed the door. She thought she heard Kay say, "I won't," but in reality Kay just offered a groan. When Fatima was gone Kay took a deep breath releasing any negative energy that threatened to disrupt the night ahead. She shook off thoughts of Walter, Malik, and Fatima and embraced the warmness that thoughts of Emanuel brought.

Chapter Sixteen

By the time Emanuel arrived at Kay's house she looked like she had just stepped off of the cover of a sophisticated magazine and he was very pleased by her vision of beauty.

"You look amazing." Emanuel could not hide his excitement.

"Thank you." Kay blinked "You look very handsome yourself, Mr. Rivers." Kay's smile melted Emanuel's heart. He leaned in and gave her a kiss on the cheek although her lips seemed to be calling him to them. Emanuel was very excited about spending a night on the town with Kay. She was smart, beautiful, and successful -- just the right caliber of woman to parade around at a Randolph Emerson gala.

Randolph Emerson was one of Philadelphia's biggest success stories. He was born to drug-addicted parents and raised in the Richard Allen Projects, one of Philadelphia's worst housing developments. He was the proverbial poor boy turned business mogul. He acquired high-end real estate in Philadelphia's Penn's Landing district in the early seventies and parlayed that success into other venture capital investments like restaurants, casinos, and hotels. He was one of Emanuel's biggest clients and a true gentleman's gentleman. Everyone from Martha's Vineyard to the Carolinas was familiar with Randolph Emerson and those that knew him respected him greatly.

The driver pulled up in front of the Hyatt Regency on the boardwalk. He opened the door and Emanuel stepped out. He extended his hand to Kay and led her out into the cool brisk night. She felt like a movie star getting ready to walk the red carpet on Oscar night. The night air was clear and crisp and a billion bright stars gathered in the dark sky to shine on her and witness the magic of the night. It only took a second for Emanuel to usher Kay into the hotel but in that second Kay took in the entire scene and made a mental note of its beauty. Emanuel gently placed his hand around her waist and escorted her towards the grand ballroom where the event was being held. Kay walked through the hotel lobby wide-eyed. She was no stranger to class, but her jaw dropped as she walked through the glass and gold trimmed doors. The high ceilings were bejeweled with several huge chandeliers that lit up the room and everyone in it. Kay looked over her shoulder at Emanuel whose eyes were just as wide as hers.

"Pinch me. I must be dreaming," she said. There she was in a grand hotel with a room full of beautiful and successful people and in the company of the man that she was quickly falling in love with.

"It is amazing, isn't it?" Emanuel cosigned not really asking a question or expecting an answer. The air was filled with music, chatter, and laughter. In the far corner of the room sat a gray haired man stroking the keys of a grand piano. His delicate fingers barely grazed the ebonies and ivories, releasing music in the air that nurtured the soul. He played a soft jazzy melody, which made Kay feel at home. His white tuxedo blended perfectly with the white piano and the picturesque room. Emanuel and Kay's eyes met and they took an obvious deep breath before they stepped, in unison, into the crowd. Emanuel received greetings and pats on the back as he walked towards the bar. Kay had never witnessed Emanuel in his element, but she could see, based on the party- goers response to him, that he was well known, well liked, and well respected. Walking with him made Kay feel even more elegant. Her confidence was through the roof, which was much needed after her earlier run-in with Malik and Heather and her talk with Fatima.

Before they could reach the bar an attractive older couple greeted them in the middle of the dance floor. The gentleman was just as tall as Emanuel but he carried a leaner frame. If it weren't for the gray hair that completely covered his head one would have guessed that he was a young man. Kay had never met Randolph Emerson but she had recognized him from the papers and the many local reports on him. He was unbelievably breathtaking and an aura of success was thick around him. She was pleasantly surprised by how attractive Mr. Emerson was; he kind of resembled Ed Bradley -- very distinguished. The woman that hung on his arm was the perfect picture of a trophy wife.

She was just as tall and lean and her hair was also completely gray. Like her husband, she did not look a day over forty. Her skin was flawless with very few wrinkles. She was simply beautiful. Kay prayed to God that she would age as gracefully as Mrs. Emerson had.

"Emanuel, I am so glad you were able to make it," Mr. Emerson said as he wrapped Emanuel in an embrace.

"Randolph," Emanuel said through his smile. "I wouldn't have missed it for anything in the world," Emanuel said with an air that Kay had never witnessed. "Claudia." Emanuel nodded before leaning in and planting a gentle kiss on Mrs. Emerson's ruby-blushed cheek.

"Emanuel. How are you?" Her eyes were kind.

"I am well."

"Are you really?" She looked directly into Emanuel's eyes.

"Yes." Emanuel nodded much longer than it took to say the word. "I am doing a lot better." He added and Kay got the sense that he really was.

"I'm glad to hear that." Mrs. Emerson held Emanuel's hand in hers as she turned to face Kay. Up until this point Kay stood by looking, smiling aimlessly. "And who is this beautiful woman?"

"This is a family friend, Khadijah Ali."

"Kay," Kay corrected as she leaned in and shook Mrs. Emerson's hand, then Mr. Emerson's. Kay felt a ting of discomfort *a family friend*. The words echoed in her head. She didn't know how she expected Emanuel to introduce her but the words family friend just didn't settle right with her. But the reality was that they were just friends despite the fact that less than twenty-four hours ago she was straddled across him. The friendship zone was okay -- it was comfortable and expectations were low. Despite the scene that unfolded on Kay's living room floor last night, they were only friends and neither of them was sure that they were fully committed to doing what needed to be done to take things to the next level.

"What a beautiful young lady. Emanuel, you are a very lucky man," Mr. Emerson not taking his eyes off of Kay. "The last time I had a friend that beautiful, I married her." He looked adoringly over at his wife; she smiled a bright tooth smile. Mr. and Mrs. Emerson laughed hard, but Kay and Emanuel just gave a polite laugh. They both thought more deeply about Mr. Emerson's words than he had intended. "Well, you two enjoy yourselves. Dinner will be served shortly." Mr. and Mrs. Emerson excused themselves and continued through the crowd greeting their other guests.

"What a beautiful couple." Kay offered, trying to move past the awkward silence between them.

"Yeah, they really are great people." Emanuel looked back and followed them with his eyes as they went from one guest to the other. He always thought that he and Jada would have been that kind of power couple when they reached the Emersons' age and their level of success, but now all he was left with were broken dreams. Without warning Emanuel reached for Kay's hand and lead her the rest of the way across the dance floor to the bar. Needing to relax and shake off their nervousness Emanuel and Kay both ordered a glass of white wine. They sipped slowly as they pointed out the many famous faces in the crowd. There were several politicians, including the mayor and Kay wondered if she introduced herself as Walter's daughter would he recognize her or was Walter's "recognition," as Fatima called it, some generic political ploy. There were athletes from each of Philadelphia's professional teams: the Sixers, the Eagles, the Flyers, and the Phillies. There was also an assortment of television and radio personalities in attendance. Mr. Emerson loved the media, as most big time moguls do. During dinner Emanuel and Kay sat at the big table with the guests of honor, the city mayor and a few other high profile dignitaries. This glitzy scene was more Jada than Kay. She could see Jada maneuvering through a crowd like this effortlessly. Despite her upbringing Jada always knew that she was a contender and deserved to be at the table among the best. Jada would always quote the old proverb, *a man's gift maketh room for him, and bringeth him before great men.* Kay looked over at Emanuel who appeared very comfortable amongst the elite bunch. He talked more than she ever remembered, and this new level of confidence that she saw only made Emanuel even more attractive. Instantly, Kay questioned her ability to stand next to a confident Emanuel amidst this type of crowd. She felt completely out of her element. Kay tried to channel Jada's confidence, but she completely lost it when Mr. Emerson's beautiful and equally successful daughter, Caroline, who was conveniently seated on the other side of Emanuel, immediately made her interest in Emanuel known. Like everything else around them, she was shiny -- jewels adorned her ears, neck, wrist, and fingers. Caroline wasn't your average girl in the room plotting on your man. She was the typical rich, spoiled, privileged daughter of a millionaire who probably always got what she wanted and Emanuel would be no different.

"Emanuel, I was very impressed with the work that you did for my father." Her voice was smooth and commanding.

"Thank you."

"I'm hoping to get in your rotation so that we can talk about some ideas for my company."

"Absolutely. Just call my office. Mona will get you on my calendar." Emanuel's response was polite and Kay really didn't get the sense that Emanuel was flattered by Caroline's interest in him. "Just mention that you are Randolph's daughter and she will give you top priority." Kay sat stiff backed too afraid to look over at Caroline. Emanuel pointed Caroline out to Kay earlier in the evening. He identified her as Mr. Emerson's daughter. Kay watched Caroline from across the room, and her beauty was almost intimidating. Caroline was tall like a model, with a smile that lit up the room. She was the perfect mix of Mr. and Mrs. Emerson. Emanuel introduced Kay and Caroline, just before they sat down and Kay noticed that she was even more beautiful up close.

"So, would you be opposed to conducting business over dinner?"

"It's not my usual practice, but for you, I will make an exception."

"Well, I will be sure to give Mona a call first thing in the morning. I would be a fool to miss an opportunity to sit over dinner with someone as handsome as you." Caroline smiled looking around at the other smiling faces. It was typical in these circles for people to hang onto Caroline's every word. They would smile when there was nothing to smile about and laugh when there was nothing funny.

"Now, Caroline," Mr. Emerson interjected, "I don't think Ms. Ali appreciates you hitting on her date right in front of her face." Everyone laughed, even Emanuel, which infuriated Kay. She felt foolish. What made her think that she could sit in the same company with these people in an off-the-clearance-rack dress, a homemade hair-do, and cheap make-up. She wished that she could just disappear. She could not have been more out of her element. She was more the artsy-type, a true dime among the down-to-earth, non-superficial poets, artists, and musicians that frequented *Soul Sistahs*. But this, the Emerson's and all of their glitz and glamour -- called for the wearing of a mask that Kay just didn't have in her repertoire.

"I never mix business with pleasure," Emanuel said coyly, "and although dinner with you would be pleasurable it would be strictly business." Emanuel's response settled the entire table, but most importantly it assured Kay. And when Emanuel reached for her hand under the table and gave it a gentle squeeze she knew that despite her insecurities, Emanuel still saw her as beautiful and worthy of his time and space -- this made Kay happy. After dinner, the night was just getting started as couples took to the dance floor and swayed to the music. Emanuel reached for Kay's hand and asked her to dance. She hesitated a bit, but it didn't take too much convincing before she was on the floor snapping her fingers and bobbing her head with the rest of them. When the band slowed the music down, Kay fell effortlessly into Emanuel's arms. He held her at a distance initially, but the more they swayed from side to side the closer they got to one another until their bodies were brushing against each other. By mid-song Emanuel had Kay in a full embrace as she rested her head against his chest. Emanuel ran his fingers slowly up and down the small of Kay's back. He thought about how good it felt to have her in his arms. Emanuel was amazed at how similar Kay was to Jada -- both 5'5,'' both very petite in frame. Holding Kay was eerily similar to holding Jada, and for that moment he closed his eyes and pretended that he was holding Jada. Neither of them said a word they just enjoyed each other and allowed their bodies to rest in this peaceful place. Kay could not ignore the intense attraction that she felt towards Emanuel. Her flesh was in complete control. She had been celibate for over four years, and it had been just as long since she even made out with a guy -- but despite all of that she was ready to skip over first, second, and third base and take it all the way home. She wanted nothing more than to make love to Emanuel. She wanted to give herself to him completely and figure out the details later. Emanuel bent down and kissed Kay on the neck just behind her ear.

"It feels so good having you in my arms," Emanuel whispered. Kay inhaled his intoxicating cologne -- that plus the warmness of his breath dancing across her neck made her weak and sent her system into over load. Her knees fell weak; her heart was beating a million miles a minute, and her breath was nowhere to be found. The room started spinning and the last thing that Kay wanted to do was pass out in the middle of such a beautiful evening.

"Lets go out to the balcony," Kay suggested and began walking in that direction before Emanuel could protest. The night was beautiful and the temperature was perfect; it was just cool enough to give Emanuel a reason to get close to Kay. The night air wrapped around her bare shoulders and sent chills throughout her body. Emanuel placed his jacket over Kay's narrow shoulders, wrapped his arms around her waist, and they both looked out into the darkness. Water could be heard in the distance, crashing against the pier. Kay leaned back and rested her body against Emanuel's stature and relaxed in his embrace.

"I could stay in this moment forever," Kay said softly.

"Me, too," Emanuel echoed. Kay closed her eyes and took it all in -- the beautiful night, the grand hotel, the music in the background, and Emanuel. She listened to the pace of Emanuel's breaths and she could hear them becoming steadier as he became more relaxed.

"The moon and stars are so beautiful against the dark sky," Kay said looking up into the heavens.

"This is the part when I could say something cheesy like - not as beautiful as you," Emanuel joked. "But I'm not going to say that because we both know that you are, without question, the most beautiful part of tonight." Emanuel said as he placed a gentle kiss on the back of her head. A chill shot through Kay's body, and, although she was sure that it was in response to Emanuel's embrace, she told herself that it was because of the slight breeze that came from being on the banks of the Delaware River. Kay struggled to pace herself, but her mind was heavy with thoughts of the night before and the kiss that they shared. She wanted more; Kay turned to face Emanuel being sure to remain in his embrace. She looked up at him, and their eyes locked. A feeling of fear mixed with passion and uncertainty filled their eyes and muted them both. The wind blew Kay's hair in her face and before she could wipe it away Emanuel reached down and brushed it away for her.

"Thank you," she blushed.

"No problem," Emanuel said still with his hands in her hair. He lowered his hand slightly, lifted Kay's chin, and kissed her lips softly. This time he kissed her with more passion than the night before; he took his time and explored her -- he studied her lips and took note of her responses. Tonight there was no lust but Kay could feel something very similar to love when they kissed. There was something about the feel of Emanuel's lips that literally took her breath away. She wasn't sure what it was that drew her to Emanuel and made her desire him so deeply, but she didn't want it to stop. She enjoyed Emanuel's every touch no matter how insignificant: the touch of his hand against her shoulder when he wrapped his jacket around her; the touch of his hand in her hair when he brushed her hair from her face; and most enjoyable was the way he touched her hand under the table when she was feeling like an outsider. Her heart skipped a beat every time he whispered in her ear, and she felt the heat from his breaths across her earlobe.

Things heated up rather quickly out on the balcony, and Emanuel couldn't seem to keep his hands off of Kay. But she had no complaints; she didn't want him to keep his hands off of her. After four hours of lavish partying Emanuel and Kay ditched the gala and jumped in the limo heading back to Kay's house making out all the way there. Kay was slightly embarrassed by her behavior, but she was comfortably planted on cloud nine. There was no place for common sense or decency on cloud nine, and, ironically, although cloud nine seems to be close to heaven, Kay never felt more in the flesh. There were some serious negotiations going on in Kay's mind. It was like a scene from one of those television police shows where a dazed and confused woman is standing on the roof top of a high rise threatening to jump and a police negotiator is waiting below with a bull horn trying to convince her not to, and Kay was playing both parts. She was working overtime trying to convince herself not to give in to her carnal desires and end the night like the God-fearing woman that she was. There were still too many details that need to be worked out, she pleaded with herself. She fought with herself the entire drive, and by the time the driver dropped her off at her house and Emanuel had walked her to the door she thought for sure that she had lost her battle.

"Would you like to come in?" Kay offered, prepared to give herself to him.

"You have no idea how badly I want to come in, but I have a meeting early in the morning and I have some work that I have to do to prepare for it. If I come in I probably won't come out for days," Emanuel joked. "I had a really great time with you tonight," He reassured, sensing Kay's feelings of rejection.

"I had a great time, too."

Emanuel leaned over and kissed her again.

"I will call you tomorrow."

"Okay," Kay said with a glazed-over smile.

"Get some sleep," Emanuel suggested as he walked back to the limo.

"I am pretty exhausted," Kay said to him as he disappeared in the vehicle and the driver closed the door behind him. *Yeah, walking in the flesh for so long tends to do that to you,* Kay's conscious responded.

Chapter Seventeen

When Kay opened her eyes in the morning she already had a smile on her face as thoughts of Emanuel played in her mind. She lay in bed with no plans of moving any time soon. She replayed the elegant scene of the night before over and over and over again in her mind: her dance with Emanuel; the time they spent on the terrace; and, the hot and heavy petting session that they shared in the limo. Instead of waking up and going into her usual early morning workout she opted to lie in her bed and daydream about Emanuel all day. The moment Kay settled on that plan her telephone rang.

"Oh-no," she sighed. She looked over at the digital clock on her nightstand and took a mental note of the nine o'clock hour. Kay looked in the direction of her telephone with absolutely no intention of answering it. It rang four agonizing times before her answering machine picked up,
Hello you have reached the home of Kay...and Khalial, Khalial's small voice sang out. *We're not home right now but if you leave your name and a brief message we'll call you back.* They finished in unison. *Beep.*

Kay waited patiently for the caller to speak into the machine.

"Khadijah, it's your mother," Eva said loudly. "I know you are home. Pick-up." Eva waited for Kay to get to the phone. Kay sighed deeply; surely she could have spent at least another hour lying in the bed relishing in thoughts of Emanuel. The last thing she wanted to do was entertain Eva. Kay rolled to her side, threw her feet over the side of the bed and stood up slowly. She dragged her feet towards the phone, which sat on a table in the corner of her room. Kay grabbed the wireless phone from its cradle.

"Hi, Ma,'" she said into the receiver.

"Hey, open the door I'm right outside." Eva announced. Kay pulled the receiver away from her ear as she reached for her terrycloth robe. Eva always spoke louder than the average person.

161

"I'm coming." Kay unlocked the door and opened it to find Eva standing there with her cell phone against her ear.

"What are you doing still in the bed this time of morning?" Eva was still speaking into the phone even though Kay was standing in front of her. Kay hung up her phone and answered looking her mother directly in the face as a clue for her to hang up her phone also.

"I'm tired, Ma,'" Kay said as she walked to the sink and began to prepare a pot of coffee. She didn't drink coffee but Eva did, and Kay could tell by her mother's attitude that either she hadn't had a cup this morning or it was time for her second cup.

"You shouldn't be hanging out all late on a school night any way," Eva scolded.

"School night? Ma, I am not in school, and I own my own business so I can pretty much show up to work whenever I want to. If you would have let me take Khalial home with me last night then I would have been up before the roosters just like always. I was trying to take advantage of the situation and so I slept in," Kay sassed. She began randomly opening and closing cabinet doors, not looking for anything in particular just not wanting to look at her mother. Kay knew that Eva was there for one or maybe two reasons only: one, to get the skinny on Kay's date last night; and or two, to talk about Fatima and the baby on the way which reminded Kay that she promised Fatima that she would try to smooth things out about the babysitting thing. Without further delay Eva revealed the reason for her visit.

"When was the last time you talked to your sister?" Eva asked as she took off her jacket and grabbed a seat at the dinning table. Kay shook the last thought of her wonderful night out of her head and prepared herself for a conversation that she really wasn't interested in having.

"I talked to her yesterday. She came by a did my make-up for me." Kay offered disinterested.

"So, I guess she told you that she is pregnant again?" Eva said with disappointment in her voice. "I don't know where she got that baby-making mentality from," Eva said and tooted her lips. "She got it from Walter, I mean Karim, -- whatever he's

calling himself these days." She rambled on, content with having
a conversation with herself, Kay was just her audience. "It
doesn't make any sense." Eva sat back and thought for a minute.
"I swear that girl is just like her father." Kay walked over to the
cabinet and pulled out a coffee mug and began pouring her
mother a cup. She knew that if she didn't get some coffee in this
woman as soon as possible she would be in for a long morning.
The fact of the matter was that Kay chose not to expend her
energy on negativity and although her father and sister were very
religious, they spent a lot of time doing a lot of stupid stuff. Kay
pulled a bag of bagels out of her breadbox, split one in half, and
placed it in the toaster. She walked to the refrigerator and pulled
out a jar of jelly, a stick of butter, and a tub of Philadelphia
cream cheese. She placed them all on the table in front of her
mother along with a knife and saucer. If Fatima was like their
father that meant that Kay was like their mother. Kay got her
good housekeeping, hospitality, and independence from Eva.
Secretly Kay really admired her mother's tenacity because she
realized that if Eva weren't as independent as she was they
would have been subjected to Walter's idiocy. Kay stood in front
of the toaster and listened to it crackle as the bagel toasted. She
watched as a stream of smoke rose from the toaster disappearing
into thin air. Kay's mind was still very much focused on
Emanuel. Every time she thought about him a flutter of
butterflies tickled her stomach and stole her breath as they
escaped through her parted lips causing her to inhale deeply.
Kay could hear her mother still going on and on about Fatima
and her poor choices. Whenever Fatima made what Eva
considered a poor choice, she would rehash every poor choice
that Fatima had ever made leading up to the latest incident.
Frankly, Kay couldn't care less how many children Fatima chose
to have -- she was married and if she and Raheem decided to
have a whole baseball team it was their business. Eva always
feared that Raheem would leave Fatima one day, and she would
be left to raise four -- soon to be five -- children all by herself
which Eva knew from experience would be a difficult task,
especially with only a high school education and absolutely no

skills. Kay believed that secretly her mother resented Fatima and the choices that she made. Eva had always tried to raise her girls to be independent and self- sufficient, to rely on no man for their survival. Kay, seemingly, learned that lesson well, but Fatima seemed to do the complete opposite of what Eva had taught them. The bagel popped out of the toaster, breaking Kay from her trance. She reached in front of her mother and grabbed the saucer. She placed the bagel on it and placed it gently back in front of Eva. Without hesitation Eva opened the cream cheese and began to spread a thick layer across each bagel half. Kay braced herself for a minimum one-hour session of Eva dogging out Fatima and her situation, but Eva threw her a curve ball when she asked,

"So, how was your date last night?" she looked at Kay expectantly.

"It was very nice." Kay blushed although she tried hard not to.

"Very nice hunh? Who is the lucky fellow?" Eva inquired. Kay wasn't quite sure if she should tell Eva that Emanuel was the guy that she went out with; she didn't want to risk her getting all philosophical, reminding her of all the obvious don'ts. But Kay relented.

"I went out with Emanuel."

"Emanuel? Emanuel who?"

"Emanuel, Emanuel... Jada's Emanuel." Kay felt uneasiness in the pit of her stomach. *Why did I say Jada's Emanuel?* She questioned herself.

"Oh, my. Okay." Eva said as she took it all in. "Emanuel." When Eva found peace about the situation she continued. "So, how long have you been seeing Emanuel?"

"I'm not seeing him." Kay sighed. "He came to the club on Friday night and we've hung out a few times since." Kay was trying to downplay her feelings.

"So, you two are just a couple of old friends hanging out?"

"Yeah, something like that."

"How is he dealing with the loss of Jada?"

"I guess he's fine. I mean he seems a lot better since Friday."

"What do you mean? How was he on Friday?"

"Well, when he first got to the club he didn't seem comfortable being there. But there were pictures of Jada all around the place and it was his first time coming to the club since that night so I think it was all just too much for him."

"And now?"

"Now he seems fine. We've been spending time together and he seems happier." Kay looked at Eva intently trying to read her thoughts. She could tell that Eva was in deep thought.

"So, how do you feel?"

"I don't know, Ma. I really enjoy spending time with him." Eva just looked on as Kay continued. "Last night we had such an amazing time. I can't even begin to explain how I felt being with him last night." Kay looked at her mother half expecting her to go off, so she braced for her wrath.

"How does he feel about you?" Eva asked calmly.

"I think he likes me just as much as I like him." Kay thought about the time that they spent together over the past few days. He was the one who kissed her first; he was pursuing her just as hard if not harder than she was pursuing him.

"Have the two of you slept together?" Eva asked the question like she was talking to one of her patients, nonchalantly. Kay, on the other hand, was embarrassed by her mother's question. She just didn't feel comfortable talking to her mother about her sex life.

"No, Ma. Didn't you hear me when I said that we just started hanging out on Friday?"

"I'm just asking, Khadijah. If I remember correctly, Emanuel is a very attractive man, and I know that it's been a while since you had a man in your life, which leads me to assume that it's been a long time since you have been intimate with a man."

"Ma," Kay stood up, "I am not going to talk about my sex life with you." Kay's face was beet red. She stomped to her bedroom as hard as her bare feet could stomp. Kay huffed and sighed as she shuffled through her drawers for something more appropriate to wear. Suddenly she didn't feel comfortable sitting at the kitchen table in nothing but a robe and panties talking about her sex life, or lack there of, with her mother. She threw on a pair of gray sweatpants and a white signature *Soul Sistahs* t-shirt. Kay returned to the kitchen to find Eva munching down on her bagel like nothing ever happened; she showed no sign of embarrassment. And without as much as a glance in Kay's direction Eva continued to speak.

"Khadijah, we are both adults. I don't know why you are acting like a child."

"Ma, I don't know why you are okay with asking me about my personal business."

"Your personal business?" Eva was surprised by Kay's statement. "Since when did your business become personal?" She questioned again, still not expecting a response from Kay; these questions were just a prelude to her dramatic conclusion.

"Who was it that listened to all of your woes about Malik for the past five-years? Ma, I can't move on; Ma, I just love him so much; Ma, do you think he will ever come back to me; Ma, pray for us." Eva mocked, piling on the evidence, in the most dramatic way that only she could.

"Okay, okay, Ma. Dang. To answer your question, no --I have not slept with Emanuel and frankly I don't plan on sleeping with him."

"Fair enough." Eva settled.

"Besides, he was Jada's husband. Is it even fair for us to try to be together?" Kay was hoping to tap into Eva's professional counseling sense.

"Why not? The way I see it, both of you are single, and knowing Jada, she is probably in Heaven orchestrating this whole thing. She probably would rather Emanuel fall in love with you than any one else in the world. Why? Because she knows you best and she knows that you would make a great woman for Emanuel." Eva popped the last piece of bagel into her mouth. "So, I say go for it." She spoke despite a mouth full of food. Kay smiled on the inside. Eva was a good mother, and

Kay knew that she was blessed to be able to call her friend as
well. Kay settled into her seat and tapped the table, on waiting
for Eva to finish her bit knowing that she was that much closer
to walking out of the door.

"Thanks, Ma. Kay smiled.

"Anytime." Eva returned the sweet smile. "Speaking of
Malik," Kay jerked in her seat,

Who mentioned anything about Malik? She asked herself.

"What is this I hear that he is engaged?" she continued,
"and why am I hearing about it from Khalial?" Just that quickly
Eva had moved onto another topic that Kay didn't want to talk
about. Eva moved effortlessly from one off limit, none of her
business topic to another without skipping a beat. Kay thought
that she would explode if she didn't exhale at that very moment;
she let out a heavy sigh and couldn't control her eyes from
rolling hard towards the heavens.

"Oh, my," Kay huffed like an embarrassed teenager. *If I
knew that she was going to be in here all in my business I would
have left her behind outside,* Kay thought to herself. "You are
just all up in my business." Kay laughed an annoyed laugh.

"Really this isn't your business. This is Malik's
business."

"Well, if it isn't my business then explain to me how in
the world it's any of your business?"

"It's not any of my business either, but I still want to
know about it." Kay chuckled at her mother's nosiness because
that was all that it was.

"Well, you know just as much as I know. They're
engaged. Khalial is going to be the best man. I have no idea of
the date, time, or location."

"You mean Khalial is going to be in the wedding and you
don't even know the date?"

"Ma, Malik will take care of everything that needs to be
taken care of."

"And you're going to just stay out of it?"

"Yup."

"Umph!" Eva huffed. "Do you think you will be invited to the wedding?"

"I don't know, Ma. I imagine that I will be."

"Will you go?"

"I tell you what, I will cross that bridge when I get to it." Kay was drained. Eva had managed to come in and disrupt her entire mood. Eva looked at her watch.

"Well, I have to go, but let me share a story with you before I leave." Eva sipped her coffee and sat back in her chair. She looked in Kay's direction but she wasn't looking at her. Her mind had already begun churning its next thought.

"Have I ever told you the story about how your grandparents got together?" Eva asked the question with a look in her eyes that told Kay that she was getting ready to tell the story whether she wanted to hear it or not.

"No." Kay nestled into her seat preparing for one of Eva's tales.

"Your Uncle Earl and your granddaddy were best friends since they were little boys. Now, your Uncle Earl and your grandmother had been courting for many years before your Uncle Earl was sent off to war. Before he left, Earl asked your granddaddy to keep an eye on your grandmother, his gal, while he was off to war." Eva laughed a hardy laugh as she thought about the way it ended. "Well, by the time your Uncle Earl made it back to the states my momma and daddy had fallen in love, consummated their relationship, had a baby on the way, and were due to get married in three days." Kay's mouth sat wide open. She could not believe that there were still family secrets that she had never heard before.

"What did Uncle Earl do?" Kay questioned like a little girl.

"Well he and your granddaddy went out in the backyard and they fought a little, and talked a little, and fought a little more, but three days later Uncle Earl stood next to my dad as his best man." Eva ended the story like the moral was obvious, but when she noticed Kay still looking bewildered she added the moral. "So the moral of the story is that love has no limits and

no boundaries. Don't be afraid to fight for the one you love."
Eva tipped her head towards Kay as if to say *So there you go*.

Kay still had no idea what Eva was insinuating. Did she
want Kay to fight for Emanuel or Malik? Based on the story
about her grandparents Kay assumed that Eva was comparing
the three of them to Jada, Emanuel and Kay -- the only
difference being that Jada wasn't gone for a little while, she was
gone forever. Then again, Malik was the one who was getting
married, so did Eva want Kay to fight for him? Kay was
confused, but it didn't matter because the only person she
wanted was Emanuel and there was no fight to have; she only
needed to love him and have him love her back.

Kwanza

Chapter Eighteen

After Kay's conversation with Eva she decided that she would allow her feelings for Emanuel to develop naturally; she wasn't going to suppress them or encourage them -- she would just be herself and just let love happen. After Eva left, Kay laid back across the bed. She snuggled up with her pillow and held on to it tightly. She wished that Emanuel were there with her. She imagined what it would be like to wake up with him next to her; she didn't have to imagine what it would be like to fall asleep in his arms because she already experienced that. Kay wondered if her friend was looking down from Heaven on all that was going on, and, if so, what was she thinking about the whole situation. They had agreed that they would never date a man that the other had dated, but did this count? Kay wondered. Did the rule stand post mortem? Kay knew that the only way to settle this was to talk to her friend and ask for her blessing. She sat on her bedroom floor, which was where she did most of her praying and meditating, crossed her legs, and began to talk to her friend.

Jada, girl, I miss you so much. I know that you are looking down at us and I pray that you are okay with the situation that is developing between Emanuel and me. You always said that life was too short and we should always seek happiness, well, I am. I am happy when I'm with Emanuel. I have tried to fight the feelings that I have for him because I didn't want to appear disloyal to our friendship, our sisterhood. But, I can see myself falling in love with him, and I need to know that you are okay with our relationship. I could never break the bond that you and Emanuel shared and I would never try to. I pray that I can make him as happy as you've made him, and that I can bring joy into his life and take away the sadness. I will never compete with or denounce the love and life that you two shared, but you know Emanuel is a good man and he deserves to be with someone who will love him and respect the relationship that you two had.

171

A tear rolled down Kay's cheek; she didn't wipe it away she just let it fall. Kay closed her eyes and rested in this state of uncertainty for a few minutes. She was torn and confused, but the desire to be with Emanuel was too great, and she wasn't convinced that what she was feeling was completely wrong or immoral. She knew right there in that moment that she wanted nothing more than to be with Emanuel. From her open window a gentle breeze blew through and brushed against Kay's face drying her tears instantly. The act was so obvious and intentional that it frightened her. She opened her eyes and looked around half expecting to find Jada sitting in front of her with a handkerchief wiping her tears. Kay put her hands against her face feeling to see if the tears had really dried up and to her surprise they had. She laughed out loud and she knew in her heart that Jada had given her blessing. "Thank you," Kay whispered to her friend.

Kay couldn't wait to call Emanuel and hear his voice. With a clear heart and open mind she dialed the number to his office. The phone rang two times before Mona answered sounding almost mechanical.

"Good morning, you have reached Mr. Rivers's office. How may I help you?"

"Good morning. May I speak with Mr. Rivers, please?"

"Let me see if he is available. Who should I say is calling?"

"Ka- Khadijah Ali." Kay wanted to sound professional despite her excitement.

"Hold on, please."

Kay heard a click then the sound of country music playing through the receiver. Kay recognized the tunes as Shania Twain's, *Still the One*. She sang the words she knew and hummed the rest, "Your still the one that I love... the only one I dream of... your still the one I want for life hmm... hmmm." In that brief moment Kay envisioned herself singing to Malik. She immediately shook that thought from her subconscious mind and focused all of her energy on Emanuel. She laughed to herself, *It was the words,* she reasoned, *just the words. I don't have any feelings for Malik,* she reminded herself.

Emanuel sat at his desk daydreaming and for the first time in a very long time he was conscious of a subtle feeling of peace in his heart. He doodled on the blank pages of his sketchbook just like he had done as a young boy in math class when the teacher introduced a new equation. He laughed at the symbolism-- here he was in real life being introduced to a new equation: *him, minus Jada, plus Kay. Could it equal happiness?* He wondered about the possibilities. Emanuel's life revolved around only three concepts -- what he knew, what he believed, and what he felt. After Jada's death he knew that he didn't want to live without her; he believed that his broken heart was terminal; and he felt that his death was imminent. He believed that he would never feel happiness again, not even for a minute, but here he was feeling something that felt a lot like happiness with Kay. Emanuel searched his mind and settled on thoughts of absolutes -- the things that he knew to be true. He knew that above anything else he loved Jada with all of his heart. He knew that on certain levels of his mind he was completely insane. And he knew the moment he was told that Jada was dead was the exact moment that his world shattered and he had yet to pick up the pieces and put it back together again. Emanuel also knew he had strong feelings for Kay. Yes, they were motivated by his desire to be in the presence of Jada's likeness, but he believed that if he kept an open mind he could possibly really fall in love with Kay and recreate the once perfect life that he shared with Jada. Emanuel wished that there were someone that he could talk to, someone who could give him some guidance or advice or someone who would just listen. He thought about revisiting Dr. Banks for a counseling session, but he was afraid that she would try to make him deal with losing Jada and the baby, and he didn't want to have that conversation with her. His thoughts were interrupted by Mona's voice coming through the telephone intercom.

"Mr. Rivers, Ms. Ali is on hold for you. Are you available or should I take a message?"

173

"I'm available. I'll take it, Mona," he said. "Mona, I need to ask you a question. Could you come in here for a minute?"

"Yes sir." Before Emanuel could think of how he would phrase his question Mona was at the door.

"How can I help you, sir?" Emanuel twirled his seat from side to side as he gathered his nerve. He wasn't in the habit of discussing his personal business in the office, but he had listened to everyone else's opinion about him and Kay so he was curious to know what Mona thought. And even though Emanuel hadn't discussed his relationship with Kay directly he was sure that not only was she was aware of it but that she had an opinion.

"Mona, what do you think about Kay and going to the Emerson event together the other night?"

"Excuse me?"

"I know you have an opinion about us going out together. I just want to know what it is? What do you say to your friends about me and Kay?"

"Mr. Rivers, sir, I don't have an opinion."

"Mona, please. When you call up your best girlfriend and you start talking about work and how big of a jerk your boss is, what do you say?" Mona smiled at Emanuel's reference to himself as a jerk.

"Come on! So, you're like, oooh girl," Emanuel began in a feminine voice, placing his hand to his ear pretending that it was a telephone, "... Mr. Rivers is seeing this new woman chile' and she..."

Mona bust out laughing, she didn't know what was funnier -- his imitation of her or the fact that she had that very conversation with her girlfriend on the phone last night. She was certain that she started out with *oooh girl*. "Why are you laughing? I'm right, aren't I? I know how you women are. So, what do you say?"

Mona couldn't hold back her laughter.

"Well, sir, honestly, I thought about you and Ms. Ali as an item when you invited her to the party. The way you came in here on Monday morning and the way you came in here this morning, I was beginning to think that maybe the two of you together isn't such a bad thing," Mona offered. "I was happy to see that you had found a woman to spend your time with. I've notice that you are a lot happier these days and that's good. When I found out that Ms. Ali was the woman in your life I was surprised at first, a little concerned even."

"Concerned?" Emanuel interrupted. "Concerned about what?"

"I was concerned about you getting hurt or getting your heart broken, but when I thought about it I realized that she was the most likely choice for you. I mean she and Jada are so similar. She's beautiful and successful. She's familiar and I think your heart needs that right now."

"You know, you are the second person to say that to me." Emanuel laughed at how quickly she jumped in to offer her opinion; he appreciated her honesty.

"Thanks for you honesty, Mona." Emanuel reached for the phone, which was an indication to Mona that he was finished with their conversation. Without a word Mona turned around and exited his office.

"Hey there." Emanuel said interrupting the music and Kay's singing.

"Hey!" Kay echoed back with giddiness in her voice.

"How are you?" he asked.

"I am wonderful. How are you?"

"Well, if you are wonderful I guess I can't be anything less than great."

"Great is good."

"What are you doing?"

"Nothing. Just hanging out," Kay said as she sat on her bedroom floor twirling her hair and pinching the carpet between her toes.

"Hanging out? Are you not working today?" he asked.

"Yeah, I'm going to go to work in a little while. I just didn't want to start my day without talking to you." Kay blushed.

"So you didn't want to start your day without talking to me. Wow, that's a lot of pressure. What if I weren't available? Then what would you have done?"

"I don't know. I guess I would have had to spend the day in bed."

"That's not such a bad idea." Emanuel flirted.

"Well, I am still in my pajamas." She lied.

"Is that an invitation?"

"Only if you say yes."

"Give me five minutes. I'm on my way," he said jokingly. "No, seriously, I have been kicking myself wishing that I would have stayed with you last night."

"Me too, but what happened to the big meeting that you had?"

"It was canceled."

"Did your friend call you to get on your calendar for dinner?"

"Is someone jealous?"

"Not at all. Just because Caroline Emerson is interested in my man doesn't mean that I should be jealous."

"Your man? Am I your man now?"

"Did I say my man? I meant my man as in my homeboy, my main man." Kay said imitating J.J. Evans or some other seventies sitcom character. "You are officially the man. Rumor has it that Caroline could have any man that she wants and the ones that don't come freely she uses daddy's money to buy them -- or ruin them."

"Well, to answer your question and ease your concern, Caroline Emerson has not called me and if she does then I will not agree to have dinner with her. Instead I will invite her to my office and have a meeting in the boardroom like I do with all of my clients."

"Yes. I think professionalism is the best approach." Kay loved the way she and Emanuel talked. He was not only someone that she was growing increasingly in love with, but he was quickly becoming a great friend.

"Yes, ma'am."

"Did I tell you how great of a time I had last night?"

"Yes, you did. But, you can tell me again." Emanuel teased as he continued to doodle on the blank piece of paper where his next big idea should have been.

"I don't think that I will ever get tired of kissing you. I dream about kissing you when I am asleep and I daydream about kissing you when I'm awake."

"Wow, that's deep," Emanuel, laughed sarcastically.

"Why are you laughing? I'm being serious," Kay whined. Emanuel was just teasing; he knew that she was pouting with her bottom lip sticking out like a kid and he tried to imagine how cute she looked, but for the life of him he could only see was Jada's face. This struggle with reality scared him a bit and he fought with himself to control his mind, but he couldn't. Kay continued to whine something to Emanuel, but he had drifted off. He heard her talking, but his mind was preoccupied with thoughts of Jada. Unconsciously he heard himself say, *"Yes, of course I do."*

"Of course you do what?" Kay quizzed.

"Oh-no, not you. I'm sorry Mona just asked me a question." He lied. Emanuel rubbed his neck in an attempt to release some tension. His palms were sweaty and he felt very anxious although he didn't understand why. *What is wrong with me?* he asked himself. Instinctively Emanuel thought to call on God but he remembered that he wasn't talking to God. So he took a deep breath instead then blew all the air from his lungs.

"I would love to see you today if you get some free time."

"That shouldn't be a problem. I had a meeting that had to be rescheduled so I'm just working on a storyboard for a commercial that I have to pitch in the morning," Emanuel said looking at the blank slate.

"Wow. That sounds interesting," Kay offered.

"It's really not that interesting," he joked. Emanuel was great at what he did. And with all that he lost after Jada's death he didn't lose, not even for a minute, his creativity. "So what time are you going to work today?"

"I don't know, I'll get there eventually."

"Are you going to be free for lunch?"

"I can make myself free. Why? Are you inviting me to have lunch with you?"

"Only if you would say yes," he laughed using her earlier words against her.

"Umm -- let me see," Kay paused for dramatic effect. "Of course I will have lunch with you."

"Of course," Emanuel repeated in jest.

"I would like that very much."

"Cool. I'm going to leave here in a couple of hours or so. I can meet you at the club and we can have lunch there if that's cool with you."

"That's fine."

"Okay. Well, I'll see you later."

"Okay. See ya."

"Kay, by the way. I love kissing you, too." Emanuel said before hanging up the phone. His words warmed Kay's heart. She placed the phone to her heart and breathed deep she was filled with excitement and looked forward to the journey that she and Emanuel were beginning.

Chapter Nineteen

Emanuel finished up most of the work that he had
planned on doing and he was preparing to leave his office for the
day. But before he could get out of the door Mona buzzed him,

"Mr. Rivers, there is a Ms. Caroline Emerson here to see
you."

Caroline Emanuel thought to himself, *I thought I told her
to call my office, not just show up*.

He reached over to the telephone and picked up the
receiver, instead of responding to Mona on speaker. "Mona, I'm
sorry, did you say that Ms. Emerson is here?"

"Yes Sir."

"Okay, you can send her in." Emanuel buttoned his suit
jacket. He scrambled to position himself. *Would it be better to
stand at my desk or sit*? He wondered, really putting more
thought into it than necessary. Just as his door opened Emanuel
decided to sit down so in one awkward motion he flopped in his
chair causing it to swivel from side to side. He gripped the arms
of the chair in his hands forcing it to be still. When he looked up
Mona and Caroline were halfway through the door. Caroline was
looking breathtaking as usual, which made Emanuel nervous on
top of the fact that he did not have time to prepare for her,
coupled with the fact that she is his biggest client's daughter.
There was really no room for error. He wished that he hadn't
agreed to talk business with her. Mona presented Caroline to the
head of Emanuel's desk. Emanuel stood to his feet, and reached
out to shake Caroline's hand, but in his awkwardness, or maybe
it was nervousness, he simultaneously knocked over his pencil
holder and the cup of cold coffee that sat on his desk. The
caramel-colored liquid started a slow destructive path across his
desk destroying sketches and notes in its way. Mona stood
frozen for a moment, surprised by Emanuel's clumsiness.
Caroline on the other hand reveled in the power of her allure--
this behavior was no surprise to her; even the most confident
men often stumbled and stuttered in her presence. Mona and
Emanuel rotated positions -- he moved to the front of his desk

and she moved behind it reaching for a stack of Kleenex to aid her in her clean up efforts.

"I'm sorry," Emanuel apologized to Caroline. "I wasn't expecting you."

"Well, I was in the neighborhood, so I thought I'd just drop by." She smiled big revealing a beautiful set of white teeth.

"No problem," Emanuel said trying his hardest to be as confident as possible. Mona shook her head at the power that a beautiful woman had over men, even a man as handsome as Emanuel. Caroline irritated her immediately; she was one of those beautiful women who used their beauty as a weapon. And Emanuel was under her spell.

"Can I get either of you something?" Mona interrupted. Emanuel looked at Caroline and said

"Would you like anything?"

"No, I'm fine. Thank you," Caroline said politely.

"We're fine. Thank you, Mona," Emanuel said looking slightly over his shoulder. Mona twisted her lips and maneuvered her way to the door. She didn't close it though, which was what she would usually do, but instead she left it cracked wide enough for her to see inside. "Please, have a seat.' Emanuel extended his hands towards the leather couch.

"Thank you." Caroline had many captivating qualities, but by far her greatest asset was her smile, which she made a habit of flashing after every statement.

"So, what can I do for you?" Emanuel asked as he took a seat opposite her on the leather chair.

"Well, I wanted to tap into your genius and hopefully get some ideas for promoting my restaurant."

"Okay. We can work on that. Usually the way it works is that we enter into an agreement, which states that I am developing concepts for you – you, being your restaurant. We would have an initial meeting where I would get a sense of the direction that you want to take and then develop strategies around that."

"So, when can we get started?" Caroline smiled.

Emanuel looked at the clock on the wall, it was ten-minutes after twelve and he hoped to be at *Soul Sistahs* by twelve-thirty.

"Is now a good time?" Caroline asked the question but given all of the underlying pressures Emanuel really didn't feel like he had a choice.

"Now is fine," he responded.

"Wonderful." Caroline leaned forward and pulled out a notebook and pen from her briefcase. "So where do we begin?"

Emanuel was completely drawn to Caroline's beauty. She began explaining her campaign ideas, and Emanuel watched her glossed lips part as she spoke. His creativity was no where to be found so he spent the next hour and a half listening to her amateur ideas and giving them praise as if they were genius.

Emanuel arrived at the club around two still feeling unsettled from his impromptu meeting with Caroline. When he walked into the club he was surprised at how packed the place was; he didn't realize how good business was at *Soul Sistah's* as the late lunch crowd was just as robust as the evening crowd. An attractive young lady greeted him at the door.

"Good afternoon, sir. Will you be eating alone?" She asked with one menu already in hand prepared to grab another upon his request.

"Actually, I am here to see Ms. Ali. Is she in?"

"Yes sir, she is. And you are?"

"Emanuel Rivers."

"Mr. Rivers, sir," he said in a stutter and way too apologetic "I apologize. I didn't recognize you."

Emanuel wondered why she would recognize him because he had never seen her a day in his life, but he wasn't in the mood for unnecessary chatter so he just let it go. "Ms. Ali is waiting for you. She is in her office just through those curtains." The young woman pointed to a set of heavy curtains in the opposite direction of the club's entrance. "Please, just go right in."

"Thank you," Emanuel said through a soft smile. When Emanuel walked into Kay's office she was in the middle of a conference call. She put a finger in the air signaling for Emanuel to give her a minute. Immediately upon seeing Kay, the thoughts and nervousness that lingered from his earlier meeting completely disappeared.

"So, what are we talking about here, Larry?" Kay asked in the direction of the telephone. Emanuel half-listened to the muffled male voice coming from the speakers; he was too busy admiring Kay. He stood slightly off to the right of her and watched her silhouette as she handled her business. He had never witnessed Kay in business-mode, and he had to admit that it was a bit of a turn on. Kat was dressed in a very sophisticated gray pencil-skirt and a silk blouse; her hair was down long and flowing with big curls settling on her shoulder. From his position in the room with the lighting that came mostly from the outside Emanuel was astonished at how much Kay really did favor Jada. He watched as she morphed into Jada right before his eyes. Her face transfigured and it was like looking at one of those holographic pictures that change when you turned it just slightly. He blinked his eyes hard and thought that maybe they were just tired and that was why they were deceiving him. He vowed that he was going to take some time off as soon as work slowed down. He knew that irrespective of the time that he was spending with Kay he still had some unresolved issues of stress that he needed to contend with. The time that he spent with Kay was refreshing, but he wondered if they were moving towards something real or if it was just as Nadia and Mona suggested, that the he and Kay were simply finding comfort in one another. He searched his heart, but there was no truth there, only confusion.

Emanuel took a seat on the couch and listened as Kay wrapped up her phone call.

"Okay, Larry. I am interested, but I need to look at the numbers. Send over everything that you have and we'll talk in a few days." Kay said her goodbyes and hung up the phone. "Hey there," Kay smiled big, turning her attention to Emanuel.

"Hey, yourself, Ms. Businesswoman." Emanuel stood to his feet and walked towards Kay.

"That was Larry, the financial advisor. He's trying to convince me to expand *Soul Sistahs*. He thinks we should open a club in either L.A. or Atlanta."

"That's exciting."

"Yeah, it is, but I'm not sure if right now is the best time. I mean this place has only been open for a year."

"Yeah, but it looks to me like business is doing well."

"I can't lie. Business is great."

"So, what's the problem? I think you should do it."

"So, without any other details fifty-percent of *Soul Sistahs* says yes." Kay laughed.

"Kay, the decision is completely up to you."

"No. Technically, the decision is up to us."

"I'm really not interested in owning any part of *Soul Sistahs*."

"Well, you do. And until you don't, you have equal interest. I should get some information from Larry by the end of the day. I will forward it over to you, give you a few days to look things over, and we can go from there." Emanuel made a mental note to himself to look into releasing his shares in *Soul Sistahs*. He understood why Jada listed him as beneficiary, but she did so not thinking for a minute that she would be gone so quickly and that he would really have to step in and make decisions. He didn't feel entitled to ownership. *Soul Sistahs* was Jada and Kay's vision; he only played the role of a supportive husband and friend.

"Have your people call my people," he joked exaggerating his importance. "I don't want to talk about that right now." Emanuel wrapped his arms around Kay then placed a gentle kiss on her lips. He took her breath away.

"Wow," she smiled. "I like closing business meetings with you."

"I have been wanting to do that since I opened my eyes this morning," Emanuel said.

"Me too," Kay said and leaned in to kiss him again. This time they kissed long and hard. "So, I half expected you to show up for lunch at lunch time," Kay joked. "I had this beautiful spread waiting for you." Kay took Emanuel's hands in hers and led him towards a Bohemian-styled room divider that decorated her office. "But since it is after two o'clock, everything is super cold. I can order something from the kitchen if you have time." Emanuel looked over at the spread: salmon, wild rice, asparagus spears, and red wine. Emanuel reached for an asparagus spear from the plate and began eating it.

"Don't go through the trouble. I like cold salmon." He smiled.

"Ha-ha-ha," Kay huffed. She walked towards the telephone to call the kitchen to order a fresh meal, but before she could reach the receiver the phone rang. "Hello," Kay whispered in the phone. She paused listening to the caller's voice. "Hi, Ma," she said into the receiver all the while smiling at Emanuel. Suddenly her expression became more serious as she paced along the length of her desk. "Oh… oh… okay. No problem. Ma, don't worry. I'll take care of it." She hung up and without saying a word she began dialing another number. She shrugged her shoulders and cut Emanuel a short smile. Emanuel could see the concern on Kay's face despite the smile, which lighted when Malik answered.

"Hi, Malik."

"Hey, Kay?" Malik responded.

"Hey. I hate to bother you at such short notice, but I have a very important meeting this afternoon that I absolutely cannot miss. Ma called and said that she is going to be caught up in a meeting, as well, and she won't be able to pick up Khalial. Would you be able to pick him up?"

"I can't. I'm completely tied up. I can get Heather to pick him up though," he assured. "If that's okay with you."

"No. I don't want to bother her. I'll figure something out -- maybe I can change my meeting to tomorrow."

"Kay, it's no bother -- she would love to help out."

"No, really," Kay said pleasantly. Kay was just getting used to the idea of Heather being in the fold, but she had yet to accept her as a backup plan as far as Khalial was concerned. "Don't worry about it. I'll figure something out. I'll give you a call later." She hung up before Malik could protest. Emanuel stood up next to Kay.

"What's going on?"

"Nothing major. My mom got tied up in a meeting, and she's not going to be able to pick Khalial up this afternoon. Malik is tied up as well."

"Well, I'm completely free. I can pick him up," Emanuel offered without pause.

"No, Emanuel, That won't be necessary."

"Actually, it is necessary. My godson has to be picked up, right? Last I checked that's part of my god-fatherly duties," he smiled at the title. "I got your back." He rubbed her back gently. Kay gave in with little urging.

"Okay. Well, he gets out of school at three o'clock and he gets really nervous if a familiar face isn't right at the front door to greet him."

"No worries. I will be there at two forty-five." Emanuel looked at his watch. "I'll pick him up, take him home, and we'll hangout until you get there."

"I really appreciate this, Emanuel."

"Not a problem. I hope that I will have plenty of chances to do a lot of really nice things for you in the future." He smiled and gave her a big hug, which was exactly what she needed. Kay lingered in his embrace and settled in to the comfort she felt having him in her life again.

Chapter Twenty

Before Emanuel left the office Kay read him a list of do's and don'ts, which included, "Do give Khalial a snack when he gets home, but don't let him play his video game until he has completed all of his home work." Emanuel took note of it all. At two forty-five Emanuel was there to pick Khalial up just as he promised, and Khalial was happy to see him. Emanuel followed Kay's directions to the letter; he took Khalial straight home, gave him a snack, sat with him at the dining room table, and helped him with his homework. Emanuel he had no idea how inquisitive six-year-olds could be and he realized that if he didn't engage Khalial in something then he would spend the next hour asking a million questions. Khalial was jazzed about Emanuel's offer to challenge him in his favorite PS2 game and after connecting a few wires, the two began an intense game of Madden. Emanuel and Khalial sat on the living room floor, shoes off, completely concentrating on the game and trash talking when the doorbell rang. Khalial jumped up out of habit and began running towards the door.

"Whoa, buddy!" Emanuel warned, "I'll get it." Khalial stepped to the side and allowed Emanuel to answer the door. "Who is it?" Emanuel asked before he opened the door taking advantage of the opportunity to teach Khalial a good lesson in safety. He tensed up a bit when he looked through the peephole and realized that it was Malik at the door. *Damn,* he said under his breath.

Malik announced himself and without further hesitation Emanuel opened the door. He knew that Malik wasn't going to be pleased with him being there so he braced himself for a tense situation.

"Hey, Malik. What's up, man?" Emanuel tried to sound normal.

"What's up, E?" Malik's tone was rough and his discomfort with Emanuel being there was obvious and immediate.

"Hey, Dad." Khalial said hugging his father.

"Hey, man." Malik bent down to hug his son, never taking his eyes off of Emanuel. "Where's Kay?"

"She had a meeting that she couldn't get out of," Emanuel said as he closed the door.

"What are you doing here?" Malik quizzed.

"She needed someone to pick Khalial up. I was in the area so I offered to help out." Emanuel's response was exact.

"You were in the area? How convenient," Malik said sarcastically. "You've been spending a lot of time in the area lately." Malik was obviously making reference to the other night when he dropped Khalial off and found Emanuel and Kay together.

"Kay should be here any minute," Emanuel said trying to change the subject.

"Well, thanks for keeping an eye on Khalial, but I can take it from here." Malik opened the door and motioned for Emanuel to leave. "How much do I owe you?" Malik asked as he reached for his wallet. His insult was intentional and Emanuel was offended.

"Actually, I was just helping out." Emanuel threw his hands in the air in surrender, a sign to Malik that he wasn't interested in his money. "I don't think that Kay would mind if you hung out until she got home, but she left Khalial in my care so I would like to hand him over to her." Emanuel pushed the door closed, basically letting Malik know that he wasn't going anywhere.

"Hey, Khalial. Why don't you go to your room? I need to talk to Emanuel alone for a minute."

"Is everything okay, Dad?" Khalial asked with a look of concern in his eyes.

"Everything is cool, lil' man." Emanuel answered before Malik could respond. Emanuel wasn't sure what kind of feelings coming to your ex's house and finding another man there watching after your child would provoke, but he was certain that anger was one of them.

"Khalial," Malik began, "everything is fine I just need to talk to E for a minute." Malik tried to hide his anger, which, based on Khalial's question, he realized he wasn't doing a good job of.

"Mom said that it was okay for Uncle E to pick me up. He took real good care of me. He was on time, he helped me with my homework…" Khalial began to explain.

"Khalial, it's cool." Emanuel wanted to stay out of it, but he didn't want Khalial to worry. "Your dad and I just have a few adult things to talk about. It has nothing to do with me and you hanging out." Emanuel made the statement partially in truth; he knew that Malik's anger wasn't about him being there with his son as much as it was about him being there for Kay. With Emanuel's explanation Khalial's concerns were eased. He gathered his books and took off towards his bedroom.

"So, what's going on E?" Malik asked in anger.

"What do you mean?"

"Look, let's not play dumb. Are you and Kay seeing each other now?" Just as Emanuel thought -- this confrontation wasn't about him being there with Khalial.

"Malik. Look, man. You really need to talk to Kay about that."

"Oh, I'm going to talk to her, but I want to hear it from you -- man to man. Are you seeing her?" Emanuel started walking towards the living room. He was hoping that Kay would walk through the door any minute.

"Is that what this is about? Whether or not Kay and I are seeing each other? Because I thought this was about me being here with Khalial."

"Just answer the question." Malik's tone was angrier than before. "Are you sleeping with Kay?" The words forced themselves through his tight lips. He asked the question appearing more concerned than an ex-boyfriend, engaged to be married, ought to be.

"That wasn't the question," Emanuel responded, unafraid.

"Well, that's my new question because the answer to the first question is obvious."

"Really? What needs to be obvious is the fact that Kay's personal life is none of your business."

"You don't tell me what's my business. Kay is the mother of my son. Who she brings around my son will always be my business."

"Well, it's not like I'm a stranger. Obviously Kay felt comfortable with me being here with Khalial and I would suspect that you would too if you weren't so concerned with whether or not we are sleeping together." Emanuel was flip.

"Don't catch a beat down, E. I'm telling you… you don't want these problems." Malik warned.

"Come on, man. Are you serious? You need to check yourself. You are engaged. Why do you think that you have any right coming at me like that?"

"Like I said, who Kay is dealing with is my business." Emanuel refused to talk to Malik any further about this and instead he began picking up Khalial's video game equipment and putting it away.

"What is wrong with you? Do you even know how close Kay and Jada were?"

"Malik, don't do that. You are completely out of line; you have no idea what you are talking about."

"I don't know what I'm talking about. So, what I walked in on the other night -- you two hanging out all comfy and cozy -- that was nothing?" Malik was beyond angry; he was being down right thuggish. When Emanuel opened the door he was prepared to give Malik the benefit of the doubt if he wanted to trip about him hanging out with Khalial, but he couldn't understand why Malik was concerning himself with his relationship with Kay.

"Look, bro'-- I'm not going to have this conversation with you," Emanuel said before he began walking back towards the kitchen. Malik followed closely behind.

"It's only been a year; you're over Jada already?"

"You don't worry about me and Jada." Emanuel turned hard with his finger pointing in Malik's face. "It seems to me like you want to have your cake and eat it, too. Did you expect Kay to just sit back and wait for you?"

"Yeah, and I guess that since you can't have your cake you'll settle for the next best thing. Kay isn't Jada." Emanuel couldn't understand why Malik was coming at him like that. *How dare he mention Jada's name. What did he even know about their relationship?* Emanuel was dizzy with anger; he wanted to bash Malik's head in, but he had to remind himself that Khalial was in the next room. Emanuel and Malik were squared-off, each with a look of fury in his eyes and neither of them ready to back down when Kay's keys rattled outside the door or when she opened it.

"I'm home," she announced as she came through the door. Kay was surprised to find Emanuel and Malik standing face-to-face in the middle of her kitchen. "Hey, guys. What's going on here?" she asked, looking from one to the other.

"Nothing. We were just talking." Emanuel relaxed his posture.

"Nothing?" Kay wasn't buying it. "It sure doesn't look like nothing to me. Where is Khalial?"

"He's in his bedroom," Emanuel said.

"Yeah, he just went in there to put his schoolbooks away," Malik said, finally taking his eyes off of Emanuel.

"Okay, so what's going on with you two? If I didn't know better I would have thought that you guys were about to brawl up in here." Malik turned his attention completely away from Emanuel and looked Kay dead in the eyes.

"What is he doing here with my son?"

"What?" Kay asked in disbelief.

"When I suggested that Heather pick Khalial up you all but flipped out. Then you turn around and let him pick Khalial up."

"Okay, what's your point? Emanuel was there -- he offered, and I needed someone to pick my child up!" Now Kay was angry. She had walked through the door excited about coming home to her men, but she never expected Malik to be there wreaking havoc.

"Our child!" Malik yelled.

"What is the problem? Emanuel is like family."

"Family?" Malik barked.

"Malik, what is wrong with you?"

Kay threw her keys on the counter and dropped her bags on the floor. She was confused. *Why was Malik there? Why was he so angry?* She looked over at Emanuel who had walked to the living room and found a seat on the couch with his head in his hands. She looked over at Malik who was staring her down like he was a scorned boyfriend. She had to remind herself that Malik was not her man. "Okay, so what is the problem?" Kay asked the question again and then attempted to answer it herself.

"You would have been more comfortable with Heather picking Khalial up. I was more comfortable with Emanuel picking Khalial up. The bottom line is that our son is fine and he was taken care of."

"No. That's not the bottom line. The bottom line is that you two are playing house around my son." Malik's voice went up in volume. "You are hooking up with your best friend's husband and now you want to confuse my son by prancing him around like this crap is normal!"

"Malik, you are really tripping, and I think that you need to leave." Kay pointed towards the door.

"You're the one that's tripping. I'm going to leave but only because I can't stand looking at you right now." Malik turned and stormed out the door, slamming it hard behind him and leaving Kay and Emanuel in shock.

"What was that all about?" Kay turned and asked Emanuel hoping that he could shine some light on the situation.

"I don't know," Emanuel answered in disbelief. "I thought that he was upset about me looking after Khalial and I was cool with that, but then he started making all kinds of accusations about our relationship. He was demanding to know if you and I was a couple, if we were sleeping together. It was crazy."

"Like that's any of his business."

"Yeah, that's what I said."

"My God. I never expected to walk in on that. I am so sorry for the way he acted."

"You don't have to apologize for him. But I do want to know what's up with you two. Are there still some unresolved feelings going on here?"

"What? Emanuel... Malik and I are over. He is engaged to be married; he's clearly moved on." Kay stated her case emphatically, but Emanuel didn't believe her.

"What about you? Have you moved on?"

"I'm trying to," Kay said exasperated. She could not believe how disruptive this whole scene was.

"You're trying to?"

"Emanuel, look. Things are unfolding rather quickly between us and I am sure that you, just like me, are trying to figure it all out." Kay stepped closer to Emanuel. "I am not going to put any pressure on this thing. I am going to be myself, not hold back anything that I feel, and let the chips fall where they may. If that means the two of us being together then that would be, in my opinion, the best possible outcome." Kay made the statement and she was convincing, but she wasn't sure that she was convinced. If she had her choice between Emanuel and Malik, she would, in a heartbeat, choose Malik -- not because she loved him more than Emanuel but because she believed that she and Malik was what Khalial deserved.

"I know what you said Kay, but Malik knows me; he's not going to be this uptight about me being here with Khalial if he has truly moved on. I think that maybe there is a conversation that you two need to have." Emanuel reached for Kay's hand and took it in his. "Kay, I'm not tripping. I just want you to be alright." Kay heard what he was saying and she knew that perhaps there were some unresolved feelings between her and Malik that needed to be discussed. Tired of going in circles about the whole situation Emanuel wrapped Kay in his arms and kissed her forehead. "So, how was your meeting?" He tried to change the subject.

"It was fine. Thanks again for looking after Khalial for me."

"It was no problem. We were having a good ole' time until your Baby Daddy came in here trippin'." Emanuel joked. Kay punched Emanuel's shoulder playfully.

"Yeah, well, don't worry about Malik." Kay leaned in and pressed her lips against Emanuel's. "He has nothing to do with you and me." Kay hugged Emanuel tightly and rested her head on his shoulder.

Chapter Twenty-One

Emanuel and Kay were spending most of their free time together and acting like lovers act, but they had not officially adopted the titles of boyfriend or girlfriend. But then again who claims those titles anyway. Besides they both were still struggling with it all Jada, Malik, and their own fragile emotions. Khalial was just as excited, as Kay was to have Emanuel around. In his young mind, he couldn't comprehend the significance of Emanuel and Kay's relationship; he was just happy to have his Uncle E around. Kay was pleased with the relationship that she and Emanuel had developed and she felt that their bond was sufficient. Emanuel, on the other hand, found peace in Kay and he reveled in every aspect of her and for him that was enough. He still missed Jada deeply, but with Kay in his life he was able to get through most days without tears; he was sleeping through the night, and he awoke most mornings to his alarm clock -- not the piercing sound of Jada's scream that shook him from his slumber for an entire year.

On this smoldering Saturday morning Emanuel, Kay, and Khalial resembled a real family. Kay was draped in an apron and her hair was pulled up in a high ponytail. She maneuvered around the kitchen methodically like she was on a television cooking show; scrambling eggs at the same time she dropped bread into the toaster. Emanuel and Khalial had their own rhythm going -- Khalial sat on a stool at the counter, feet dangling, and Emanuel was standing closely beside him. Emanuel was slicing oranges in half, and Khailial was pressing the halves firmly against the juicer, with all of his six-year-old might, trying to make fresh orange juice.

"Look, Ma!'" Khalial cheered, "It's almost filled up," he said as he squeezed harder.

"Good job, baby," Kay smiled. She and Emanuel caught each other's eyes and they smiled. Kay felt like the universe was balanced, the stars were all aligned, and for the first time in a long time she enjoyed the idea of being in love. They had planned to spend the entire day together -- breakfast was just the beginning. After enjoying a matinee the three geared up for an afternoon of games and fun at Dave and Busters. Malik was supposed to have Khalial this weekend but he was working hard on a big case and he couldn't get away. So Kay and Emanuel vowed to make the day all about Khalial so that he wouldn't miss his dad too much. Malik still wasn't jazzed about the idea of Emanuel hanging out with Kay and Khalial, but with a little convincing from Heather, an unlikely ally, Malik agreed to allow Khalial to hangout with Kay and Emanuel for the day. He would pick Khalial up in the morning so that he could go to Sunday service with him and Heather. Kay agreed. They hadn't had "the talk" yet but Kay was doing a good job of moving on. She stopped waking up to Malik's picture in the morning and instead she began her morning with thoughts of Emanuel.

Dave and Busters was filled with its usual Saturday evening crowd. Children were running off from their parents to find their favorite games. Laughter and chatter filled the air. Khalial was beating Emanuel for the fifth straight time at *Super Shot* as Kay stood in the background laughing and cheering on her two men. Just as Khalial threw the game winning shot at the buzzer Emanuel's cell phone rang. Emanuel stepped off the video game's platform in laughter; he reached in his jacket's inside pocket and retrieved his cell phone.

"Hello," Emanuel said through his laughter. Kay and Khalial slapped each other high-fives in celebration of his victory. Emanuel placed a finger in his opposite ear and his face turned serious as he listened intently to the caller. Kay noticed his change in demeanor, and, without alarming Khalial, she watched Emanuel closely. She felt nervousness in her stomach, and although she could not hear everything that he was saying, she could clearly make out he was constantly asking *What? What?* over and over again in disbelief.

Kay heard the anguish in his voice and immediately went to his side.

"What's going on?" Kay asked, but Emanuel didn't respond.

"Nadia, where is he?" Emanuel asked.

196

Kay gathered that something was wrong with either Mr. Rivers or Khadir because they were the closest men in Emanuel's life. By this time Khalial had come to Kay's side and with a look of concern on his face he began to inquire about what was going on.

"Ma, what's wrong?"

"Nothing, baby." Kay said, trying to assure him although she wasn't too sure herself, "It's okay."

Emanuel hung up the phone and looked in the opposite direction of where Kay was standing as if he forgot that she was even there.

"Emanuel, what's going on?" Kay asked as she reached out for his arm. Emanuel turned and looked at her like he didn't recognize her and in that moment she realized that despite the laughter and fun they shared Emanuel was still an emotional mess. Kay felt like she had to remind him that she was on his side and that she was there for him. "What is it?" she pleaded.

"My dad is in the hospital; they think that he may have had a heart attack." Emanuel said, voice shaky and visibly anxious. "He was rushed by ambulance to University Hospital." He continued. University Hospital was the same hospital that the ambulance rushed Jada to after the accident; the same hospital where she died.

"I have to go." Emanuel turned and walked away without another word-- no question about how she and Khalial would get home; no offer for her to go with him -- nothing. Kay didn't know what to do; she wasn't sure if she should run after him or give him his space. She reached in her purse, pulled out her cell phone, and pressed the button that dialed Eva's number.

"Hey, Ma," Kay breathe into the receiver.

"Hey," Eva greeted. "How are you?"

"Not good, Ma. Emanuel's dad was just rushed to the hospital. They believe he had a heart attack."

"Oh my! Is he okay?"

"I don't know. Emanuel raced over to the hospital. I want to go with him but I don't want to take Khalial with me."

"Say no more. Bring my grandbaby over here and go see about Emanuel." Kay was half way out the door of Dave and Buster's and whistling for a cab before Eva could get the words out of her mouth. She tried to convey her concerns to Eva without alarming Khalial, but he quickly picked up on her energy and knew that something was going on.

"Ma, what's going on?" Khalial questioned. One minute everyone was laughing and joking and the next Emanuel was rushing out the door. Kay knew that it wouldn't take long before Khalial started asking questions.

"Emanuel's dad isn't feeling well. He had to go see a doctor. Emanuel's just a little concerned about him so I'm going to go over to the hospital so that Emanuel doesn't have to be alone." Kay rambled on hoping that Khalial understood what she was saying.

"Can I go with you?" Khalial asked, sitting straight up in his seat, trying to show his mother that he is a big boy, strong enough to handle a hospital visit. "I don't want Uncle E to be alone either."

Kay smiled at her baby boy whose maturity never ceased to amaze her. "Well grandma wants you to come and spend some time with her. She doesn't want to be alone either." She wrapped her arms around his little shoulders, "But I will tell Emanuel that you are thinking about him." Khalial in his six-year-old wisdom thought for a moment then announced proudly,

"No, Ma. Tell him that I am praying for him and his dad." Kay was proud of her boy. *Out of the mouth of babes* she thought to herself. Children always have a way of reminding grownups of what they ought to do. Kay thanked God for Khalial's wisdom and immediately she began to do what she should have done first -- prayed. Kay reached for Khalial's small hand and in the back of the cab she began to pray.

"Father, we thank You for Your love Lord. We thank You for Your grace. You said in Your Word that you would never leave us nor forsake us; that You would never put more on us than we can bear, and we trust in Your Word. Lord, touch Emanuel and his family this day. Keep Your Angels encamped around them. Fill them with Your precious peace Father. Remind them that you are with them even now, Lord. Touch Mr. Rivers's heart, Lord; heal him right now in the name of Jesus. You said in Your Word that where two or more are gathered in Your Name there you are in the midst of them." She squeezed Khalial's hand tighter. The cab driver looked at them from his rearview mirror and smiled.

"Khalial and I are asking that You heal Mr. Rivers right now, Lord. We declare, according to Your Word that by Your Stripes he is healed. We thank You for Your Grace and Mercy and for what you have already begun to repair in Mr. Rivers's heart. Thank you for your amazing grace, Lord. We will be forever careful to give you all the glory, honor, and praise. In Jesus' name we pray. Amen."

"Amen," Khalial echoed.

"Amen," the cab driver co-signed.

Chapter Twenty-Two

When Kay arrived at the hospital, she found Emanuel, Mrs. Rivers, Nadia, and Khadir all settled in the waiting room. Emanuel sat close to his mother with his arms around her; Nadia sat across from Emanuel looking solemn; and, Khadir sat slouched in an uncomfortable chair with his head resting on the back looking towards the ceiling. The thick smell of illness in the air nauseated Kay; hospitals were by far her least favorite place. She was hesitant as she approached them. She wasn't sure how accepting anyone would be of her presence. She had not seen Mrs. Rivers or Nadia since the disastrous brunch a few weeks earlier. And although Emanuel should have been okay with her being there she wasn't quite sure where his mind would be, especially considering that he all but walked out on her after getting the news of his father's health. Kay wasn't too concerned with Khadir because he was almost always accepting.

"Hey." Kay spoke cautiously.

Emanuel looked up towards her and she instantly recognized his sad eyes. No one really said anything -- they all looked towards her, their individual sadness was easy to read on their faces.

"How is Mr. Rivers?" Kay inquired with her eyes wide with anticipation. She was certain that he was well or at least that he would be well. God had given her peace in her heart immediately after praying for him in the cab. She heard the same words that Jesus said to Mary concerning Lazarus, "*his sickness will not end in death,*" and she was assured.

"He will be fine." Mrs. Rivers responded.

Kay was surprised that she would act as the spokesperson for the family -- she thought that Emanuel would have responded. But she could tell by the look on his face that he was not present mentally or emotionally. There was something in his eyes the just read void. Kay tried to connect with him with a look, but she could not -- he seemed to look beyond her. The wall that he had hidden behind was too thick and high and she couldn't get past it. Kay leaned in and touched Emanuel's hand before she sat down in the empty seat next to Khadir.

Kay's heart was racing; she thought about the last time she was here in the very same waiting room -- it was the night Jada died. She remembered that night so clearly; she was cleaning things up at the club when Khadir called her on the cell phone. She could still hear his voice as he spoke the words that would forever change her life: "There's been an accident... it's Jada." That was all he had to say. Kay immediately dropped everything and rushed over to the hospital praying hard. Visions of city lights flashed by as she raced through the city streets to University Hospital. The entire trip was a blur. Kay regained focus as she entered into the bright, sterile emergency room entrance. She couldn't seem to walk fast enough down the long, cold hospital corridor to the waiting room. Kay could see the doctor talking to Emanuel as Mr. and Mrs. Rivers stood on either side of him. She couldn't hear what he was saying, but by the look on Emanuel's his face and his broken posture -- steady tears flowing and his head shaking constantly from side to side -- she knew that whatever the doctor was saying wasn't good. She was thinking that perhaps Jada was seriously injured and would require an extended hospital stay, or perhaps she lost the baby, in which case she had already begun to rehearse her, "You can get pregnant again" speech. But the thought had never crossed her mind that Jada was gone especially since Emanuel was standing on his own seemingly uninjured. When she heard Emanuel cry out and saw him snatch away from his parents and begin pounding his fist against the wall it was only then that Kay feared the worst, but she only allowed her mind to go there for a brief second. She immediately began to reject even the notion of Jada being killed in the accident. Her walk quickly went from a long stride to a slow jog. The short hallway suddenly turned into a marathon mile. She ran straight to Emanuel and fell to the floor with him. She rocked him instinctively still not aware of the fact that Jada was dead.

"It's okay," she tried to assure him, but it wasn't okay, in fact it seemed that things would never be okay again - and she was so right. The mere memory of that night suffocated her; she couldn't imagine what Emanuel was feeling, having to be in this place again with uncertainty lying in the balance. Everyone sat in the lobby in silence. Time ticked by slowly. After what seemed like forever, a short dark-skinned doctor entered the waiting room. His approach ushered them to their feet in anticipation. No one dared to ask the obvious question; instead everyone watched and waited for the doctor to speak.

"Mrs. Rivers," he began in a heavy accent. "Your husband is recovering. We were able to unblock his arteries and he is doing fine now."

"Thank God!" Mrs. Rivers said towards the heavens. Kay looked for Emanuel's eyes again, wanting to share in the hope, but Emanuel turned away from the group, walked towards the window and stood alone. Khadir wrapped his arms around Nadia's shoulder and kissed her head. "Can we see him?" Mrs. Rivers asked.

"Yes, but not for too long. He will need his rest tonight."

"Okay," Mrs. Rivers agreed. She looked over at Emanuel, but he was unresponsive so she took Nadia's hand in hers and walked towards the recovery room. Kay and Khadir's eyes connected and without saying a word it was agreed that Kay would approach Emanuel. She walked towards him slowly with her hand outstretched.

"Hey, Thank God your dad is going to be okay."

Emanuel didn't even turn to look at her. The very mention of God caused pain in his heart; he wanted more than ever to curse God. But before he could open his mouth and spit out his fury the soft words that Kay spoke weeks earlier came to him in a whisper:

"*If only my anguish could be weighed and all my misery be placed on the scales! It would surely out weigh the sand of the seas.*" Those words continued to echo in his head over and over again. He could not silence the soft voice in his head.

"Are you okay?"

"Yeah," Emanuel answered and nodded, but he did not turn to look at Kay.

"Khalial wanted me to tell you that he is praying for you and your family," Kay said offering a nervous laugh, but Emanuel didn't acknowledge her or her statement and Kay didn't press. Emanuel had mentally disconnected the moment he walked through the cold steel doors of the hospital. He could not find a space in his mind that would allow him to be conscious in the moment. He knew all that was going on, but he could not afford to feel any of it. Neither his mind nor his heart would allow it and so he went through the motions. He was physically there, in the waiting room, but mentally and emotionally he was absent. Emanuel was happy that his father was well; he just couldn't let go of the anger that he felt towards God which seemed to only grow with every disappointment. Emanuel was tired of being reminded of how fragile life was and how we had absolutely no control over it. Khadir recognized Emanuel's state and gently encouraged Kay to give him some time alone in his corner of the world. Kay backed away from Emanuel. His behavior frightened her. She could not contend with the idea of someone being completely connected, conscious, and happy one minute and totally shut down the next. She was no psychiatrist but she was sure that Emanuel was suffering from some kind of psychosis. Kay sat back in her seat and watched Emanuel for what felt like hours, the silence was terrifying. And so she did the only thing that she knew to do – pray. She prayed for his emotional healing; his restored faith and his happiness. Kay closed her eyes and willed her tears to dry up. No one in the waiting room moved -- Khadir stood in a corner opposite Emanuel, and Kay sat across from where he stood each with a close eye on him. Mrs. Rivers and Nadia's return to the waiting room caused a stir snapping Emanuel out of his fog. Mrs. Rivers walked straight up to Emanuel and wrapped her arms around his waist.

"Your father is going to be fine son. He is going to be fine." She rubbed his back gently. Emanuel turned, placed his hand around her shoulder, and kissed her on the top of the head.

"I know, Mom."

"Thank God." Mrs. Rivers said and again the very mention of the name ached Emanuel's heart. "So we all can go home, get some much needed rest, and come back in the morning." Mrs. Rivers took control and started dispatching everyone. "Emanuel you make sure Kay gets home safely; Khadir you can drop me and Nadia off."

"Mom, I will get you home. I'm sure Kay will be fine," Emanuel said without even as much as a look in Kay's direction. He was right Kay though, she would be fine, but she would have been better if he took her home.

"No, Emanuel." Mrs. Rivers walked towards Kay forcing Emanuel to look at her. "Kay is here to support you; the least you can do is make sure she gets home safely." Mrs. Rivers was an unlikely advocate, but she was happy to have her.

"Well, Khadir can take her home, and I will take you and Nadia home. I'm going to stay with you tonight. You shouldn't be alone."

"Why don't Khadir take me and mom home? I'll stay with mom and you can make sure Kay gets home safely," Nadia chimed in.

"No. If something happens to Dad then you two are my responsibility," Emanuel said angrily.

"You're right," Mrs. Rivers assured, gently, "but your father is fine. Khadir will make sure that Nadia and I get home safely."

"Mom is right," Khadir co-signed. "You take care of Kay and I will take care of Nadia and Mom. You could probably use some taking care of yourself." Khadir offered and gave Kay a wink. Kay was surprised at how kind everyone was being to her. She realized just how the threat of mortality helped people refocus. "Go home get some rest," Khadir continued as he patted Emanuel on his back. "I'll swing by in the morning, pick everyone up, and get us all to the hospital nice and early. We'll be here first thing before Dad even opens his eyes." This was the most mature Kay had ever seen Khadir; usually he was cracking jokes and trying to make light of every situation. Khadir was like Mr. and Mrs. Rivers's third child and Emanuel trusted that he would take good care of his mother and sister and get them home safely.

"Are you sure?" Emanuel asked.

"Yes. Khadir will take care of us." Mrs. Rivers wrapped her arms around her son and hugged him long and hard. "Kay, you take care of my baby," Mrs. Rivers said as she reached in and gave Kay a hug as well.

"Alright man..." Emanuel shook his hand.

" I will see you first thing in the morning," Khadir reminded.

Emanuel gave his mother and sister departing hugs before he took Kay's hand in his and walked down towards the elevators. Emanuel had barely looked at Kay all night, but him taking her hand was enough to make up for it all; this was the connection that she was looking for. As they walked out of the hospital Emanuel instinctively did all of the things that a gentleman would do -- he rested his hand on her lower back as he guided her to the car, and he opened and closed the car door for her; otherwise he said nothing.

Emanuel's mind felt numb, as if all thinking had ceased, he couldn't make sense of anything. All he knew was that he was unbelievably sad; his heart didn't ache like it had before and his head didn't throb, but he was aware of a sadness lurking about in his spirit. The trip to Kay's house was filled with silence. They both thought about what could have happened, and, without a doubt, they both were haunted by thoughts of what did happen just a year earlier. Emanuel pulled up in front of Kay's house, put the car in park, and sat there in silence with the car still running.

"Thank God your dad will be okay," Kay stated again. She knew that Emanuel was still on spiritual hiatus, but she refused to ignore God's grace and insisted on pointing it out to Emanuel every chance she got. Emanuel said nothing he just shook his head in agreement. "Do you want to come inside?" she offered. This moment felt like dé jàvu; it reminded her of the day Mrs. Rivers made hurtful comments, which left Emanuel in a similarly detached state. Kay turned sideways in her seat to face

Emanuel; she forced him to look at her. "Hey," she said
adoringly, "will you stay with me tonight?" Emanuel was still
emotionless. Kay leaned in and kissed his lips hoping to get a
reaction out of him. To her surprise Emanuel didn't hesitate or
resist her offer; he turned the ignition off and leaned in to kiss
her back. His tongue was warm and sweet; and he swallowed her
up with a deep forceful kiss. She slowed him down and
suggested that they go inside; she didn't want to make out in a
car like lovesick teenagers. Kay and Emanuel burst through her
front door intertwined in heavy petting and kissing. Emanuel had
begun undressing her from the door. He was very anxious
groping and grabbing her more aggressively than he ever had.
They worked their way through the dining room, down the
hallway and into her bedroom.

This was the moment that Kay had been yearning for.
Her body unfolded like a flower at Emanuel's slightest touch.
They tangled in a passionate embrace as Emanuel undressed Kay
feverishly, losing her jacket at the front door, her shirt in the
hallway, and her bra on the bedroom floor. Emanuel was eager
to make love to Kay; his mind was cloudy and his heart ached.
There were many different emotions running through his mind:
pain, fear, lust, loneliness, passion, anger, and frustration. He
was not in the right emotional state to be with this delicate
flower, but he yearned for her, to touch her and to be touched by
her despite the ache in his heart. Emanuel wanted and needed to
release his stress and perhaps along with it he would release
everything else that he was feeling. He wanted to feel *Jada* in his
arms so much so that her face was all he could see. Tears filled
his eyes as he reached for her, kissing her deeply and more
passionately than he ever had. Kay fell back on the bed, and
Emanuel lay gently on top of her. Neither Kay nor Emanuel
were sure exactly how far they were willing to go but neither had
the desire to control his or her flesh. Emanuel slipped his hands
between them and unbuttoned Kay's jeans; she didn't resist. He
began kissing her deeply causing her to lose her breath; she
moaned, completely surrendering herself to him. Emanuel
pressed hard against her body. She wanted nothing more than to

feel him inside her. She imagined that her first time with Emanuel would be gentle and perhaps would come after they had become husband and wife, but Emanuel was aggressive and this made Kay uncomfortable, but still she didn't want to deny him. She tried to slow things down so she pressed her hands against his chest and pushed him to his feet. "Slow down," she panted. She could see Emanuel stiffening. Afraid that he would leave, Kay sat up on her knees in the bed and began stroking his face until their lips connected again.

"I love you so much," Emanuel breathed in between their kisses.

"I love you, too."

With those words Kay forgot all about her vow of celibacy; she wanted to give herself to Emanuel no matter the cost. Wearing nothing but her panties, she slowly began to unbutton his shirt. She placed sweet kisses along his chest and neck. Emanuel moaned deeply as he ran his fingers through her hair. Kay reached for the collar of his shirt and gripped it in her fists. She pushed it over his broad shoulders and down his muscular arms, dropping it to the floor. Without skipping a beat Kay reached for his pants and began to unbutton them. She repositioned herself, sitting on the edge of the bed, with her feet firmly planted on the floor and his pelvis at eye level she kissed and nibbled at his stomach. His scent was intoxicating; Kay breathed him in as deeply as she could until she felt dizzy. Her mouth watered as she entertained the many unbecoming desires that raced through her head. Her lips trembled as she methodically placed soft, wet kisses down his stomach. Emanuel was completely gone by this point, his once cloudy mind had turned delusional, and he was back at *Soul Sistahs* on opening night. In his mind, he and Jada had made it home safely from the party and now here he was preparing to make love to his *wife*. His emotions ran high and he could not control the intense passion that ran through his veins. He ran his fingers through Kay's hair and lifted her head so that he could see her. There, in the darkness with only a small glimmer of light coming in from the hallway, he could see Jada's beautiful face almost clearly. He was overjoyed and his heart raced, pounding like heavy knocks against his chest. He felt dizzy with desire, and he wanted nothing more than to make love to his *wife*.

"Jada," Emanuel whispered softly but not softly enough. Kay immediately pushed away from him, and in the same motion she flicked on the light. She knew what she heard, but she didn't want to believe it.

"What did you say?"

Emanuel focused his eyes. For a split second he was almost certain that it was Jada in his arms. But when he focused he realized, not to his dismay but to his confusion that it was Kay that he was about to make love to.

"Emanuel!" Kay called out in fear. "What did you just say?" Kay demanded; her tears were instant. Emanuel adjusted his pants and stepped back from her. "Emanuel, open your eyes and see me." Kay begged as tears rolled down her face. She didn't know exactly why she was crying; there were so many reasons. Emanuel was speechless.

"Ja- Kay I-I'm sorry," he stuttered.

Kay pushed passed him, and in one scoop she grabbed her jeans and his shirt and ran into the bathroom locking the door behind her. Emanuel had, in that moment, lost his grip on reality. He wasn't a raving lunatic, but for a brief moment in time his reality was completely out of line with the reality that was going on around him. He felt certain that it was Jada that he was kissing, holding, and undressing. He stood in the middle of the floor with his hands on his head in absolute and utter confusion while Kay sat on the cold bathroom floor, sick with sadness. She was ashamed and embarrassed by the turn of the night's events. She believed that the time she spent with Emanuel over the past month was special; he gave her no indication that his mind was filled with thoughts of Jada. In the confines of her tiny bathroom a million thoughts danced in the air, *The many times that Emanuel kissed me was he thinking of Jada? Was he using me to add substance to his fantasy of pretending that Jada was still with him? Had he always looked at me and seen Jada?* But most importantly she wondered if *he lost his mind?* Her thoughts consumed her, but none of them made sense of her confusion. They attempted to suffocate her forcing her to breath deep.

Chapter Twenty-Three

Emanuel finally decided to let himself out of Kay's house after knocking on the bathroom door for nearly an hour, begging and pleading for her forgiveness. He said sorry over and over again, but Kay couldn't hear him; her pain had taken on a life of its own leaving her deaf to his pleas and apologies. As Emanuel cried out to her she cried in silence, both of their hearts aching all the while. In all of his apologies he said nothing that would explain to her why or how he could have made such an error in judgment at that crucial moment. How could he have hurt her in the very moment that she was ready to give herself to him completely? Kay was devastated and all he could say was sorry. She wanted to curse and scream at him, but she knew that it wouldn't change the reality that Emanuel had not come to grips with Jada's death. Kay knew that Emanuel would never stop loving Jada -- she didn't expect him to, but she never thought that he would be incapable of loving her. Kay sat on the bathroom floor until her legs fell asleep and tingled. Thirty minutes had past since Emanuel sighed his final, "I'm sorry," but still Kay wasn't ready to open the door because as much as she prided herself with being a realist she wasn't ready to face this new reality -- so she sat there lifeless on the bathroom floor. Even then she didn't have the energy to deal with anything or anyone so she slid out of her jeans and crawled into her bed. And curled herself into a big protective ball where she cried and rocked herself to sleep.

Kay could still feel the pressure of Emanuel's body pressed against hers. The scent from his shirt that she was wearing was strong in the air, and although she was angry with him his essence comforted her. The sound of Emanuel's voice calling out Jada's name haunted her as his words echoed in her mind. Her body ached for him. She held her pillow tightly not really imagining that it was Emanuel she was holding but secretly wishing that she had a man in her life who loved her just as much as she loved him. Kay squeezed the pillow tightly desperately trying to get a sense of security. She felt horribly rejected and this made her both sad and angry. The rejection reminded her that she was alone, and no matter how smart, beautiful, or successful she was she had no man to call her own. She was having a fancy pity party complete with a monologue of whys. "Why doesn't he love me?" she sobbed. "Why doesn't Malik love me?" she sniffed. "Why can't anyone ever just love me?" Kay cried out. Her body shook and she pounded the bed in her fit. "Emanuel, I loved you so much. Why wasn't that enough for you? Why couldn't you see me?"

Chapter Twenty-Four

Emanuel's heart was heavy when he left Kay's house; he wished that he could have taken his words back. He could not figure out why his mind had deceived him so. How could he have forgotten that Jada was dead and that it was Kay that he was holding? For the first time his delusions scared him. He simply couldn't see Kay no matter how hard he tried or how much he blinked he just couldn't see her. His delusions started when he was in the hospital the moment Kay came into the waiting room -- all he could see was Jada, not Kay, and for that reason he couldn't look at her. He knew then that he was losing his mind. His vision was cloudy, but he didn't question it. He believed that cloudy was his hospital vision. He knew with all certainty that it was Jada he was with tonight, and it was that feeling of certainty that helped him realize just how unstable he really was. He sat in his car for a few minutes after he left Kay's apartment as he tried to get himself together. His breathing was shallow again, and he thought that he would lose consciousness. "Come on, Emanuel. Get it together," he begged himself. "Get it together." He flipped his visor down; the light from the tiny mirror allowed him to get a partial view of his reflection. He looked into his eyes to see if they appeared wild, believing that insanity always showed up in the eyes first. His reflection did not reveal the eyes of a mad man, but they did reveal the eyes of a sad and lonely man. He wondered if he would ever live a normal life -- one that didn't include so much heartache and pain. He turned the key in the ignition and began his thoughtless journey from Kay's house to his. Before he knew it he was pulling into his garage; time raced by swiftly. He had not remembered any part of the twenty-minute drive.

Feeling emotionally drained Emanuel half wanted to sit in the garage with the car running and fall asleep knowing that in doing so he would not wake up. But beneath the sadness and confusion he could feel a faint desire for life so without another disparaging thought, Emanuel turned off his car's ignition and sat in silence. He never believed that he could feel any more depressed than he had felt over the past year, but here he was feeling a deeper sadness; but this time his sadness competed with a conflicting feeling of hope. The feelings resonated in his soul, and he found himself once again in this dark and lonely place. His heart ached for loss and love; it ached for the loss of Jada and a love for Kay. Emanuel eased from his car sluggishly and dragged into the house. He only got as far as his living room before his legs buckled beneath him, and he collapsed on the couch. It was in that moment that he realized just how cold and empty his house had become. "God," he called out and shook his head in disbelief, "what do you want from me?" Emanuel threw his head back and closed his eyes. He hadn't noticed that he had called out to God. With a weary mind and a body weakened by emotions he went into this back and forth thinking; he was hopeful when he though about spending the rest of his life with Kay, but that hopeful feeling was quickly consumed by feelings of guilt. He had a strong indication that he was in love with Kay because she was all that he could think about, mostly. His thoughts always began with Kay, but inevitably he always ended with thoughts of Jada. He could not see Kay without seeing Jada and that was his twisted reality. He went to sleep thinking about Kay and he woke up thinking about her times when his thoughts use to be reserved for Jada. He felt like he was in love with Kay, but given the circumstances he wasn't sure that he could trust his feelings. He wished that he had not hurt Kay, and he wondered if he would ever have an opportunity to make it up to her.

Emanuel searched his mind for answers to how he could make things right, but he came up with nothing. He peeled off his jacket and sitting there in his t-shirt he remembered how good it felt to have Kay undress him. Emanuel rubbed his hand across his hard chest; he tried to catch the flutters that danced about. His mind replayed the many different scenarios of the past month - he and Kay laughing and spending time together. He laughed as he thought about the night at the club when she played interference and pretended to be his girlfriend; even then he realized how good it felt to have her in his arms. There was no denying that the past few weeks he spent with Kay were amazing. He enjoyed every minute of being with her; he enjoyed kissing her, touching her, and falling in love with her. *So why...,* he wondered, *is my mind so confused now?* He knew that if there was a way for him to give himself to Kay completely then he would, but he also knew that in his mind there was disconnect between what he was feeling for Kay and what he wanted to feel. Emanuel closed his eyes and hoped to find peace in his dreams. The words of DMX sounded off in his head, "LORD give me a sign." He had heard the words only briefly while running that morning, but often without him realizing it those words blared in his subconscious, "LORD give me a sign." He didn't remember DMX's plea before or after those words, but in that short time those five words were forever etched in his subconscious. Again the poetic words from Job spoke to him, *"If only my anguish could be weighed and all my misery be placed on the scales! It would surely out weigh the sand of the seas."* Then for the first time Emanuel wondered what happened next? *Did Job die of a broken heart? Did God restore him?* All of these questions filled his mind until he fell asleep.

Kwanza

Chapter Twenty-Five

The early Sunday morning sun warmed Kay's face; she blinked her aching eyes as she tried to adjust to its brightness. Her body was still soar from the crying fit she had the night before which reminded her of her sadness. She lay listening to the birds chirping in the distance -- that was the only outside noise she allowed herself to hear as she searched for her peace. But in this space and time, peace was nowhere to be found. She felt unbelievably empty. Rejection was the one thing that could shake her to the core and take her off balance. She remembered the first time she experienced this feeling of rejection; it was the day her father left for what she knew would be for good. Kay lay staring at the ceiling as she remembered that day almost fifteen years ago. Despite the beautiful sunny day Kay remembered how dull and desolate the house felt. Her parents had been arguing most of the day, and Kay witnessed first-hand their exchange -- the name-calling, the accusations, the disrespect. She sat on the stairs but her parents didn't seem to notice that she was there despite the fact that they walked past her time and time again. Usually one of them would be concerned and say, "Not in front of the kids," or "Are you okay honey?" "Don't worry mom and dad are just talking." But not on this day. Neither of them noticed or cared that she was there in the midst of it all. Fatima stayed in the bedroom playing with the paper people that she cut out of an old Sears catalog. Kay sat with her hands pressed against her ears but not pressed hard enough to block out the voices because she secretly wanted to hear every word so that she could tell the whole story to Jada later on -- including the bad words. The last thing she remembered was Eva calling Walter a momma's boy. Eva's opinion of Walter hadn't really changed over the years; if Kay had a nickel for every time Eva called Walter a momma's boy then she would have had enough to buy all of her favorite things. Kay had heard it all many times before, but this time the anger in Eva's voice cut through everyone in earshot, and Kay knew that things would be different.

"Go ahead and leave," Eva yelled. "Go back to your mother's house like you always do -- live in her basement like the good-for-nothing-low-life that you are. You're nothing but a momma's boy." Walter storming down the stairs and out the front door followed her harsh words. He brushed past Kay in his haste; he never looked back. He didn't say goodbye to Kay or Fatima, but most importantly to Kay, he never asked the one question that she long to hear,

"Do you want to come with me?"

Even in her thirteen-year-old mind she knew that she would have never choosen Walter over Eva, but, still, she wanted him to ask the question. She wanted him to at least pretend that he wanted her. The memory of that day combined with the fresh scars of rejection from last night was too much to bear. Kay rolled herself into a tight ball, tucking her knees into her chest and her head to her knees. She just wanted to disappear if only for a moment. She wanted to close her eyes and only open them when all of the pain and sadness was gone. She thought about her father; she thought about Emanuel; and, she thought about Malik -- the mere thought of them left her feeling empty and afraid. Insecurity had begun to set in and suddenly she began to feel vulnerable and unworthy of love. Her body yearned for the touch of a man -- a man who would hold her, love her, and make love to her. She thought about Emanuel's touch and remembered how beautiful he was standing over her last night. She rolled herself into an even tighter ball trying desperately to let go of thoughts of him. Her mind shifted from thoughts of Emanuel to thoughts of Malik. He, too, still held a piece of her heart and she could not deny the fact that she was still very much in love with him. She loved his long, lean, muscular body, his athletic build. She thought about his smile, which revealed the most perfect set of white slightly bucked teeth; he had the same smile that Khalial had. She laughed regrettably as she thought about how easily he used to make her laugh. He was the funniest guy that she's ever known. He was always animated when he talked no matter what he was talking about. Kay thought about how he would tell her stories about the academy and how hard the sergeants were on the cadets, especially the ones who they knew were weak. She used to dream about growing old with him; the two of them sitting in their rocking chairs on the porch -- her laughing at the many stories he would tell. She found comfort in her thoughts of Malik, and she wished so desperately that things had not changed. She wanted to go back to the days when she, Malik, Jada, and Emanuel would spend time together playing cards and listening to music or when they would spend a night out on the town at one of Philly's hottest clubs. With emotions all over the place Kay finally realized just how much her life had changed. As she continued her chain of thoughts each reminded her of her loss, and each memory left her feeling less and less like her confident self. Her thoughts had gone full circle and there she was again entertaining thoughts of last night, Emanuel, and his words. Heart aching and still very sad she tried to sink deeper into herself. Unable to roll any tighter into a ball she wrapped her arms around her knees and pulled them closer into herself.

Her ringing doorbell interrupted her thoughts, and for the first time since she began seeing Emanuel she was happy to have her thoughts of him interrupted. She rolled to her side half hoping that maybe it was Emanuel coming back to her with an excuse better than, *I'm sorry*. Kay slid out of bed and walked slowly towards the door wearing only her panties and Emanuel's shirt, which fit her like a dress. She looked through the peephole and let out a heavy sigh when she realized that it was Malik at the door. Her thoughts kicked into gear, and she remembered that he was picking Khalial up for church this morning. She forgot to call and tell him that Khalial had stayed with her mother last night. Kay opened the door listlessly. She had no energy to expend on him; he was just another reminder of her disastrous love life.

"Good morning," Malik said with a huge smile on his face.

"Hey," Kay said as she turned her back to him and started walking towards the refrigerator. Usually Kay would have tried to keep it together and hide her sadness and pain, but she was emotionally drained.

"What's wrong with you? You look a mess," he joked, unaware that she was truly not in the mood. Kay ignored his question and statement and chose to only deal with his reason for being there, which was Khalial.

"I meant to call you. Khalial stayed at my mom's house last night." Malik took a mental note of the scene – Kay dressed in a man's shirt and Khalial at Eva's, which in his mind could only mean one thing, so he asked,

"Oh, am I interrupting something?" he questioned looking in the direction of the bedroom. With the refrigerator door completely ajar Kay followed Malik's eyes and also looked towards the bedroom. It took a minute for her to realize what he was insinuating, and when she finally realized what he was suggesting she rolled her eyes and her head simultaneously,

"No. I'm alone," she huffed before she started to explain. "Emanuel's dad had to be rushed to the hospital last night and instead of me taking Khalial to the hospital and freaking him out I took him over to my mother's."

"He was rushed to the hospital? What happened? Is he okay?" Malik asked with genuine concern.

"He had a blocked artery or something. The doctors said that he is going to be fine." Kay rambled on still looking in the refrigerator, not giving the news the attention that Malik thought that it warranted. She closed the refrigerator and headed towards the cabinets.

"Aww, man. How is Emanuel dealing with all of this?"

"Fine. I guess." Kay shrugged her shoulders. Her eyes lit up when she spied a box of Tension Taming tea; it was definitely a Tension Taming tea morning. She reached for the teapot, which was resting on top of the stove. Kay filled it half way with water and placed it on the burner without extending an offer to Malik.

"Naw, I'm cool. I don't have time for a cup of tea or coffee or anything," he said sarcastically. Usually Kay would have offered him something to eat or drink within minutes of him walking through the door. But, the truth was, she didn't want him to stay there any longer than he had to. She didn't respond to his comment; she didn't even acknowledge the fact that he spoke -- she just stood staring at the blue and yellow flames that illumed under the teapot. Malik studied her behavior and knew that despite what she was saying there was something going on with her. "So, Kay, what's up? You don't seem much like yourself this morning. Is something bothering you?"

"Nope," she sighed, her attention still on the flames. Malik knew better. Kay was much too smart to give half responses like 'nope.' Whenever Kay gave monosyllabic responses he knew that she was not her usual centered, focused self, which almost certainly meant that she was unhappy. When they came to the end of their relationship, communication was nearly non-existent -- in fact the only time they seemed to talk was when it had to do with Khalial. Otherwise, everything that Malik asked was answered with a yes, no, maybe, or whatever.

"So, what time are you going to the hospital? I can keep Khalial all night or until you get back. Whatever you need."

"That won't be necessary. I'm not going to the hospital. So, you can bring Khalial home at the usual time."

"You're not going to the hospital?"

"Nope."

"Why not?"

"Why should I?"

"To support Emanuel and his family."

"Emanuel will be fine." Malik looked at her in disbelief. It was not like Kay to be so uncaring and disinterested in the pain or suffering of others. She was always extending herself to those in need even if it was nothing more than sitting in the hospital with the family while their loved one was having surgery. He remembered that shortly after the two of them called it quits his mother was diagnosed with breast cancer. Kay was there everyday cooking or cleaning -- whatever was needed just to take the smallest burden off of the family.

"So, what's up? You two aren't...," he paused looking for the right word, "kicking it like that anymore?" Malik knew that the topic was off limits for him but he asked anyway. Kay cut a look that could have sliced right through him, but he stood his ground and gave her a look that told her that he wasn't going to back down.

"No, we are not kicking it like that," she replied with an attitude. Kay brushed past Malik and reached for the telephone that hung on the wall. "I'll call my mom and let her know that you are on your way to pick up Khalial. You don't want to be late for church." Malik intercepted her reach and placed his hand on top of hers with just enough pressure to signal to her that he wasn't going anywhere until they got to the bottom of her woes.

"Man, what's wrong with you?" Malik asked annoyed.

"Nothing, Malik. I'm fine." Kay snatched her hand from under Malik's and brushed past him again this time towards the cabinet.

"It doesn't seem like you're fine to me." Malik reached for her arm and turned her to face him.

"Malik, just let it go, please," Kay said through clinched teeth. Her voice cracked as she tried to hold back the tears, but she was unable to. "Everything is fine," Kay said, but the tears in her eyes told him otherwise.

"Hey," he turned her to face him and lifted her chin so that he could look into her eyes. "What's up?"

Kay couldn't hear the sincerity in his voice nor could she recognize it in his eyes because she was consumed by her sadness. *How could she open up and share her feelings with him when he was in part to blame for her loneliness* she thought to herself.

"Kay I know that I am probably the last person that you want to talk to about this right now, but I hope that you still think of me as a friend, and I hope that you know that I will always be here for you."

Kay sighed deeply. There were so many things that she wanted to say to him but she realized that it wouldn't do any good; she would probably just look like a fool. How could she tell him that four years later she was still holding on to the hope that he would come back to her? When she thought about her response, tears filled her eyes and the lump that already invaded her throat had begun to swell.

"Malik, I'm fine." And with that, a single tear crept down her cheek.

"Kay, you're not fine," Malik said as he wiped the tear away.

"I'm just not feeling well," Kay offered. She was a horrible liar.

"Okay. That's allowed, but that doesn't have anything to do with you crying or coming to the door looking like crap." Malik's comment wasn't meant to hurt her but it did. "What's wrong? Is it Emanuel?" he asked with trepidation.

"Malik, really I'm fine. Really. It's nothing that you need to concern yourself with."

"So, are you fine or is it nothing that I need to concern myself with?" Malik quizzed not about to let her get away with a dual response.

"I'm fine," Kay said through her tears. Once one tear dropped it was like a waterfall and others quickly followed. He wasn't as concerned about her reasons for crying as much as he was about the fact that she was crying, and without thought he reached for her and took her in his arms. Kay was angry; she did not want to cry over Emanuel especially not in front of Malik. She jerked away from him, "Why do men have to be such jerks?" she asked suddenly feeling more like expressing anger rather than sadness. "Do you guys not realize that I am a person with a heart that aches every time you say or do something stupid?" Malik was caught completely off guard. He expected her to talk about Emanuel and whatever the situation was between them. He did not expect her to bash the entire male species.

"What are you talking about?"

"What am I talking about? I'm talking about you and Emanuel and every other man that ever came into my life. You're standing here trying to console me over something that you think Emanuel did, but you aren't any better. You come up in here out of nowhere announcing your engagement to Heather like it was all good with absolutely no concern for my feelings or what I thought."

"Kay, I thought you didn't care that Heather and I are getting married."

"What did you expect me to do? Beg you not to marry her and ask you to come back to me?" Kay huffed, "Why couldn't you just see that I was still in love with you, that I still needed some time to get over you?"

"Kay, it was four years," Malik reasoned, or so he thought.

"I know. So, how were you able to move on so quickly? What was she able to give you that I wasn't Malik?"

"Kay, I thought that things were good between us. I thought that we ended in a good place."

"You didn't even try to make things work, Malik. You just walked out and moved on without looking back." Kay threw a volley of verbal darts at Malik. She didn't care if he answered her questions or not; she just had to ask them.

"Kay. It was over between us. I thought you agreed. You didn't try to fight for us either," Malik threw back.

"I was always the one fighting for us; trying to give you exactly what you needed to make your dreams come true."

"And I didn't support your dreams?"

"You didn't make the sacrifices that I had to make, Malik."

"What sacrifices, Kay? We both made sacrifices. I gave you everything that I had and I still do. You and Khalial mean the world to me. You don't ever have to want for nothing as long as I am around. I made that promise, and I try to do everything that I can to keep that promise to you."

"Well, that's not enough, Malik. I never wanted to be a single mother. Khalial deserves to have a mother and a father."

"He does have a mother and a father. Just because I'm not living under the same roof with Khalial that doesn't make me any less of a father." Kay couldn't deny that statement -- Malik was a great father. They both knew that they had to have this conversation; it was the only way that they could truly move on, but neither of them expected it to turn into an argument. Malik knew that Kay's frustration wasn't really about him, so he decided to step back from his anger and allow her to vent. "Kay, I will never stop loving you. You are an amazing woman, a great mother, and friend. I love you, and I always will." Malik meant every word that he uttered, and she knew that he did, but she was too angry to let it go with the ole' I-love-you-but -- it was all very cliché. She didn't know what she expected. In her rational thinking Malik was right -- four years was more than enough time to move past a relationship, but she wasn't in the mood for rational thinking. "Kay, I'm sorry if I hurt you," Malik apologized. He knew that he hadn't done anything recently to get on her nerves, but he was certain that he had contributed to her sadness. He knew that the words that she spoke were coming from somewhere, and all he wanted to do was ease her pain. Malik reached for her hands and took them in his. "I love you." He leaned in and kissed her on the forehead. Kay breathed in Malik's scent, and her heart swelled. She prayed to God in that short moment that He would free her from the strong feelings that she still had for Malik.

"I'm sorry, too, Malik. This isn't about you. I just had a really rough night and I guess I'm kind of trippin'," Kay forced herself to smile.

"It's all good, Khadijah," Malik said with a twist of the neck. He called her Khadijah whenever he felt like she was in "baby momma drama" mode; whenever she was in full touch with her ghetto, which was nothing like the sophisticated, centered Kay that he knew and loved. They both laughed. He gave her one last squeeze. "Kay, I really am sorry that I hurt you," Malik said.

" I know, Malik. It's really not about you or Heather; I just have some things that I need to work out with myself. I guess in all of my centering I forgot to toss some old baggage. I will be fine, but thank you for caring."

"I will always care, Kay. Believe me, that is never going to change. You are the mother of my son -- that role is important to me."

"Believe it or not, I am really happy that you and Heather are getting married. She's a good woman, and I'm glad that she's in your life and Khalial's life. Plus, you guys look so cute together," Kay said playfully.

"Well, I'm a good looking brother. You can stand me next to a mop and we will look cute together," Malik joked. "Naw, but seriously, Kay, you were my first love and my best friend for like ten years. You know me better than anyone." Kay's tears returned to her eyes. "I will always have your back. And although I don't completely understand your relationship with Emanuel, I will respect it because I know that you are a smart lady." The boiling teapot screamed demanding Kay's attention. Kay took a deep breath, wiped her tears, and tried to get herself together.

"I'll get it for you. You just relax." Malik left Kay's side and focused his attention on giving her a small bit of relief. Kay continued to try to get herself together. She sucked in a deep breath and pushed it out hard.

"Kay, get yourself together," she demanded.

"Do you want sugar or milk in your tea?"

"Neither. Just give it to me straight," she responded attempting to lighten up. Kay held her teacup in both hands and breathed in its relaxing aroma.

"I'll call Eva and let her know that I am on my way to pick up Khalial," Malik offered then walked towards the telephone. Kay knew that she needed to clear her mind and get her thoughts in order. She had no time to cry over Emanuel; she felt foolish. "Whatever will be will be," she chimed.

"What's that?" Malik called out from the kitchen.

"Nothing. Just finding my center." Kay smiled as she took in another deep breath and closed her eyes in search of peace. She began her meditation with an old Chinese proverb,

"To the mind that is still, the whole universe surrenders."
And with that, she found her center. She turned to Malik with renewed focus, took a deep breath, forced a smile on her face, and looked directly in his eyes. "Malik, I appreciate you being here and for all of your words of encouragement. I feel so much

better. Thank you," she declared. And this time she really meant it.

"Kay, I know that things have changed between us, but I hope that you still think of me as a friend and know that I'll always be here for you." Kay smiled this was the Malik that she fell head over heels for when she was fifteen. He had always been a good friend; his loyalty was unmatched, and she knew without a doubt that he would always have her back. She smiled at him, leaned in, and kissed his cheek.

"I know, Malik."

"After all, you were my first love. You'll always hold a special place in my heart." Kay smiled at the thought. *His first love*. She hadn't thought about it like that, but it was true no matter who he dated or married she would always be his first love, and the special place in his heart that she held could never be replaced by anyone. As was the case with Emanuel, she knew that Jada would forever own a portion of his heart, but she hoped that he would have tried to love her just a little bit. She wasn't angry with Emanuel, she was angry with herself for falling for him so hard and so quick. She felt like maybe she was asking for too much from him. When she took the focus off of herself and her own pain she realized that Emanuel had lost Jada in the most tragic way, and it was obvious that he had not learned how to deal with that loss. In her clarity she knew that Emanuel loved her, but she believed that he just hadn't learned that it was possible and even okay to love her and Jada. She realized that that was something he would have to come to terms with on his own.

Kay was all right with her conclusion, and although she secretly wished that Emanuel would discover that he could love her she decided that she would give him the space that he needed to heal. This was one of those life moments when she had to consciously decide to be happy despite her circumstances. Kay decided that she would spend the day in meditation and let God work things out.

Chapter Twenty-Six

Khadir arrived at Emanuel's house bright and early just like he promised. He rang the doorbell a few times but he got no answer. He peered through the window and tapped against the pane gently. He noticed Emanuel sprawled out across the couch with one foot thrown over the back of the couch and the other dangled over its edge; the couch could not contain all seventy four inches of him. Khadir knocked on the window again, but still he got no movement from Emanuel.

"Hey, E!" Khadir called out as he tapped the window for the third time. Emanuel was in a deep sleep, and nothing that Khadir could have done short of shaking him out of his slumber was going to wake him. Khadir stepped onto the stony [something] beneath the window and retrieved the spare key that was hidden under a perfectly blended artificial rock. He let himself in. "Hey, E," Khadir called out as he shook Emanuel's foot, "wake up, man." Emanuel opened his eyes slowly and stretched his arms over his head.

"Hey. What's up? What are you doing here?" Emanuel asked confused.

"What am I doing here?" Khadir repeated the question. "I'm here to take you to the hospital, remember?"

"What time is it?" Emanuel asked looking at his wristwatch. It was shortly after nine o'clock in the morning. With all of the drama that unfolded with Kay he hadn't even thought twice about his father's health scare and with that memory came another reason to be distressed. Emanuel tried to sit up but he was too tired. He threw his head back on the couch and closed his eyes. Khadir sat in the chair across from him and watched as he struggled to get himself together. Emanuel's head was heavy with thoughts of his father, thoughts of Kay, and thoughts of Jada -- each thought fighting for his undivided attention. He did not want to deal with the activities that awaited him on this day. He didn't dare have any expectations for the day because he could not take one more disappointment. Emanuel let out a heavy sigh as he struggled to sit up.

"So, how are you doing this morning?"

"Tired," Emanuel exhaled the word. Tired was his escape phrase; whenever life was too hard and his burden was too much to bear his response to life was *I'm tired.* Anyone who knew him or took the time to learn him over the past year knew that meant that he was completely tired -- mind, body, and soul.

"Tired, hunh?"

"Yup." Khadir felt his friend's heaviness; it was thick around him. He wished that there were more that he could do to help lift his burdens, but even he understood that Emanuel's heaviness required a different kind of lifting, something that man just couldn't provide; he needed spiritual restoration. Emanuel held his hands to his face unsure of how he would even convince himself to begin the day. He wished that his father had not fallen ill because then he could choose to close himself off from the world. But here he was forced to deal with one more thing that life threw at him.

"Well, your mom and sister are going to be expecting us soon so why don't you go get showered, and I will call and let them know that we will be there around ten." Emanuel nodded his head in agreement and staggered towards his bedroom. Khadir was never regarded as the sensible one between the two, but he knew and understood brokenness and he knew that the only remedy for it was prayer. So with his eyes closed and his head bowed; without eloquence or fashion he prayed a simple prayer for his friend, "Great is your faithfulness, Lord. I know that you are with him. Remind him that you are with him. Show him that you are with him. Heal his heart, Lord, and I know that healing for his spirit will follow." Khadir remained in his posture of prayer, head in his hands, and heart open, waiting to hear from God.

Emanuel moved slowly and mechanically through his routine, mindless in his actions. He knew that he needed to talk to Kay, and although he didn't want to plan anything for fear of disappointment he decided that he would make it a point to talk to her today. After getting dressed, Emanuel sat on the edge of his bed. He reached for the phone on his nightstand and dialed

Kay's number; he had no idea what he was going to say to her -- he just knew that he needed to say something. The phone rang several times before Kay and Khalial's voices announced, "*You have reached Kay and Khalial sorry we aren't available to take your call but if you leave your name and a brief message we will get back to you. Thank you for calling and have a blessed day.*" - *Beep*. Emanuel stuttered, "Hey, Kay. I-I just wanted to talk to you t-to tell you again how sorry I am. I know that I really messed up last night. If you're there, please pick up the phone. I really need to talk to you." The sadness in Emanuel's voice could not be denied. He listened to the dead air for a moment; concentrating as if he listened hard enough he could hear Kay walking to the phone. A loud beep echoed in his ear indicating that time was up for him to leave a message. He hung up the phone gently determined to keep his emotions in check. Emanuel immediately dialed Kay's number again convinced that perhaps she was just about to pick up the phone when the call was disconnected. Maybe she was in the shower, he thought as he imagined her running from the shower to the phone but again the machine answered his call. Emanuel left another message. "Kay...hey, it's me again... I'm about to head out to pick up my mom and Nadia to go see my pops in the hospital... I was hoping to catch you before I left. Well, I have my cell phone with me; give me a call when you get this message or the first message... well, I guess it won't be until you get this message because in my first message I didn't tell you that I was leaving or that I had my cell phone," he babbled on. "Well, call me... we need to... " *Beep*. He was disconnected. Emanuel pressed redial calling Kay for the third time -- this time he was prepared to speak to her answering machine. "Hey, I got cut off... I was just saying that we need to talk so call me," he said and hung up quickly, as if he were racing against time.

Emanuel sat on the passenger's side of Khadir's BMW. He half listen as Khadir went on and on about the latest chick that he had his eyes on. Emanuel was convinced years ago that Khadir loved nothing more than to hear himself talk so he took advantage of the situation and sat in silence only interjecting a word of acknowledgement every now and then. Emanuel could not escape his own thoughts, wondering when, exactly, did he lose his mind and how would he ever find it. He looked out the window as Khadir maneuvered through the congested city streets, whipping around double-parked cars and fearless pedestrians crossing through moving traffic trying to get to the other side. Khadir was heavy on his horn at times causing Emanuel to step out of himself and step back into reality. He looked up just in time to see a dusty old man with checkered teeth give Khadir a vulgar hand gesture, but Khadir was completely unfazed. He continued to talk about himself. Emanuel looked over at his friend with a strange admiration; he wished that he could find just a portion of the joy in his own life that Khadir seemed to have in his. Emanuel sank in his seat trying to muster the energy necessary to get through this day. How would he resolve things with Kay and contend with his father's health? If Emanuel had his choice he would have locked himself in his house and never come out again. Emanuel gripped his chest trying to sooth his aching heart. Mr. Rivers was the one who had the heart attack but Emanuel couldn't understand how he had not gone into cardiac arrest himself with all of the pain that plagued him.

Khadir entered the Rivers's horseshoe-shaped driveway just before ten a.m. He could see the curtain move, and he knew that Mrs. Rivers had probably looked out the window a million times wondering where they were. Emanuel stepped out of the car, and in the same moment stepped back into reality. He knew that despite his feelings he needed to appear strong for the women in his life. Mrs. Rivers and Nadia came out of the house ready to go before Emanuel or Khadir could make their way to the front door.

"Good morning, gentlemen," Mrs. Rivers greeted.

"Hey, Mom." Emanuel leaned in, hugged his mother, and kissed her cheek. He greeted Nadia the same way.

"So, are we all set?" Khadir asked with one foot back in the car.

"Yes, we are." Mrs. Rivers stepped swiftly towards the car causing Emanuel to shuffle to get to her door in time to open it for her. He then rushed to the other side to open the door for Nadia who waited patiently for him to do so. When they arrived at the hospital Mr. Rivers was propped up in his bed. Emanuel had expected him to be sedated with tubes and such hanging from every orifice – but he wasn't. He was just as bright eyed and alert as always . Everyone took their turn greeting Mr. Rivers, followed by Mrs. Rivers's lip lock and long embrace. Mr. and Mrs. Rivers spent very few nights apart since their wedding day. Neither of them believed that absence made the heart grow fonder; they were fond enough of one another and absence only made them miss each other like crazy.

"Hi, Daddy," Nadia said in her daddy's-little-girl-voice that carried no hint of maturity. Nadia climbed in the bed with her father, curled up, and laid her head on her his shoulder. Mr. Rivers kissed her forehead.

"Hey, baby girl." Neither of them was concerned with how they appeared to anyone watching. Nadia would always be Mr. Rivers's baby girl and she played the part well. Emanuel met Mr. Rivers on the other side of his bed and kissed him on the cheek.

"Hey, Pops."

"Hey, son."

"How are you feeling?"

"I feel great!" he exclaimed. "I'm ready to go home."

"Do you think they will let you go home today?" Khadir questioned as he leaned in and gave Mr. Rivers a hug and a handshake.

"I don't know, but it doesn't change the fact that I'm ready to go home." Everyone laughed. All Emanuel could think about was his mortality and how fragile life was. He sat quietly as everyone enjoyed light conversation and laughter. Laughter was a sign that all was well, but not for Emanuel because he still had some unfinished business to take care of. He looked admiringly over at his parents whose love seemed renewed by Mr. Rivers's near-death experience. As everyone sat around in the hospital room remembering the circumstances surrounding the scare yesterday, Emanuel sat by the window waiting and hoping for his cell phone to ring, but he noticed that he had no reception in the hospital. He wanted to call Kay, but he didn't want to have this very necessary conversation over the phone, and he didn't want to initiate it with his family within such closeness. Emanuel offered to make a coffee run, using it as an opportunity to excuse himself. With two orders requested Emanuel's first stop was outside of the hospital where he could get a cell phone signal connected again and see if Kay had called. But he had no new messages and worse than that no missed calls. He knew that Kay was upset with him, but he never imagined that she wouldn't call to allow him to make amends.

Emanuel dialed Kay's number but still no answer. Emanuel was beginning to feel desperate; he did not want to lose his connection with Kay, but he was terribly afraid that he had. He dialed her number again; he could not resist the urge to talk to her. When her answering machine answered his call again he hung up. And each time he hung up he found himself immediately dialing her number again. He imagined that she had just missed his call by seconds and with that he dialed her number again and again. He didn't leave a message; he was just finding comfort in hearing her voice. He listened intently to the message as she announced,

"You have reached Kay and Khalial sorry we aren't available to take your call but if you leave your name and a brief message we will get back to you. Thank you for calling and have a blessed day." Each time the life-like sound of her voice was interrupted by a loud beep, which indicated that this was the time to leave a message and this time, after seven straight calls, Emanuel decided to leave a message,

"Kay… it's me again… Emanuel," he reminded her in case she wouldn't recognize his voice. "I-I just want to say that I really am sorry about last night. I don't know what came over me… well, I think that I know, but still there is no excuse that I can give you. I have just been under a lot of pressure and my mind… I guess it just couldn't take it any more," he continued,

"I guess I just lost focus an-and I'm sorry." The machined beeped one final time telling him that his time was up. He hung the phone up in frustration, feeling like he had not said all that he wanted her to hear. Emanuel pressed the button to disconnect and get another dial tone.

Kwanza

Chapter Twenty-Seven

Kay decided to spend Sunday in complete solitude. She thought about going to Sunday service, but she decided to just spend some one-on-one time with God. After she called her mother to let her know that Malik was coming by to pick up Khalial she turned off each of her telephones and turned down her answering machine. Kay retreated to her bathroom. Making it her sanctuary, she spread out a blanket on the floor along with a few candles, some meditation music, and Christian literature. She brought along a few bottles of water and her journal just in case she was inspired to write. Kay settled into a posture of meditation, she closed her eyes, and just listened -- heart, mind, and spirit clear and open, ready to hear from God. And faithful to His promises God began to speak and Kay's heart received and understood all that was imparted. Kay spoke the promises Jesus spoke in Matthew 7:7, *"Ask and it shall be given you; seek, and ye shall find; knock, and it shall be opened unto you."* Tears filled Kay's eyes as she began to ask for the things that she wanted. She asked for continued wisdom and strength; she asked for a love of her own; and most importantly she asked for forgiveness of her sins and that the anger and bitterness she carried towards any man be removed. Kay sealed the prayer with thanks and praised God for His continued faithfulness as she immediately felt her burdens lifted. God had set an atmosphere, in the tiny space of her bathroom that allowed Kay to be free. In that place she didn't have any of the pressures that everyday life brought. She didn't have to concern herself with pleasing anyone, dealing with anyone's insecurities, or trying to figure out anyone's emotional state -- and that was exactly what she needed. She lay with her back on the floor and her feet propped up on the cold resin bathtub. She could not control the sporadic thoughts of Emanuel that managed to creep into her head every now and then, but with each thought she asked God to bless him. She wished that she and Emanuel could be together, but more than that she wanted him to find his own peace -- the peace that only God could give -- and that's what she prayed for. Knowing that God's plans were greater than our own, and resolving that if it was God's will for the two of them to be together then His will be done.

Kay enjoyed her day. She did all of the things that she loved; she read and she wrote; she dance and she sang. By the time Malik brought Khalial home at around eight o'clock her mind was clear, her body charged, and her spirit renewed. She knew that God had truly done a work in her because when Malik arrived at her house she was completely absent of any desire for him. Kay put Khalial down for the night before she turned her telephone back on and checked her messages. She guessed that Emanuel would have called to apologize again, but she had no idea that he would have called her house twenty-six times according to her caller i.d. and left sixteen messages. She listened to his choppy messages one after the other; she could hear the sadness and confusion in his voice. Kay's heart began to ache for him but she remembered that God was already working in his life, and with that assurance she thanked God. By Monday morning things in the Ali household were back to normal. Kay woke up at the crack of dawn for her usual prayer, meditation, and yoga, followed by a hot relaxing shower. She woke Khalial up singing one of her quirky morning songs just as she always had. They exchanged playful taps before Kay disappeared to the kitchen to prepare breakfast. The atmosphere in Kay's house was quiet and peaceful -- just the way she liked it.

However, in Emanuel's world things were just as befuddled as ever. He struggled to sleep peacefully, and the nightmare of Jada's death continued to haunt him. Her screams echoed in his head even when he was awake. He went to work super early just as he had during his pre-Kay days trying to find solace in the superficial. He tried to focus on the work that was before him, but he was unproductive. Emanuel wasted hours looking out of his office window from his chair; his bird's eye view revealed only a cloudy sky. He entertained thoughts of opening the window and stepping out into the clouds, but an image of him lying on the dirty concrete in a puddle of blood and brains was frightening. But his weary mind continued to play the scene in his head over and over again. He swirled his chair from side to side feeling relatively comfortable in this space of insanity. He wondered what an insane life would look like for him. Would he live his life on the streets or would he spend his days in a white padded room? Maybe, he thought, he would be so heavily sedated that he would sit in a wheelchair mindlessly staring out into space. An image of the old man that Khadir nearly ran over the other morning came to his mind and suddenly he saw himself. He swirled his chair faster from side to side. He could feel a ball of rage rising up in him, forcefully, but the only way to express it was through tears. He wanted to scream and yell, but he didn't even want to give that to God. He didn't even want to give Him his anger. When Mona arrived in the office shortly before eight-thirty she was concerned to find Emanuel sitting in the dark, the scene was eerily familiar. Mona's head dropped to her chest she left the office without saying a word and returned with a bible in hand. Mona flipped through the pages as she pulled the empty chair in front of Emanuel's desk closer. She sat down and without introduction she spoke,

"Blessed is the man that hears God's word and keeps it." She did not have to see Emanuel's face to read his reaction because she was not speaking to the man but to the heart of the man. She knew that Emanuel's heart was hungry for God's word and so she continued to flip through the pages. "Come unto me, all ye that labor and are heavy laden, and I will give you rest." Mona continued, "Wait on the Lord: be of good courage, and he shall strengthen thine heart: wait, I say, on the Lord." Comfortable with the scriptures that she shared Mona closed the bible but continued to speak to Emanuel. "Mr. Rivers, you asked my opinion once before and I appreciate the fact that I can be honest with you," Mona continued despite the fact that Emanuel still had not turned his seat to face her. "Sir, I really think that you ought to talk to someone... a professional, a therapist, or spiritual advisor, someone who can help you sort out the things that are heavy on your mind." Mona leaned forward in her seat and reached for a notepad from Emanuel's desk. She began to scribble information on the blank page. Mona slid the notebook back towards Emanuel. "Here is the name and numbers for Dr. Banks and my pastor, maybe it will be helpful for you to talk to them," she said upbeat. "I can call them if you want." She paused offering him an opportunity to comment, but he did not. Mona tapped the sheet of paper. "Well, your calendar is clear today maybe one or both of them could get you in today." Emanuel still had not turned to face her. She knew that he was angry with her for even suggesting that he speak with a professional. He swung his chair feverishly from side to side.

"*Just leave. Just shut up and leave. I don't want to talk to anyone-- not you and especially not a therapist or a pastor. Just leave me alone,*" he thought. If he weren't so tired and worn he would have told her just that. Mona continued to speak to his back.

"Emanuel," she said trying to reach him on a personal level, "I'm no doctor, but I am certain that being this sad is not healthy; you can't live with such heartache." Mona's voice began to crack "... I want to see the man that I came to work for two years ago. The confident man that was charismatic and strong. That was the man that was able to convince me to leave Fisher and Greene and come work for you in your small start-up company, and now here were are," she said spreading her arms out like and eagle, "flourishing." Emanuel continued to stare out of the window, but his chair swinging had ceased and Mona knew that he was listening to her. "I just want so desperately for you to find happiness." Emanuel could hear the sincerity in Mona's voice -- he heard her sniffling. He wanted to turn around and console her, but he didn't want her to see him crying. She got him with the scripture, "*Come unto me, all ye that labor and are heavy laden, and I will give you rest,*" because that was what he wanted more than anything in the world at that moment -- rest. He didn't want to be unhappy, and he didn't want to live in a state of constant mourning, but he didn't know how to get past those feelings. He hated the man that he had become, but he didn't know how to save himself from the hell on earth that was his life. Emanuel's tears traced down his face and settled just under his nose causing it to tickle; he didn't want Mona to see him wipe his tears away so he dropped his head to his chest and wiped his tear on his shoulder. Emanuel cleared his throat, and still without turning to her he dismissed her they way he always did,

"Mona, thank you for stopping in, but I have work to do." Mona dropped her head and let out a sigh. She was confident that a seed had been planted, and she knew that God would take care to water and grow that seed. Without another word, Mona got up from her seat, walked around the desk, and stood directly in front of Emanuel. She placed her hand on his shoulder.

"Emanuel, don't ever forget that God loves you."

She looked deep into his eyes, which made him slightly uncomfortable. Having her that close to him witnessing the fresh track of tears on his face made him feel weak. Emanuel's shoulder was warm under Mona's hand, and he could feel something stirring in his belly; he dropped his eyes as feelings of embarrassment hung over him. He placed one hand to his face and met his tears as they escaped against his will. Mona lifted his chin and looked directly into his eyes. She wiped his tears away with her thumbs, "Emanuel, your very name means that God is with you." She smiled. "Know that He is and will always be with you. Rejoice, find peace, be happy, and live. Live for Jada, live for Kay, live for you, but most of all live for God." The stirring in his belly got stronger and it felt like his whole body was shaking. Mona balanced on her tiptoes and planted a soft kiss on his forehead; she leaned back and traced a cross on his forehead like his mother and grandmother use to do just before they were about to pray over him. Emanuel grabbed Mona's hand before she could start the two-step process.

"Thank you, Mona." Emanuel didn't want her to pray for him he wasn't ready to make amends with God. He stopped her action but he did not stop her words because her prayers had already begun their journey from her mouth to God's ears. And with that Mona turned and walked away.

Emanuel sat at his desk and studied the notes that Mona inscribed the pad which he had propped up against his keyboard. Dr. Banks's number and address were written neatly on the first four lines of the paper and Pastor Riley's name, number, and address were written directly below it. He knew in his heart that this was one of the crossroads that people spoke of.

Chapter Twenty-Eight

Emanuel wiggled nervously in his seat as Dr. Banks prepared herself for their one-hour session. She crossed her long legs, slid her reading glasses on her face, and with a click of her pen she began, "So how have you been?"

"I'm okay."

"Just okay?" she quizzed. Emanuel searched himself and concluded,

"Yes. Just okay."

"It's been over a year now. Tell me what have you done to cope with your loss?"

"I have done absolutely nothing. Actually, I was doing a really good job of ignoring it all, but then I was forced to face it." He spoke through a lump in his throat that seemed to appear out of nowhere.

"Explain." Dr. Banks sat erect leaning into Emanuel, and like a balancing scale Emanuel leaned back, sitting further away from Dr. Banks. He tried to get a grip on exactly what it was that he was feeling. He wanted to get beyond the anger and the sadness and somehow tap into the pain. He knew that his heart was sick with grief, but he wanted to say more. He wanted to pour his whole heart out to Dr. Banks, throw it all on the table so that she could fix it. He wanted her to remember all that she learned in her studies, and show him why she was worthy of carrying the title doctor.

"I became close to someone. Without trying to it just happened, and before I knew it I wanted nothing more than to be with her."

"So what did that relationship force you to face?"

"I had to face the fact that my mind was splintered."

"Splintered?" Dr. Banks repeated, then paused for effect, as a way to lore Emanuel to talk further on that point.

"It was like in my mind I knew that I was talking to…" he paused, debating if he wanted to say Kay's name or not, then deciding not, "her, but somehow I pretended or believed, maybe even wished, that I was talking to Jada."

"Did you pretend that you were talking to Jada or did you believe that you were talking to Jada? There is a very real difference." Dr. Banks refrained from taking physical notes, but her mind had already begun to process the things that Emanuel was saying to her.

"Sometimes I pretended that I was then other times I guess I believed that I was." Emanuel thought about the times when in his mind Kay had become Jada. Even thinking of it in that moment gave him a weird sense of pleasure.

"Tell me about a time when you believed that she," Dr. Banks said clumsily, "was Jada." Emanuel's mind immediately went to the other night. He could not bring himself to retell that story to Dr. Banks; he was certain that she would stamp him certifiably insane, so he gave her something less dramatic.

"Well, one day we were together looking at pictures, and she was telling me stories about her and Jada growing up." He paused and replayed his words back in his head. He did not want to give Dr. Banks any indication that the woman he was talking about was a friend of Jada's although he knew that bit of information would be important. He hoped that Dr. Banks didn't pick up on his words, but when she began writing on her note pad he figured that she had in fact made the connection. Emanuel swallowed hard. "She and Jada are so much alike." He frowned causing his forehead to wrinkle. "Their laugh, their sense of humor, their lips." He laughed a nervous laugh. "I couldn't take my eyes off of her. I watched her lips as she spoke; I was completely enthralled. Then on her shoulder there's this tattoo of a butterfly. It was the same tattoo that Jada had." He licked his lips as he remembered how sweet she tasted against his lips.

"What happened?"

"All I could see was Jada. I knew that it wasn't her, but she looked and felt exactly how I remember. She even smelled like her. I wanted her to be Jada. I needed her to be Jada because my mind could no longer pretend. I was forgetting what she looked like. The small things like the way her lips curled when she smiled and how her nose would crinkle when she was embarrassed. Kay has each of those characteristics and it was beautiful -- more beautiful than anything that I had witnessed the entire year. I needed it." His words drifted as he recalled that night. "I needed it," he repeated. Emanuel didn't even realize that he was crying until his salty tears seeped between his lips. He took the back of his hand and wiped his eyes. Next to Jada's death, his greatest fear was that he would forget her, and it scared him when he realized that thoughts of her were in fact fading.

"What happened?" Dr. Banks asked again.

"I leaned in and kissed her shoulder, then her neck, and before I knew it I was kissing her lips. I felt so alive, like she was what I had been missing."

"And with those feelings, she became exactly what you had been missing. Jada."

"Yeah, without her even knowing it."

"Then what happened?"

Emanuel looked at her a little bewildered, *"Did she really want to know the details of that night?"* he wondered to himself.

"Were you intimate with her?"

"If you're asking if we slept together, the answer is no, but I would say that we were intimate. More intimate than the act of intimacy itself because I felt her more deeply and emotionally than I could ever have managed physically. She opened up her heart to me, and I allowed her to get beyond the walls that I had constructed, even if it was under the pretense of her being Jada." Emanuel was surprised that he was able to articulate his feelings and thoughts so clearly. He was slightly proud of himself, and Dr. Banks was proud of him too. They both realized that a year ago was too soon for them to try to tap into his grief and have the conversation that they were having. Emanuel had not begun to take note of his life. Everything was very much one-dimensional; the only thing that he was experiencing a year ago when they first sat down was sadness -- deep, unreachable, unexplainable sadness.

Chapter Twenty-Nine

Kay sipped a hot cup of green tea while she looked over the real-estate information that Larry sent over by courier. She had settled on opening a new club in LA and had even begun entertaining thoughts of relocating. The way she figured, Soul Sistahs in Philly was successful and it was pretty much running itself; she really didn't have to live in Philly to oversee the day-to-day business activities. The thought of starting a new life in LA was exciting -- Kay was completely over her drab life in Philly and LA was just what the doctor ordered, at least she hoped. She had not made any final decisions, but she had made plans to fly out to LA and not only take a look at the commercial properties that Larry had proposed but also to test the nightlife to check out the competition both professionally as well as socially. She could not imagine that the men in LA could be anymore difficult than the ones in Philly.

Kay looked over the past year's financial earnings. By all accounts, new businesses generally struggle during the first year and many of them call it quits before the year ends, but *Soul Sistahs* had done exceptionally well over the past year, and she knew that if things kept going the way that they were then expansion was the next logical step. She could not deny how blessed she was professionally. She knew that God had greater plans for her than she could ever imagine, and she believed that Jada was in Heaven advocating hard on her behalf. Kay imagined her friend in Heaven being just as popular as she was on earth, speaking to everyone in her soft, sultry voice, "*hey family*" which was how she greeted almost everyone. That thought made Kay laugh. She wished so desperately that she was contemplating this expansion with Jada the way that it was suppose to be. In their minds, they were going to grow old in this business perhaps one day making Soul Sistahs a historical landmark in art history. The kind of club that would birth great artist who would come back and talk about their days at Soul Sistahs the way many great groups talk about the early days at Motown. The clicking and clanking sound of high heels against the club's tiled floor interrupted Kay's thoughts. She peered up to find Eva dressed to the nine in a pin-stripped navy blue suit.

"Hey, lady," Eva chimed with excitement. She gave her daughter a kiss on the cheek and sat in the empty chair across from Kay. "How are you today?"

"I'm really good, Ma. How are you?"

"I am fabulous," she announced. And she was. Eva had the beauty of Lena Horne, the elegance of Diane Carroll, and the grandeur of Diana Ross all rolled into one. Kay smirked at her mother.

"So, what brings you by here?"

"Nothing, I had some free time between clients, and I thought I'd drop in to see how things are going with you."

"I'm fine. Just tracking my next move."

"Your next move, which will be?" Eva asked.

"Well, for one thing I decided to move forward with opening a new club," Kay beamed causing Eva to scream for joy.

"Kay, that is wonderful. If I had a glass of wine I would toast to that. So where have you decided to venture? Atlanta or LA?"

"LA."

"Yes!" Eva clinched her fist in the air. "This is very exciting, Khadijah."

"Yes, but a little frightening as well."

"Yeah, well, you know what I always say, fear is just an additive that keeps you moving forward." Kay thought about what her mother said trying to recall if it was something that she heard her say before, but she had not. Eva was good for throwing out new one-liners, which in her mind encompassed some great message. Eva looked over her shoulder and called for one of the waitresses. "Hey, can we get two glasses of wine over here. We are having a celebration." Eva smiled approvingly at her daughter. Kay was very grateful for her relationship with her mother. She was happy to have her in her corner always supporting and encouraging her. The waitress returned with two glasses of white wine filled to the rim. Eva reached for her glass without saying a word; her mind was too busy constructing her toast. Kay reached for her glass,

"Thank you very much, Angel," she said addressing the waitress by name.

"You are very welcome, Ms. Ali."

"Here's to pushing beyond fear towards your greatness." The two clanked their glasses, shared a smile, and took a short sip of their noonday libation.

"Thank you, Ma. It really means a lot to me to have you here to celebrate with me."

"I love good news, Kay, and one thing's for sure you always have good news to share. Unlike your little sister." Eva said with a toot of her lips.

"Oh no, Ma," Kay interrupted. "Please let's not get on Fatima."

"You're right. This is a happy occasion." Eva took a long swig from her glass. "So, how is Emanuel's father doing?" Kay did not know the answer to that question. She prayed for Mr. Rivers and God gave her peace concerning his health, but in her attempt at giving Emanuel his space she failed to check in with the Rivers family to get an update on his father's recovery. Kay made a mental note to herself to have flowers sent to him.

"I haven't talked to the family to get an update."

"You haven't talked to the family?" Eva quizzed suspiciously. "How about Emanuel -- have you talked to him?"

"Nope," Kay answered this time taking a long sip from her glass.

"What happened now?" Eva sat with her hand on the stem of her glass ready to drink if she had to, to stop herself from saying something out of order. Kay breathed a heavy sigh. She wasn't in the mood for advice, especially not Eva's fly-by-night philosophy.

"Nothing happened." Kay lied.

"The last I heard you two were really into one another. Catching feelings and what not. What changed?" Eva was relentless; she demanded transparency from everyone that she chose to talk to. It was annoying at times especially when one wasn't ready to be transparent.

"We just decided to take a break," Kay stuttered.

"Take a break?" Eva didn't believe that for a minute. "Well, whatever the case. I just suggest that you take care of yourself and not use LA as your escape from dealing with the truth." Kay acknowledged her mother's words with a simple head nod. "Women sometimes tend to run away from the pain instead of confronting it head on." Eva was exact in her thinking at least as far as Kay was concerned. Running away, although she didn't call it that, was her way of coping. She wondered if Eva was so familiar with this approach because it was her approach of choice.

"So, is that how you chose to deal with Walter, I mean Karim?" Kay said jokingly, because that's how Eva always referred to him, when she chose to use his name. Eva laughed in lieu of a response. "Were you ready to let go of him when he left?"

"Which time?" Eva questioned in a very serious tone. "The last time that Walter, I mean Karim, walked out of my life I was over him. If I hadn't been he would have been right back in my life just as he had so many times before. When you come to the end of a chapter in your life it is sealed with a peace that you can't even describe. You see, we often think we are at the end of a chapter, that we are over something or someone, because we've said good-bye, but then we spend weeks, months, and sometimes years asking ourselves *what if*, wondering if we could have done things differently, and wishing for an opportunity to have that last conversation all over again, so that we could have said this, that, or some other thing. But for me and Karim," Eva smiled a kind smile, "it was really over that day he walked out, and like it or not, that's what made it possible for each of us to move on. It was totally out of our control. Without any urging from either of us our hearts had moved on." Eva never ceased to surprise Kay with her wisdom. That was the perfect answer. It left no room for debate or even a follow-up question. Kay was envious of Eva's wisdom concerning moving on and in that moment she prayed to God for that same wisdom and understanding, that she too could walk away from every situation with a spirit of peace.

Chapter Thirty

Emanuel was exhausted when he left Dr. Banks's office. He contemplated whether or not he was going to go to see the Bishop, but with not much fight he decided that he had enough enlightenment for one day. His experience with Dr. Banks was more than he had expected. He left her office feeling lighter and his thoughts were less cloudy. When Emanuel entered his home for the first time with this newfound freedom he noticed that not only was his heart and mind lighter but his home appeared brighter, like a dark cloud had been lifted. Emanuel picked up the photo of him and Jada that rested on the console. It was the last photo that was taken of the two of them together. Emanuel placed the photo to his lips and kissed the glass. "This has been the worst year of my life," he said to the photo -- not out of anger but from a place of absolute honesty. Emanuel sat the picture on the coffee table in front of him and picked up his stack of mail. He flipped through each enveloped until he came across one that read *Essential Retreats*. Emanuel recognized the name of the resort that he and Jada had planned to visit the day after the opening of Soul Sistahs, but because of the accident it was a trip that neither of them ever made. Immediately after hearing about Jada's death *Essential Retreats* offered Emanuel a rain check on his visit and said that he was welcome anytime, all he had to do was call. Emanuel opened the envelope. He looked past the beautiful scenery of tall mountains and green pastures; his eyes settled on an image of a log cabin set out by itself amidst the "wilderness" – thick heavy trees. The serenity of the scene translated through the brochure, just as it was designed to do, and without thought he searched the pages for a number to call to make reservations. Emanuel reached for the phone and dialed the number. He had no idea what his schedule looked like for the week, but if they would have him he was prepared to fly out to Colorado first thing in the morning. The woman who answered the phone at *Essential Retreats* was very accommodating; she searched their database and within minutes she had made provisions to accommodate him for a week in a private log cabin, beginning in the morning. He was given the option of how he wanted to spend his week. The woman explained in a very polite way that he could either spend his time at *Essential Retreats* alone, scheduling his own activities and events, or he could be placed in a group based on his needs, whose activities were carefully planned and designed. Emanuel opted to spend it alone -- not out of depression but out of necessity. He felt that it was very necessary for him to tap further into the peace and freedom that he found after his conversation with Dr. Banks. And oddly enough he thought that this would be the perfect place for him to have his long awaited discourse with God.

Emanuel rested relatively well that night and first thing in the morning he packed his suitcase and headed to the airport. He called his parents from the airport as he waited for his flight to take off. Of course Mrs. Rivers was more concerned than she needed to be and asked a million questions, but Emanuel assured her that all was well, and he expected all to be much better by the time he returned. Emanuel didn't call Kay although he desperately wanted to. But there was nothing more that he could say to her besides I'm sorry, and somehow at this stage of the game I'm sorry was not enough. He had no idea what he needed to say and hadn't even begun to entertain thoughts of what he needed to say. He was hoping that he would have greater clarity on the other side of his retreat. Emanuel's next call was to Mona. He asked her to reschedule his calendar for the week; she did so without question. Mona was very happy to clear his calendar so that he could take some time away to clear his mind.

When Emanuel arrived at the airport he was pleased to find that the resort had arranged for a limo to pick him up and drive him to *Essential Retreats*. The one-hour drive from the airport to the resort was a series of desert-like basins turning into plateaus, followed by alpine mountains and grasslands. Emanuel knew that he was in for an amazingly relaxing week. He thought about how significant this trip was when he and Jada scheduled it a year ago. He could only imagine how in awe Jada would have been as they drove up to the resort. He could see her now --

mouth open wide and her eyes as big as silver dollars. Emanuel took in the beauty of the scene enough for the both of them, and he couldn't help but take a long deep breath. *Essential Retreats* was more beautiful than their brochure could express. The driver stopped in front of a mid-sized log cottage. He opened the door for Emanuel and commenced to gather his bags from the trunk. Emanuel stepped out of the limo and into a dream. The scene of tall trees and mountains as far as the eye could see was awe-inspiring. His heart was instantly at peace, and he knew that this was the only place in the world that he needed to be right now. He felt the presence of God all around him as he stood admiringly at His magnificent wonders. Emanuel was almost ashamed at his ignorance and attempt to deny God. He knew that he had to make amends with God and looking at all of the beauty that surrounded him he knew that he could not be closer to God on this side of life than he was at that moment.

Emanuel didn't waste anytime starting his week of purging. Emanuel unpacked his suitcase then showered and relaxed in a pair of sweats and a t-shirt. He sat on the couch, pulled out his Bible and turned to the book of Job. He had wanted to explore this beautiful story every since the day Kay mentioned it to him, but he could never bring himself to pickup a bible, let alone read it. Now with his heart open and his spirit hungry for answers he read through each of the forty-two chapters as if he were reading poetry. His eyes filled with tears on occasion and rested for a little while on versus in the book that he found familiar including the poetry in the first verse of chapter six, "If only my anguish could be weighed". He connected completely with Jobs anguish and cried with him through his words. He continued to read. Like Job, Emanuel had spent way too much time questioning God and measuring his despair against his perceived faithfulness. The burning question that they both shared was how could God justify such an outcome for their lives, despite their faithfulness?

Emanuel had loved the Lord; he gave his life to Him. He gave to the poor, just as it was commanded of him, and showed love to all of those who he came in contact with, but what was his reward? -- a life absent the one that he loved most. The one that he stood before God and the world and promised to love and cherish through sickness and health until death parted them. Who knew that day, besides God, that death was imminent?

Emanuel was embarrassed by his lost of faith in God, but he was overjoyed when he found it again somewhere around the thirty-seventh verse, "*The Almighty is beyond our reach and exalted in power; in His justice and great righteousness, he does not oppress.*" Emanuel's heart had begun to turn around, and there was a churning in his belly that inspired a change in his thinking. He was conscious for the first time since giving his life over to Christ of the presence of God that lived within him. Tears continued to fall but for reasons completely opposite of anger or sadness. Emanuel cried with a new understanding of God's power. Within three short hours of arriving in Colorado, Emanuel had found peace and made amends with God; something that he was unable to do over the past year. After reading the beautiful story of a man named Job, who was considered blameless and upright before God, Emanuel had found himself again and fell back in flow with God's rhythm for his life. By the third hour Emanuel was confident in knowing that there is no love greater than the love that God has for His children, and for that, Emanuel was grateful.

Chapter Thirty-One

Kay thoroughly enjoyed her trip to LA. It took only minutes of her being on ground before she decided that she would give LA a chance. The weather alone was worth the move. She looked at the beautiful scene from her hotel room. She was on the fifteenth floor of the Sheraton in beautiful downtown LA. Her plush suite was as comfy as home; she kicked off her flip-flops as soon as she got settled in her room. Kay was scheduled to begin her tour of a few commercial properties at two o'clock; she looked at her watch, which automatically converted to West coast time, it was only ten o'clock. She was exhausted; the three-hour time difference was already taking a toll on her. She did the math in her head -- she awoke at four a.m. to catch her six-thirty flight; she arrived in LA at just after nine a.m., but her body was experiencing noon. She gained three hours that she really wasn't in need of. She was a busy woman and often wished she had more time in the day to do the things that she needed to do, but this was a bit much. Kay yawned and stretched her arms above her head. She thought about taking a nap before her meetings, but she was too anxious. She thought about all of the grand possibilities that awaited her if she only she would keep moving. She knew what Jada would say if she were here,

"Just show up." Jada was always the one who encouraged Kay to take chances, to fight against all odds, and with Jada beside her Kay was fearless. But now here she was, all alone, expected to make such an important decision. She wished that Emanuel had made himself available to her so that he could exercise his partnership power. She could not bring herself to call him for any reason, but she never stopped wishing that he would call her. Since his marathon calls the day after the incident he had not called her. She managed to busy herself with work which filled her mind most of the day. She fought to hold back thoughts of him at night when she laid in her bed restless. Kay's heart ached each time she thought about Emanuel and their last encounter. She wished she knew what would become

257

of their relationship; her desire was to be was to be his lady, but she knew that God would plant her exactly where she needed to be. Kay pressed past her fears and decided to spend her free time talking to God. She found a space on the floor, crossed her legs, and prepared her heart for what the day had in store for her. Kay sang a song of praise. Without thought the words came to her, *"All to Jesus I surrender all to Him I freely give. I will ever love and trust Him...I surrender all...I surrender all...all to thee my blessed Savior...I surrender all."* Kay rocked in silence as she meditated on the words of that beautiful hymn. She was reminded of her grandmother who would sing that very song over and over again as she went about her daily chores. That memory alone was enough to usher Kay into the presence of the Lord. Tears streamed down her face as she talked to God. She prayed for the boldness to be obedient and walk towards the blessings that God laid out for her. She hadn't realized how comfortable she was in her little bubble. She couldn't deny how much hard work she put into *Soul Sistahs* over the past year given the circumstances, going from a joint venture to practically running everything on her own. Now she was preparing to open a second club all the way across the country. Jada would be proud. Kay was sure of it. In fact, she could hear Jada cheering her on from Heaven,

"Work it, Ma'ma!"

Chapter Thirty-Two

After his weeklong hiatus Emanuel returned to work completely restored. He had a whole new perspective on life and was excited about his new found energy and focus. Although he hadn't realized it before he was reminded that his happiness was not solely tied into his life with Jada, and for that reason it wasn't completely lost with her. Through the story of Job, Emanuel was awakened to the ultimate truth, which was spoken by the great young prophet, Elihu, *"God is mighty, but does not despise men; He is mighty, and firm in His purpose... He does not take His eyes off the righteous: He enthrones them with kings and exalts them forever."* So inspired and encouraged was Emanuel by those words that he typed and framed them on his desk -- words that he could and would refer to whenever he was feeling heavy by life's demands. Emanuel sat at his desk dissecting a long list of things to do. First on his list was to complete the legal paperwork relinquishing any interest that he had in *Soul Sistahs*. He understood Jada's thinking behind leaving her shares of the club to him, and he knew that she did it out of respect for their marriage and their partnership; but he recognized that the creation of *Soul Sistahs* was more about the bond between Kay and Jada, as evidenced by the name. And for that reason he couldn't rightfully accept any ownership of the club. He hadn't had the conversation with Kay that he knew he would have to have. It had been over a week, and he was sure that she had moved on, but he still felt that he owed her an apology. He hoped that she would be receptive to it. The way he treated her was unfair. He was ready to accept it if she cursed him and demanded that he never talk to her again. Emanuel had just finished signing the final legal documents when Mona buzzed him on the intercom.

"Mr. Rivers, I just want to let you know that Ms. Caroline Emerson is here for your eleven o'clock." Emanuel picked up the receiver,

"Thank you, Mona. Please make her comfortable, and see if she needs anything. I will be out in a minute."

"Yes, sir." Mona turned her attention to Caroline who stared admiringly at the office space. Mona gave her the once over; she was so incredibly beautiful that it was almost unreal. Everything about her was perfectly in place. She was slightly taller than the average woman and that in and of itself made her intimidating. Caroline was dressed in an expensive business dress, heather grey, form-fitting. Mona calculated and concluded that she was probably five-seven, one-hundred forty-eight pounds, a perfect 36-C, maybe a twenty-seven inch waist, and a rear-end that was perfectly perky and round -- not a dent or dimple visible. Suddenly Mona felt awkward and embarrassed by her full figure. So she decided that instead of standing to greet Caroline as she would do normally, she would address her from her seat. Mona leaned forward over her desk, "Ms. Emerson, Mr. Rivers will be with you momentarily. Please have a seat." Mona smiled. She hoped that Caroline didn't want anything extra because she really didn't want to be put on display. Mona believed if she got up in her cheap suit and round figure that Caroline would watch her and judge her harshly. "Can I get you something to drink?" she asked hesitantly hoping that she would say no.

"No. Thank you. I am fine." Caroline responded in a way that only exaggerated her elegance. She looked at the seat nearest her, cuffed her clutch under her arm, and smoothed the back of her dress before taking a seat. Mona remembered how clumsy and gauche Emanuel had become when Caroline last visited; she eagerly waited to see how he would respond to her today. Emanuel's office door opened and he stepped out looking most professional -- suit jacket buttoned, tie fitting snug around his neck -- he was all about business and appeared unmoved by Caroline's bright smile. He walked directly up to her, and for the first time since entering the office Caroline appeared unsure and off balance. She fumbled awkwardly from her seat, dropping her clutch, which laid, across her lap in the process. Without thought she reached out to shake Emanuel's hand and bent down to pick up her clutch at the same time leaving her looking quite amateurish. Caroline stumbled over her words, saying hello and apologizing for her clumsiness. Mona cut a curt smile full of attitude. This was the Mr. Rivers that she was used to; he had the natural ability to trip up any woman, even bourgeois Caroline Emerson.

"Caroline. How are you?" Emanuel ignored her little fumble and took her hand in his. "Please, follow me." He directed her towards his office. "Mona, could you please hold all of my calls, and buzz me in exactly thirty-minutes I have another appointment that I must keep."

"Yes, sir." Mona smiled at the fact that Emanuel was back to his naturally confident and in control self but even more laughable was Caroline's reaction to it all.

Emanuel moved quickly through the meeting with Caroline. He was prepared to show her four different designs and discuss a different approach for each. He had gone over the conversation in his mind a million times, and each time he concluded that the meeting shouldn't take any more than twenty-minutes including questions. Just as he had planned Emanuel went through his entire pitch in just under eight minutes; he was fourteen-seconds ahead of schedule.

"What questions do you have?" Emanuel concluded. Caroline was undoubtedly impressed with the work that Emanuel presented before her, but she was more impressed with his demeanor. She hadn't heard a word that he said about any of the designs because she was too busy admiring him. Emanuel's dimples played peek-a-boo when he spoke, and Caroline watched his handsome face to catch a glimpse each time they appeared. Caroline hadn't stopped thinking about Emanuel since the night of the Emerson gala. She knew that her father adored Emanuel and she could see why. She didn't want her thoughts to get ahead of her, but she couldn't help but think that he would make a great husband for her. She knew that he came from a successful family of course the Rivers's money didn't measure up to the Emerson's, but Caroline was confident that Emanuel would compliment her well. Caroline wanted to spend some time with Emanuel outside of business so she looked for the perfect opportunity to ask him out.

"I- um- love all of the designs," she stuttered. "But I think I would love them even more if you would join me for dinner," she asked, flashing her beautiful smile. Emanuel knew that Caroline was beautiful, he would have had to be blind not to notice, but he was very hesitant to mix business with pleasure and that was exactly the reason he gave when he turned her down. "Okay, well, I will take my business somewhere else." She smiled as she stood from her chair across from Emanuel and made her way to the couch where he was sitting. "Emanuel, I really like you, and I would really like to spend some time getting to know you. My father thinks the world of you, and I would like to see that awesome and amazing guy that my father always speaks of." Caroline's eyes caught Emanuel's and he smiled. It would have been easy for him to deny her, but somehow he knew that wasn't a part of the approach towards the new life that he was looking for, so without further debate he agreed.

"Dinner is so many hours away," he said looking at his watch for affect. "Why wait when lunch is but minutes away." They laughed together.

"Lunch sounds great."

"So, are you really going to take your business somewhere else?"

"Only if you insist." Caroline reached her hand out and placed it on top of Emanuel's knee. Emanuel was pleased that a woman like Caroline was interested in him. She was the kind of woman that any man would want to call his own. She was the kind of woman who just by having her on his arm would increase his stock. She would make any man better, and right now Emanuel was all about the better. At exactly eleven-thirty Mona buzzed Emanuel to make him aware of the time. He gathered his documents and placed them in a folder and prepared them for Kay. Before lunch, Caroline agreed to ride with him to *Soul Sistahs* to drop off the documents. As Emanuel sat in the back of Caroline's chauffer-driven Bentley he couldn't help but think of how easy it would be for him to get use to the kind of good life that Caroline Emerson could afford him.

Chapter Thirty-Three

The Emerson's black Bentley pulled up curbside in front of *Soul Sistahs*. The driver stepped out first and opened the door for Emanuel. Emanuel had given Caroline the short version concerning his mid-day visit to the club. She knew that *Soul Sistahs* belonged to his late wife, and he had inherited her portion of the club after she passed. He also shared with her his intentions of signing all rights over to Kay. He hadn't bothered to share the details of his relationship with Kay; he figured he'd save that for another time. Caroline gave him a gentle rub on his back as he exited the vehicle. The light misty rain was refreshing on this warm May day. Emanuel was sure that the flowers needed the rain, but he preferred sunshine. With his head tilted slightly forward he ran towards *Soul Sistahs*. Once in the club he instinctively looked to his left towards the main lounge area. At that very moment a tall thin waitress appeared from behind the curtains offering Emanuel a short glimpse of the light afternoon crowd. He wondered, but not for long, if Kay was sitting in her office or if she was in the lounge.

"Good afternoon, sir. A table for one?" the waitress inquired.

"No. Actually I am here to see Ms. Ali."

"Oh, certainly. Who should I tell her is visiting?"

"Emanuel Rivers." With no additional reaction the waitress turned towards Kay's office and disappeared down the corridor. "She must have missed the be nice to this guy memo," Emanuel joked to himself. Emanuel stood in the entranceway looking nervously at the information posted all about. There were bulletins all around about up and coming acts, where they are performing, and which acts are coming soon to *Soul Sistahs*. There was an announcement of a poetry slam on Friday night, asking that interested artists sign their names on the list. Emanuel counted fourteen entrants already signed up; he laughed at the artsy names that made up the list, names like Black Poetry and The Lyricist. Emanuel thought what would he call himself if he were the poetic type? He raised his eyes towards the sky and thought *E. R.* – he laughed at how silly that would sound. "Coming to the stage," he mimicked, "E.R." he over-emphasized, "it must be an emergency." Emanuel laughed at his silliness. He missed that side of himself. Kay turned the corner; she was nervous. She was not prepared to see Emanuel today. She hoped that he would have given her a courtesy call to say that he wanted to meet with her, at least then she could have channeled her peace, but now she was nervous. Dressed in a pair of sweats and a signature Soul Sistahs t-shirt she immediately felt like Emanuel had home court advantage despite the fact that he was in her territory. She had been cleaning her office preparing for her big move to LA. Her hair looked a mess pulled back into a ponytail, adorned with an assortment of pencils and pens randomly tucked. As she cleaned she tacked the writing instruments in her hair. Kay patted herself in place in an attempt to not look so disheveled. Emanuel turned and smiled at Kay's reckless appearance -- even dusty and unkempt Kay was still as beautiful as ever. He knew that she was kicking herself for looking the way that she was looking, and he wished that he would have called in advance to give her a chance to clean up, but he didn't want to risk her hanging up on him and denying to take his visit. So here they were, neither Emanuel nor Kay had really prepared for this moment.

"Emanuel. Hi," Kay's mouth instantly became dry, nervousness always did that to her.

"Hey." Emanuel ran his eyes from the pencils in the top of her head to the brown, red, and green Gucci sneakers that were on her feet. He smiled, "Is this a bad time?"

"Um, no. I was just in the middle of cleaning," Kay offered. "But I could use a break." She tried to appear calm as she removed the writing instruments from her hair.

"Is there somewhere we can go to talk?"

"Sure. My office is free. It's a little messy, but." Kay concluded with a shrug of the shoulders. She turned and walked slowly towards her office. Her heart was pounding as she wondered what Emanuel might say. Was he there to tell her that he loved her and realized that he really wanted to be with her?

Or did he decide that he didn't really love her and that he didn't want to be with her at all. Her heart raced. Once in the office Kay attempted to reposition some things so that they could have a clear, clutter-free space to talk. She reshuffled a few boxes and transferred stacks of paper from one side of her desk to the other. Emanuel sat on the edge of the couch next to several stacks of papers, and Kay leaned against the edge of her desk. She laughed at how ragged she looked. *"Of all the times to look a mess I choose today,"* she thought to herself. "So what's up?"

"Well, first of all, I owe you a huge apology. Since the last time we were together," Emanuel paused as he was reminded of that disastrous last meeting. "I had a chance to do some thinking, a little soul searching, and I even got an expert opinion." Emanuel laughed trying to lighten the moment but there was no space for laughter, at least not yet. Kay's stern expression didn't allow it. "I guess what I'm trying to say is that I am sorry for hurting you. I was really broken on the inside, more so than I even realized. Apparently I didn't really walk away from the accident unscathed." Emanuel offered. "My brain was really scrambled long after the accident, and I wasn't thinking clearly. That night when I called you Jada I had completely lost touch with reality. I called you Jada because she was who I saw when I looked at you. In fact, I had looked at you many times before that night, and all I could see was Jada's face." Emanuel gripped his hands together and stretched his arms out in front of him. He dropped his head. This was far more difficult than he imagined. "I never realized how much the two of you looked alike, especially to someone who desperately needed to see her and feel her." Kay held her breath; this was the only way for her to hold back the tears and the anger that suddenly rose up in her. "I am so sorry." Kay could not speak though her mind was full of questions. Emanuel reached into his blazer pocket and pulled out a brown letter sized envelope. "I wanted to give you this." He handed Kay the envelope. "I understand if you are still angry with me. I pray that one day you will forgive me." Kay opened the envelope and unfolded its contents. She read through the documents. Her eyes met

Emanuel's; she was mute with heartache. She licked her dry lips hoping that the moisture would help her lips move and allow her to speak, but still she could not. Emanuel stood to his feet; he leaned into Kay and gave her a gentle hug. "Take care of yourself," he whispered in her ear. And with that he walked out. Kay's mind was dizzy with thoughts, questions, and confusion.

    "What does this mean?" she said to herself. *"Is it over? Was this his way of saying that it was over? Was he in love with me? Is this it?"* Kay sprung to her feet; she had to ask those questions of him, and he owed her an answer to each. She rushed towards the door to catch Emanuel before he drove away. As Emanuel walked out of *Soul Sistahs,* there Caroline waited with an umbrella in hand and as if it was natural and their relationship was already established, the two embraced. Kay reached the glass doors just in time to witness Emanuel in the arms of Caroline Emerson, and that was when her heart shattered. The driver stood outside of their car and held the door open for Emanuel and Caroline, and just that quickly they disappeared into the car and drove away.

Epilogue

Two years after the grand opening of *Soul Sistahs* Kay was doing it again -- this time in LA. Kay raised her champagne-filled glass to the sky. LA in the springtime offered the perfect setting for a new life and a new venture, *Soul Sistahs LA*, grander than the first. All of the key players were there: Eva, Emanuel, Caroline, Malik, Heather, Khadir, Nadia, and all of the staff from *Soul Sistahs Philly*. Kay stood on the stage of *Soul Sistahs LA* dressed elegantly in a creamed-colored mini dress. Her Jimmy Choo pumps helped her to step comfortably into her brand new life. And what was a brand new life without a brand new look. She cut her hair in a sharp short razor cut, tapered around the sides, with a heavy bang that fell on her right side, and her make-up was very pronounced -- big heavy lashes and glossy red lips. She was LA glam -- ready to do it big. She looked out into the crowd at her family and friends, all excited to celebrate this moment with her. "Tonight is a very special night for the *Soul Sistahs* family. Not only are we extending our family, but we are embarking on a new adventure. A dear friend said to me once, that life is but a series of adventures; some adventures make great stories like the one of two skinny girls from West Philly who dared to dream and imagine. We imagined that we could be businesswomen; we imagined that we could be successful. We imagined that we would find love, and we imagined that we would find happiness. We started this adventure with a grand vision, and *Soul Sistahs LA* is but a piece of that grand vision." Kay squinted her eyes to avoid the tears -- she was stronger now and tonight she refused to cry. She swooshed her heavy bang from her eyes and pressed her glossy lips together. "Here is to my family and friends, my mother Eva," Kay made eye contact with her and gave Eva a nod and a wink. "Emanuel," Kay smiled at him and Caroline who was firmly pressed against Emanuel with her arm wrapped around his, positioned just so to flash her almost blinding engagement ring. "Malik and Heather," Kay continued smiling at the couple. Heather rested her hand on her protruding belly. Kay was excited for them and their soon to be new edition, a baby sister for Khalial. Kay also thanked Khadir and Nadia, though she knew that their visit was more about having some California fun and *Soul Sistahs LA* was just one stop on their club tour. "And of course my *Soul Sistahs* family both in Philly and LA." In an instant Kay was reminded of the great path that God had set before her, and she was overwhelmed with the blessings. She blinked her heavy lashes trying to push back the tears. Kay recovered and with a slight raising of her glass she continued with her speech. "And last but most certainly not least, Jada, thank you for encouraging me to dream big and for helping to make my dreams come true. I love you Ma'ma. God Bless you all and God Bless *Soul Sistahs LA.* " Everyone cheered and sipped from their wineglasses. Kay handed the microphone over to a tall, dark, and handsome vocalists, and as she made her way off stage he belted out the famous words to a song, which thanks to Jada, had become everyone's anthem *"I was born by the river in a little tent and just like the river I've been running every since, it's been a long time a long time coming but I know a change gone come."*

The End

A Special Note From The Author:

I hope you enjoyed reading No Greater Love, and I pray that it was not only entertaining, but inspiring. Please visit my website: www.firstfruitspublishing.com and share your thoughts with me. If you are a member of a book club or are interested in hosting a book reading and would like to have me, Kwanza, make a special appearance to discuss the book then please visit my website or email me at firstfruitspublishing@gmail.com.

I thank God for each of you and thank you for supporting me.

In Him with Love,

Kwanza

About the Author

Kwanza is a native of Philadelphia, Pennsylvania. She is just one of many successful Overbrook High School Alumnae. She received her Undergraduate degree from Bowie State University and her Graduate degree from the University of Maryland both in Public Relations. Kwanza is currently pursuing a second graduate degree in Theological studies.

No Greater Love is her first novel, published under her publishing company, First Fruits Publishing. Kwanza knows that when God spoke the words First Fruits Publishing in her ear that He had already completed the plan, that He had fulfilled the promises and He had already provided the people – she must only continue to listen to God's instructions and say yes. Kwanza looks forward to a very successful career in writing and publishing.

Kwanza lives in Owings Mills, Maryland with her husband and two children.

No Greater Love

Kwanza

No Greater Love

Kwanza

Kwanza